3

20.00
80E

|||||||| |||||||||||||| ||||||||
D0850333

Bilingual Press/Editorial Bilingüe

General Editor
Gary D. Keller

Managing Editor
Karen S. Van Hooft

Associate Editor
Ann Waggoner Aken

Assistant Editor
Linda St. George Thurston

Editorial Consultant
Jennifer Hartfield Lawrence

Editorial Board
Juan Goytisolo
Francisco Jiménez
Eduardo Rivera
Severo Sarduy
Mario Vargas Llosa

Address:
Bilingual Review/Press
Hispanic Research Center
Arizona State University
Tempe, Arizona 85287
(602) 965-3867

Pilgrims
in Aztlán

Miguel Méndez

Translated from the Spanish by
David William Foster

Bilingual Press/Editorial Bilingüe

TEMPE, ARIZONA

Spanish editions © 1974, 1979, 1991 by Miguel Méndez M. and 1989 by Ediciones Era, Mexico. 1991 edition published by Bilingual Press.

ISBN 0-927534-22-3 (cloth)
ISBN 0-927534-23-1 (paper)

Library of Congress Cataloging-in-Publication Data

Méndez M., Miguel.
    [Peregrinos de Aztlán. English]
    Pilgrims in Aztlán / by Miguel Méndez : translated by David William Foster.
        p.   cm.
    Translation of: Peregrinos de Aztlán.
    ISBN 0-927534-22-3 : $20.00 — ISBN 0-927534-23-1 (pbk.) : $12.00
    1. Mexican-American Border Region—Fiction. 2. Alien labor, Mexican—United States—Fiction. 3. Mexican Americans—Fiction. I. Title.
PQ7079.2.M46P4713   1992
863—dc20   92-23636
                                                                CIP

PRINTED IN THE UNITED STATES OF AMERICA

Cover design by Christopher J. Bidlack

Back cover photo by Dolores Bahti

Acknowledgments
Partial funding provided by the Arizona Commission on the Arts through appropriations from the Arizona State Legislature; additional funding provided by a grant from the National Endowment for the Arts in Washington, D.C., a Federal agency.

Preface

I wrote this book with a plan and structure in order to move exquisite sensibilities, with the additional desire to win a smile of approval from among the many academicians of the Spanish language, as many of them as there are devoted to ridding words of their fleas. I confess that my preconceived plan failed, not by design but because of a strange rebellion on the part of the words. I chose ones that were soft and well shaped, like stones that have been polished for centuries by the currents of the rivers. But others, inopportune and ugly by virtue of being rough-hewn and deformed like the sharp stones of crags or the ones that abound along the rocky roads, began to strike me insistently on the forehead and to get stubbornly in the way of my pen. With understandable justification I tried to ridicule these words that kept getting in my way, laughing at and scorning a language to be found in the mouths of those who speak poorly. But the rebellious words assured me that they would impose themselves on my text to tell the sufferings, feelings, and anger of the oppressed. In the first place, they argued that they are the faithful expression of the majority and that a living language bestows greater life on a story than does a fossilized one, which sublimates what is dead in beautiful marble sculptures. In the end I read my work and congratulated myself on the success of the joke at the expense of this bastard speech. I truly laughed when I saw that the words of the down-and-out struggled to reach the sacred stage of literature with dirty faces and the torn and tattered clothes of peasants. Nevertheless, we came away heartsore and depressed, the hunger-filled words feeling dejected and impotent, and I knowing that my abiding childhood dream of becoming a writer in a world without greenery and without literature is only that . . . an infantile dream riding the back of a runaway horse galloping through uninhabited realms and along the vast plains of an untutored desert. There where the echoes that produce cries of anguish fall, overcome like walls of sand, felled by a murky wind. There where every soul is petrified history.

I write this humblest of works from the suffering domains of my Indian forebears, reaffirming the great faith that I profess in my Chicano people, exploited by human perverseness. They are cut off from the bilingual education that is appropriate for them and scorned in their demands for help by the ignorance of some and the indifference of others, and in particular, by the malevolence of those who seek to dominate Chicanos permanently and maintain with Chicano poverty the superiority of the white man.

My goal has also been to listen to the good humor and the joy that paradoxically are to be found in our most suffering humanity.

Read this book, reader, if you like the prose dictated to me by the common speech of the oppressed. If you don't, if it offends you, do not read it, for I will consider myself well paid just by having written it in my condition as a Mexican Indian, a wetback, and a Chicano.

Four editions of the Spanish original, *Peregrinos de Aztlán*, have appeared so far, three in the United States and one in Mexico. And now this volume constitutes the first publication of *Peregrinos* in English. The critical response in periodical articles and doctoral dissertations prepared at various universities has been extensive. I feel that I should note that the novel had been completed by 1968, although its first edition was dated 1974.

I wrote the novel while I was employed in heavy construction and working in the fields. It was important to me to lay bare the thoughts and feelings of those who suffered the most on both sides of the border and to comment, among other things, on what in those days were common occurrences. Since then certain changes have taken place in the laws affecting immigration and education. Even the language itself, which in the novel manifests itself on several linguistic levels, has undergone notable development. I am making this clarification in order to avoid confusion concerning what the circumstances were in those days, in contrast to current conditions. But even taking that into consideration, the similarities between the past and the present are probably greater in number.

The Author

Part One

One morning, as he always did, he set out down the street with his half-filled bucket of water. He'd already put the soap in, and with the sloshing around, the bucket was foaming like an angry camel. The rags draped over his shoulder looked like a load of fright-dazed hares. He walked along a ways with his arm aching from the weight of the bucket, stopped to take a breather, rubbed his leg a little, breathed in the dirty haze mixed with oxygen, and continued on. Overhead, hiding the sky, thick dark clouds swirled in circles. The soothing rain would certainly not take long in coming or, bad luck, a torrent of water of the kind that washes people and animals away with it. He was hopeful as he watched the lightning that would bring with it vein-like streaks of blinding light, along with an ephemeral design that would engrave a phosphorescence of capricious, phantasmal maps, the traces of continents swallowed up by the seas. He stopped again, thinking he heard the rush of rain in the distance, beating on the hollow crust of the earth like the furious hoofbeats of Pancho Villa's men on the attack. Rivers and streams would swell like the strings of a harp stretched over the skin of the earth, taut from rain. For a moment he thought he heard the buzz of the gullies and the crazed whistling of the washes. For a few seconds he looked at the sky with that gesture of disdain that stretches the lips into a simulated smile, and he spit with energy. The rainfall he thought was on the way was nothing more than seas of gasoline and oil, converted into clouds of poisonous gases. The smoky haze of brutalizing factories, foul-smelling smoke, dirty smoke, smoke and more smoke from the exhaust pipes of cars, from the exhaust pipes of human beings, smoke from the cursed cigarette, gasifier of sorrows and lungs. The smoky haze of legions of marijuana smokers who saw themselves as saviors. All this junk in the atmosphere did not exclude the breath of alcoholics whose nighttime libations impregnated their awakening with the stench of shit. Nor is it any wonder that the same swill-filled atmosphere bore the curses of so many frustrated individuals: veterans of the dirty wars, whoring and the unemployed rumbling with chronic hunger.

Loreto walked with the difficulties experienced by ants after someone's sadistic footstep has stepped on them. Agh! What suffering: life clung stubbornly to sick limbs that ached with the light and air; his heart leapt around like a rock-and-roll toad, and his brain bubbled capriciously with episodes of his life without his having evoked them. The complicated need to arrange his memories in a chronological order was now of no use to him. He lived with his soul turned like a telescope toward the living things of the past. Wash your car, mister? He didn't have any energy left to venture a smile, only pretending to smile with a grimace that outlined the pull suffered by his muscles, now definitely experiencing decay. In bygone times he had enjoyed letting his gaze drift over the green meanderings of the fields in harmony with the rebirth of April and the materialization of the spirit in the flowers of May. Spring! Eternal youth . . . No! The days were the same; he could see that in the young. It was he who had changed by growing old, tired, navigating like a falling star, lost in the immutability of space. He was off to offer his energy to wash parked cars in exchange for whatever the owners might give him. For old Loreto Maldonado, living meant struggling unto death, as if the fluidity of his temporal condition were a black colt, the wildest of the wild, determined to whip him off his slippery back against the outcroppings of rocks. The struggle against such a monster had become the biggest incentive of his mornings. The face of the old Yaqui revealed the wounds that his people had suffered in genealogical succession. Destiny's cruel hand, in the form of a sculptor, had worked his physiognomy with anvil and chisel. Yet, smelly, raggedy, and ugly, he was the complete antithesis of feigned dignity. As he turned the corner onto Madero Street, he came upon the tender light of a sun emerging newly born from a parting in the purplish clouds. He almost ran into a very elegant couple on their way to church. She wore a very filmy black veil over her face and a hat of the sort called a cloche on her head. Her left arm bore as many bracelets and rings as are found on an aging snake. Her makeup was very thick, enough to smooth out the ruts left by the ploughs of time. The man, for his part, had the dapper appearance of a bastard prince, and a look of arrogance and disdain poured from his eyes. His checkbook allowed him to write out any sum of money. Nevertheless, his wallet was always stuffed with hundred-peso notes. It was obvious they were going to pray for something big; otherwise, there would be no need for them to give alms. The aristocratic lady placed a five-peso note in Loreto's hand, and at the same time her face glazed over with beatitude, she prayed to him: "Help yourself with this humble gift, good man." "No!," he answered haughtily. "I have a job, and I don't accept charity from anyone." They saw him walk away under his thousands of hardships, stumbling under his shouldered dignity. The man with the mouth slightly twisted sideways touched his tie and vomited with rage: "Bums, sons of bitches, hunger strikes them down and pride lifts them up."

The man in question had made his fortune by combining the activities of politicians and thieves. Since the woman had once been very attractive, he had used her as bait, bedding her with prominent men in order to win promotions, and now he was a distinguished millionaire industrialist. They were to be seen much in church of late, and they never let a week go by without going to communion. Their dress was impeccable, and they wore the finest of clothes. They were both fastidious. He went so far as to bathe four times a day, one hour after each meal and at midnight. She only bathed once a day, but would spend an hour splashing around in the tub, festooning herself with Santa Claus beards and little hats of suds. The bathroom was lined with mirrors because they both enjoyed seeing themselves naked. He contemplated his profile, sucking in his stomach and thrusting out his chest, with a little enigmatic smile on his lips that said: I look just like Napoleon, but with the advantage that I am tall and strong, and he was a miserable little runt. She would pretend that the mirror revealed a lady of great nobility and would curtsy to her image, laughing with pretended farce and even exclaiming, hello my dear! The soap they used smelled so good that you could distinguish their aroma, the aroma of the Dávalos de Cocuch. She wasn't much interested in perfumes, but he was obsessed by them and even discretely perfumed his underclothes.

On Sundays it was their pleasure to mingle among the poor. They admired themselves deeply. On many occasions in which they wandered among the ragged and hungry people, they complimented themselves with the most poetic symbols: "You shine like a sun, my dear"; "You glow like the moon, my beloved." They were aware of the astonishment that they evoked, and they secretly wanted to be taken for monarchs. The woman caked herself with whatever powders and creams she found in the beauty shops and decked herself out with jewels. Beneath these the rich matron could hide the formerly young woman who had made an ambitious future for herself on the basis of a calisthenics that obliged her to spread her legs anytime a man showed her some money.

The man had had a different beginning in his efforts to forge a successful future for himself. He had become the aide-de-camp of a military man given to massacres. But just to vary the pattern, and this long after the Revolution, he had emerged as a true revolutionary with the credentials of a veteran. He became a prodigious acrobat on the trapezes of politics and an expert manipulator of the levers of the machines of the influential. The magnificent suits he changed daily concealed a painful illness. On one of his campaigns in which they were going after a rabble-rouser hiding in the sierras, he had had to ride a horse bareback. The backbone of that ignoble brute was so lean and sharp that he looked like he had been painted by El Greco. What was worse, the horse liked to gallop and they had given him the name of "Machete." The campaign, which lasted fifteen days, won the officer a promotion, but it caused him to lose control over his sphincter. From that day on he was always getting his underclothes dirty, but since his pants were waterproof, they were protected.

On another occasion, when old man Loreto was slicing through the mist that had plastered itself all over the dirty face of the city, looking high and low for clients with mud-splattered cars, he ran right into Malquerida, who sprayed him with her high voice: "Look here, old man, go over to the drugstore and buy me some things I need and I'll give you the money."

So much pride showed in the face of the Indian and so much bitterness shone in his eyes, an indefinite something that inspired profound respect, that the woman shrunk back intimidated, a muttered "excuse me" caught in her teeth. Nobody knew what Malquerida's real name was. She was called the "unloved" because her aggressive character kept her from making friends. According to the women, the best she deserved was isolation and disdain because she was a hog-tied mule and no mother had given birth to her. She'd been born of an aunt. The bad-tempered youngster had the bearing of those women who have been blessed with all the attributes of beauty. Her harsh character was nothing other than a deep bitterness that occupied the place of her large congenital tenderness, ruined by such an unjust fate that, instead of giving her the place of a queen, had turned her into a hapless whore.

That was about the same time the unfortunate Indian had gone three days without a bite of food to settle his guts. His insides declared themselves an entity alien to his organism, and his guts meowed sharply like cats being raped in the dark. They made such a scandalous uproar that they were like snakes in heat, knotting together and thrashing around furiously. There were moments when the old Yaqui cocked his ears with intense curiosity, thinking that he was hearing his guts speaking in imploring voices that begged for food with a piteous tone. He was very upset with himself because he had violated his own code of honor.

It was like this. Several little kids dying from hunger, barefoot, underfed, and dirty, had set themselves up with their offer to wash cars in exactly the spot he usually occupied. The little shitheads were doing a miserable job, but they looked so down and out that people were paying them without even bothering to haggle. More than pity, they scared people with what is called "social crime," which the snot-nosed kids preached with their depressing appearance. As Loreto's clients vanished into thin air, he confronted the kids with his right hand in his pocket, blind with anger and yelling at them: "If you don't get out of my spot, I'll cut the balls off the three of you bastards! Get going!" The raggedy kids were scared to death, but they didn't budge from the spot they had taken over. The old man held his ground, confident that the guardians of order would whisk away from the sight of strangers the depressing spectacle of the starving infants.

He only picked up one peso in those three days, and the result was that he was out of sorts. Without a prior agreement with its owner, he washed the luxurious rolling palace that seemed to smile it was so shiny. The owner returned, a libidinous gringo everyone called Tony Baby, an unbalanced sort who spent his weekends roaming the nightclubs along Revolution Avenue, enjoying the originality of the variety of striptease joints. The aforesaid barbarian strutted along like he had springs in his shoes, and slime dribbled from his filthy mouth like silver streamers.

The old Yaqui approached him with his hand outstretched to be paid.

"I washed your car, sir. That'll be fifty cents."

The man uttered who knows what ugly things in his language, and finally grudgingly gave him twenty-five cents.

The madman turned into the antlike traffic where there were so many cars that there was barely room for the gaze of the old Indian, who idly looked after him for a long while. He then looked down at his hand, strangely open like a spider, holding the leaden coin, round like a blob of spit.

Tony Baby was the owner of a string of restaurants that he'd inherited from his grandmother, a hairy-chested woman who had worked like a horse selling Mexican food and exploiting wetbacks. The teeth of this bitch of a "business woman" were so sharp that on more than one occasion she had turned in the hapless wetbacks to the immigration authorities so she wouldn't have to pay them the kitty's piss of a wage they were hired for. She left him a huge business that had started out with a hotdog stand. Tony Baby liked to enjoy money, but he considered that work, more than a curse, is the greatest stupidity that mortal man can commit. He was so cynical in this regard that he maintained that only burros, oxen, and fools are patient enough to subject themselves to the bridle. When he spoke about his generous grandmother, he would add: "The old devil of a bitch is probably sliding around hell on her ass over a field of burning coals."

Her heir married a shapely woman who, once she got her hands on the rights accorded by matrimony, turned out to be as frigid as the island of Greenland in the middle of winter. That sharp woman had two hobbies: Sitting around talking on the phone and collecting dollar bills in the bank. All her affections were devoted to the majesty of a white and fluffy cat who slept in the warm nook the forgotten husband so coveted. As a bit of curiosity, the woman had joined a separatist feminist movement that prattled on about liberation and other such things.

THIS UNUSUAL CITY with pretenses of a "dubious reputation" awakens redeemed with the noise of school children and the pealing of the bells calling people to mass, the bustle of the workers who earned a handful of coins, stubbornly paying with poverty the tribute demanded by honesty, and the occasional visit of goodwilled foreigners who descend to buy inoffensive objects. But as the lights of day go out and those of the night come on, the city decks itself out in the finery of a flirtatious whore to seduce the unwary. Like a mythological goddess, cynical and shameless, the city takes advantage of human weaknesses to fill its farthest corners.

"In here, in here, you marijuana smokers and drug addicts, come on in, come on in. Poor dogs! But the majority are foreigners. What's the matter, little gringos? Your poor consciences are being tortured, it shows in your faces. Ah! They have just returned from those cruelest of endless wars, wars that serve to fashion new arms. What a pity! They saw children being burned on pyres of napalm. Poor dogs! They saw blood washing over walls and forests. Come on in, I will comfort you. And what's the matter with you? Come on! You find such wars loathsome. And what's wrong with you? You've got money, but can't love. That's an old, old tale, but one that's always in fashion. Hi! Got the blues, huh? You're out of both love and money? Well, for those of you who are frustrated, especially you young ones, there are drugs by the bushel. That's the beauty of supply and demand. Knock on that door over there. That guy there walking down the street. I forgot something. You got greenbacks? Yeh, dollars. Because if you don't, you're out of luck, sweethearts."

Thus the nocturnal city draws out the bitter: shamelessly, pants down, butt hanging out, with no sense of modesty; its cocktail dress adorned with neon letters, clapping its hands at the revelers like a damsel off her rocker.

"Drunks, souses, come on in, come on in! Come drink at the fountains of alcohol like they were young ladies' breasts. There's a lot, tons of alcohol, a lot of places where you can get a drink. There's nothing to worry about, nothing to hide, the law's broad-minded. These are the clubs for the wealthy. Over here, big spenders! You'll have to pay a little bit more, sure, but come on in, you wealthy drunks; they'll call you sir and treat you with respect. Yes, yes, of course! It doesn't matter if you're assassins, thieves, slave drivers or dirty social climbers. They'll treat you like emperors, but you've got to be splendid. Right? Remember that the waiters will light your cigarettes and the owners of the rivers of alcohol will bow down before you. How pretty! Right? Oh, my most faithful lovers! Right this way, my dear poor drunks. I know that you are dying of hunger and that you love me passionately.

Follow me, I am the goddess of drink, leave your wives and children crying with their stomachs empty. I have cozy little corners for you, like this bar that I'm pointing to. Do you see it? It's called the Happy Day. There's room for everybody here, my sons. Come on in, come on in, all of you who are confused, disdained, husbands without character. What? That's right, the boys too. Let those with frustrated talents come in. Humanity is very stupid, refusing to recognize that you are all little geniuses. Also you, all of you, gays in the making, come on in and drink your booze, you queers. Also you day laborers, come and rest your weary bones, loosen your tongues at will. Here you can shout that the foreman or the chief himself is a son of a bitch. Make room for the vulgar types who enjoy telling dirty stories, that's what the Happy Day was built for. That's it, come on in, come on in to the Happy Day to really tie one on.

"HEY, YOUNG MAN, how about another drink? I'll bet you this'll be the best business we've ever had. We'll have to start right now."

"But you'll have to wait another day. I have to tell my partner."

"Set me up two more, please."

"Just a minute, just a minute and I'll get to you."

"I want a big worm."

"Sure, sure. Christ! The mister wants a worm."

"Don't be gross, he's asking you for a double tequila, Worm brand."

"Bring me a beer, please, bartender, but not 'Exes' brand."

(Take these glasses over to those dumb drunks at that table, while I serve these bastards at the bar.)

"Yes, sir, whatever you say, right now."

"Damn, what a lot of customers!"

"This friend's been at it with the mariachis for six hours and he's in a real funk."

"Well, tell him to change the record."

"The bad part is that he's the one who's paying so he can play whatever he wants."

"Listen, buddy, get that beer over here. My mouth's been hanging open for a hour."

"That guy likes to dance to the jukebox by himself."

"Heh, do you get good broads in here?"

"Sometimes they all come in at once."

"Well, get them in here, that's the only way to tell."

"Bartender! Two screwdrivers, please."

"Whatever you say, sir." (*That old scumbag sure gets on my nerves.*)

"That's what they say, that this is the biggest cantina in the world."

"Do you hear that? And what's the biggest mountain in the world?"

"How the hell do I know? Which one is it?"

"Go mountain your mother!"

"Damn mariachi! Change it. Better yet, play 'The Dove' for me."

"We don't know that one."

"Then play 'The Snake' for me."

"Get your grandmother to play with it."

"Look who just walked in."

"What's up, man? Long time no see."

"Good for you and good for me."

"Come on, give a proper answer."

"Good for you and your cancer."

"Hell, this guy's a nut."

"And you've got hair on your butt."

"Just ignore him and he'll stop acting like a jerk."

"Fine, I just won't talk. Come on, don't play games with me!"

"You're all wet."

"Hey, look at the dude who's just come in."

"He looks more like a dud to me."

"These three dames have been drinking and showing off their stuff since we opened and someone's gonna get lucky."

(*Damn, I've been all over the place, brother, setting up drinks for all these bastards. Pipe down, it's a miracle I haven't dropped like a stone, because it looks like every goddamn son of bitch in town has dropped by.*)

"Bartender, three more over here."

"Whatever you say, my pleasure, you're the boss."

"One isn't enough, not even two, the bad part is the habit."

"That's the way it is with everything, friend. Excess is what gets you in the end."

"I'm here to tell you, friend, just tell them that a madman said so. Those that don't drink, it isn't because they don't want to. It's just that they're too damned tight or their old lady won't let them."

"That's for sure. I had a neighbor once who'd get back a dime each payday."

"Boy, now that was one tight woman."

"Well, no one studies to be a jackass."

"The true businessman has to know how to lose money in order to be able to earn it."

"Now you're talking, my friend. Right on, man!"

"We can sit over here, come on."

"I prefer the strong stuff, thanks."

"According to my research, if there's a special motive, yes."

"Certainly, if it's pure alcohol, it's cheaper to drink at home."

"Look here, the drunk drinks more to find himself than for any other reason."

"Or to escape?"

"Well, yes, to escape from reality."

"Yes, sir, they find themselves from the inside, but only here in public taverns, believe me."

"Explain yourself."

"Because they sit in front of a mirror, and since the majority of them suffer from narcissism, between one glass and another, they shoot themselves tender looks."

"I'm not convinced. The majority of them are real ugly, and besides they drown themselves in alcohol."

"That's the key right there. They love themselves, but hate themselves because they know they are ugly. And each drink helps them overcome the conflict. After sitting there drinking for hours, they see themselves as so beautiful that they are capable of drowning themselves in booze just to find their own arms in the mirror."

"Great! What an original hypothesis!"

"Thanks. I just got my doctorate in sociology."

"Where'd you study?"

"In Tucson. . . . "

(*"Listen, are these glasses all clean?"*

"So what if they're not? Nobody's paying any attention."

"Why do we get paid nothing, but they still want us to wear fancy clothes and look like penguins?")

"Hello, what a miracle!"

"Here I am, man. . . . Yes, in a bottle, please."

"I know what's up with you."

"Hey, you look half tired."

"I'm waiting on that dude over there dancing to the jukebox by himself. He's stinking drunk."

"Yeh, right! So he's going to come out fighting."

"He's not bothering anybody, until all of a sudden he jumps his leash. He doesn't attack, but he sure knows how to cuss."

"Listen . . . I know that guy. . . . Yes, no question about it. . . . That's him alright."

"You don't say. Where did you meet him?"

"We worked together in the States. He's a swell guy, a great fellow to work with."

"Well, he's all yours. Do me a favor."

"Chuco! My friend. I'll go say hello to him. We've got a lot to remember together."

THE RUINOUS COMPETITION that resulted in the crazy old coot's empty stomach ended in misfortune for one of the kids: Chalito, the skinniest of the bunch, the one who never stopped trembling, the one whose laugh was as pretty as the bells of Christmas. Chalito's tender mind got the idea that no one in the world earned as much money as he did. He took pleasure in listening to the clink of the coins he dropped in his pocket along with the ones he already had. Something made the innocent fellow believe that in a few days of washing cars he would amass enough to free his family from the terrible poverty in which they lived. That was why he didn't even realize himself that because he insisted on washing more and more cars, he was getting all soaked with water, and after a little while his chest and back were dripping. During the day he was feverish with enthusiasm, and he didn't realize it until it was dark and he was on his way home, when the strong wind plastered his wet shirt against his body. . . .

His little brothers, more resistant, did not get sick. The first day, there were little isolated fits of coughing. By the second afternoon he was hacking hard, as though his throat contained sheets of sandpaper rubbing together. By the third night Chalito showed all the gravity of a mature man given over to meditation. He was being felled by millions of ferocious, microscopic bugs with all the determination of an army of fire ants out to devour him. And devouring him they were! The walls of his respiratory tracts gave off a damp red liquid. Nothing or no one helped him to defend himself!

"It is easier for a camel to pass through the eye of a needle than for a doctor to go out at dawn to see a desperately sick man at the begging of very poor nobodies."

The one who said this was Lencho García y del Valle. Before reciting it, he deliberately looked both ways to make sure there were people listening.

Lencho García y del Valle was the father of poor Chalito.

Hospitals charge a lot of money and do not accept the needy. The last resort with which they tried to save Chalito consisted of giving him piping hot cinnamon tea to drink and rubbing his chest with Vicks. They also gave him two aspirins, and his mother kissed his forehead with the words, "You are going to get better, my little sweetheart, right?" In the middle of the little face shining like a ripe apple his eyes gleamed like drops of black ink. The same day that Loreto the carwasher found his business free, he felt a certain amount of remorse and a dark foreboding. At that very moment the little kid was showing off a splashy coffin, blue in color, painted the same blue as the sky, with little white wings on the side and made from very pretty cardboard. It also sparkled with some very pretty little drawings that looked like bunches of stars. The lining was made from the same cloth used to make shirts for the well off. His mother grabbed the other two kids under her arm like a clucking chicken, and at the cemetery his father swore never to get drunk again and to give himself over to working for his other children.

"Hey, Chuquito, my friend, it's a real miracle to see you around here."

"Nah, pal, just over here in Mexico having a beer, you know? I'm really blue, so stand me one, maybe it'll make me feel better."

"Sure, it's on me, Chuquito. Let's grab a couple and talk about the good times, I bet you're still the champ when it comes to picking."

"Hell! Cut that crap out, okay? I can't hack it, pal. My hands are no good anymore, and my back's all gone. I've gotten old and been to hell and back. This guy's all broken down."

"Yeh, time doesn't go by for nothing, what with the work so hard, we're all washed up quicker than a wink, Chuquito."

"What would you gentlemen like?"

"A beer for me."

"Bring us two beers, fellow."

"Chuquito, Chuquito, you're still the same old hellraiser."

"Nah, kid, we're just broken-down donkeys, see? You bray so the others won't think you're a she-mule, right?"

"Hah, ol' Chuquito. What are you living from these days, friend?"

"Not a hell of a lot, brother, just barely holding it together. Sometimes I think it'd be better just to shove off out of this life, because all they do is squeeze you dry without even giving a shit for you. Anyway, I've been hanging out in Tijuas, dragging my butt through the mud, you know how it is. . . . I don't give a damn whether I eat or not, because there's always someone to buy you a drink."

"Damn, Chuco, you're really something for drinking beer."

"Hell, yes, now that we've got this one taken care of, let's see if we can get another set up real fast."

"Don't worry, Pachuquito, don't worry about it for a second."

"No problem, friend, I'm not looking for trouble, only when the jerks get to me. You know something, pal? Keep an eye on my beer for a second and don't go away. Hold on tight and I'll be right back. I'm just going to lift my leg for a minute."

"Careful there, Chuco! Watch you don't fall. Okay, he's over it now."

"It's okay, it's okay, no problem, I'm okay now. Just playing! I'm going to the john."

"I don't think I'll serve your friend Pachuco any more beer. He's as drunk as a lord."

"Look, man, you should know him by now. This guy wouldn't bother a soul. I've known him well since we worked together on the other side."

"Yeh, well look, you're right, we've got to deal with all kinds here. But that guy's far gone. Not that he'd hit anyone, but he's real abusive. He spends weeks here drinking one after another. I run him off when he starts to insult me, because I know that after me, he starts in with the customers. So as soon as he swears at me for the first time, you get him out of here, or you'll get the same treatment. If not, someone'll beat the shit out of the two of you, just like the other day. . . . "

"You've no idea what these poor fellows are carrying around inside."

"It's none of my business sticking my nose in those things. So, you've been given the word—the first insult, and you get him out of here. Look! There he comes, stumbling all over the place, barely on his feet."

"Come on, come on, pal, give us a beer, waiter. Let's play us a song, give it a whirl, pal."

"It'd be better for us to go for a walk, Chuquito."

"Hold on! Just calm down for a minute. I'm just starting to feel good."

"Tell me about your family, your mama and your brothers."

"I feel like shit, pal, real down. . . . My old lady took off. The kids are just getting by, doing watermelon, lettuce. You know what? I used to get out there good and early because I was a real dude in the fields. Now that I'm all broken down, I think about things, because, you know, when you can't take it anymore, well, you're like a dull knife. And if you ask for help, they just dump you on the garbage heap. You know what? Now it's almost like I felt ashamed, always scrounging around like an animal. You know what I mean, you've read a lot of comics. Are we just a bunch of slaves? It's just like they went and cut your liver up into pieces. You're nothing but a greaser, a spick, and then you come over here and you're nothing but a pocho. It really makes me happy when they call me a Chicano, pal. You don't have any idea what a thrill it gives me, brother. A man's somebody, not just a greaser or a pocho, right? You've read a lot of funny books, pal, what are we?"

"Well . . . , Mexican Americans."

"That's a bunch of crap. Mexican to shove you down in the dirt, in the mines, to fuck you over more. American just so they

can sign you up to fight their dirty wars. Isn't that right? Give me
another beer, you're sure a real pal."

"Two more beers, bartender."

"You remember that time we went over to the cathouse? I
wanted to stick it to that little gal who was with her boyfriend,
and he beat me up? Remember?"

"Yes, I sure do, Chuquito, and also that time the police picked
us up in Los Angeles."

"Damn L.A. cops. They picked me up and I really told them
where to go. They ended up beating the shit out of me so much I
was like a drunken mule. They stuck me in the can for a month.
Damn it, pal! What's up, boss, you hiding the beer? What's going
on?"

"Please don't hit the bar."

"Little piece of shit, I'll take you on barefisted or with a knife,
you know that, bartender? You motherfucker!"

THE FACT OF THE MATTER was that old man Loreto had a head full
of cobwebs. Grand ideals and dignity were the threads that time
kept half intact, woven halfway, unraveled. Although if you
looked at it from the other side, he'd probably inherited his behavior from the very ancient dignity of his race, a pure-blooded
Yaqui with the regal appearance of a statue struck from the very
roots of granite.

In recent years he crisscrossed the streets of the growing border
city like one of the many unfortunates no one pays any heed to,
those individuals who bear their hunger and abandon as if their
only purpose were to bear witness to how everybody else was fortunate enough, beyond the simple fact that it is easy to get lost in
a whirl of people of so many differing conditions and occupations
as different as they were strange.

Loreto was a strange guy. How many times had he seen his
reflection in the panes of glass of those buildings, where so many
things are for sale, without recognizing himself, until after a few
seconds it would strike him that that blackened and wrinkled face
was his own? He, who at times persisted in the idea of being the
sprightly youth, the terrible warrior, would smile upon seeing himself changed into such an ugly old man, remembering the story of
the country fellow who found a mirror and when he picked it up,

exclaimed: "Shit, they had good reason to abandon you. You look horrible!" Old man Loreto was already close to eighty, of an age when a man has already buried a world of people and goes on living, or better, dreaming that he's on an unknown planet and confined to oblivion like a foreigner without a country, ashamed of taking up someone else's space.

The old man refused to give up his concept of honor which was in direct conflict with his chronic hunger, and his subsistence became more problematical each day. He gave up washing cars to continue in another line of the same business, that of guarding cars at night while their owners raised hell in one of the many whorehouses or gambled or ran after drugs, which, just like in a drugstore, were always available in every variety. He picked up some loose change that he barely managed to get by on, while the moment approached in which time gnaws at the carrion with the tiny mouths of worms. When exhaustion and his aches and pains kept him in, he would spend his few coins on cans of soup and juice because all he had left were two teeth, although it's true that on occasion he would try out a piece of sponge cake. There he was in a hut that looked like a cave, which he had built he didn't know how or with what. When his provisions ran out, he would drag his humanity forth, burdened under the tools of his trade. Poor trade, the mere pretext for not begging for a living.

The ancient Yaqui could barely haul himself around as he worked with the iron will of a post. He worked hard and his gestures were determined, despite how dry his shell was, tanned like a mummy's hide. He squinted his eyes, blackened by a lot of sun and wind, as though crossing an abyss sunk in a very remote time. . . . Often when he walked through those streets, it was as though he pretended to move. He felt himself suspended in space, as though already caught in the cold annals of yellowing pages like a delicate, desiccated butterfly. What wouldn't many princes with idiot faces have given, their stupidity dangling from their aristocratic smiles, for the solemn regality of the destitute Yaqui. By contrast, other individuals of the same dimension who surrounded him basked in his glory like parasites, paying homage with grotesque clownings. Now, there's Kite: fat like a butcher shop cat, with his little dancing eyes surrounded by puffed cheeks, an indifferent flat nose and a shiny forehead overhung with hair that served as trapezes for the lice that engaged in heated acrobatic tournaments. He wore high-waisted pants, heaving with dirt and grime, held up by a single suspender. This "Wanderer" had permission from the gut pusher, who said his name was Mussolini, to help himself to the delicious fried pig drippings that stuck to the bottom of the pan. As much as Kite was an enemy of shoes, his feet were more in the shape of two huge sponge cakes. Once in a blue moon, he would take up the whole sidewalk, striding around the streets with a buzzing hoard of kids behind him. Kite had been the forerunner of the hippie style in clothes and his hair wouldn't dream of knowing a comb. According to his own words, he had an aversion to barbers because they're always arguing with you and stick their noses in other people's affairs. In reality, his phobia dated from when a barber with a wagging tongue had shorn him. He had put him to sleep by massaging his ears and face with padded hands, all the while trading gossip with the other barber who worked alongside him and who also liked to wallow in the valley of snakes. The gossip was so juicy that, in a gesture overcome with emotion, he ran into one of Kite's ears. The poor clown had the momentary sensation of his ear being sliced off. They patched it up, but the aforesaid Kite took better care of himself by uttering the well-known "Go fuck your mother." From that time on, the insistent fellow shed all hygienic habits, and his beard and mustache were one snarl of snot and drivel. They gave him the nickname of Kite because he had the patience to tie to his clothes dozens of tails of every color. When the wind blew, he would take to the streets with a flying tail, with the kids pursuing him shouting and pulling them out one by one, just like they were plucking a game cock. When they were almost on top of him, he would turn around shaking in a rage, shouting with his fists clenched and gritting his teeth: "God damned sons of bitches!" Then he would collapse crying like a little kid who's just lost his ice-cream cone. The hoards of kids would fall silent when they saw him, and Kite would be left alone in a pose as pensive as the picture of a philosopher. Kite was very popular. They would give him food, even if it was only scraps. Sometimes he would pick up a coin. Nevertheless, when he didn't have his public of vandals around, he would settle down with an air of profound desolation, like a tired actor resting between acts.

Among the whole gamut of crazies, Ruperta the madwoman would turn up at all hours digging through the cans full of garbage looking for food. She was tall and thin and always wore a bride's veil made out of whatever she could find. Her mouth was always rimmed with remains of cast-off tasty morsels. Yet, she bore herself with elegance, with all the airs of a ballerina.

The insistent beggars were a whole legion. Some had learned with consummate skill how best to extend their hand and to show their profile, assuming the pained face of saints in a trance on the verge of suffering the flames of the stake or hot tongs ripping at their flesh. The children, trained to the tune of the whip, marked by terror and hunger, begged for help with such persuasive little voices that the stones would turn to jelly just to hear them. From afar they were spied on from their lairs by creatures related in spirit to reptiles awaiting the fruit of the infamous industry.

There were also pimps in abundance, young types who would soon get used to the path of perfidy. And kids who were as boisterous and loud as gaggles of parrots, pestering, washing cars, or simply begging for alms. Some of them were only five years old. These kids came from families that were so large they seemed like onion patches; in the end, only two or three would survive.

In front of the same shop windows, walls of temptation, Loreto looked at himself again, with his smooth skin, his brilliant cheekbones, his spring-like muscles, capable of propelling him wherever he chose. From his elastic youth, there shone the remote gaze of many ages. The man was reviewing his experiences insistently, as though looking for the error that by some accident had altered things, transforming what could have been sublime into something ridiculous and absurd. Some people saw the raggedy old man as ecstatic, even when wandering around. Some came to feel the rare presence that emanated from his forehead.

"GENERAL, SIR, we've lost the waterhole."

"Damn it to hell. Where are the soldiers who were defending it?"

"All dead. They're full of holes and the ground has sucked up all their blood."

"Shoot all the officers so they'll learn to act more like men."

"They were all killed too, sir."

"Shit! Well, we'll have to take the waterhole away from those cowards no matter what it takes. Don't you know there isn't another one on this whole plain for a hundred miles around? Now that's a fact!"

"They are well dug in in front of us."

"Look, at dawn we'll send them fifty men to break their ranks. And while they're busy killing them, we'll come up behind them with two hundred more, and then we'll kick the shiiiiiiit right out of them and take the waterhole back. Are we a bunch of kids or what? Tell Captain Moreno, the one they call Thinker, to go with fifty of his men. . . . "

"But that's just like sentencing them to death."

"Well, now! And just what do you think military strategy is all about, huh? Christ, what a help you are!"

Captain Moreno was a great guy, with heart and brains besides. Once he was in power that bandit of a general turned into a real hound and stole even the air.

The men crawled along in a file, bunched together, looking like crocodiles or something similar. The federal troops over at the waterhole acted distracted and pretended not to see them. But you can bet they saw them! Some of them got thorns in their foreheads because the place was filled with cacti. Damn what a lot of thorns! Their chests, hands, knees, every part that touched the ground ended up covered with needles. God damn! A rattlesnake this long slithered by them hissing, running away. He crawled over Loudmouth Beto's neck. He didn't bite him, but the guy's stone face blanched with fright. With the roar of the firing you couldn't even hear the skulls crushing under the impact of the lead buzzing like bees. The first bodies were used to make a trench. There's not much to tell about Captain Moreno. Whatever the dogs left (damn hounds, they got fat in those days), they cast in a hole a few days later, thrown in along with some federal troops. Only four men were left alive: Tadeo Rosas with a bullet in his shoulder and another in his ankle, Loudmouth Beto with his shank all beaten up and with bad diarrhea, Maldonado the Yaqui with a graze on his head, and Chayo Cuamea without a scratch, despite the fact that he had acted as lead man.

The terrible Yaqui Chayo Cuamea came out of the fray unscathed. The fierceness of his squinty little eyes and the stony gesture had given way to a profoundly melancholic look. The crazy passion of the frantic Indian began to germinate. He sought the thickest part of the brush in

order to contemplate—Her!, his beloved "Slim." Not much time went
by without. . . . What a fearsome Yaqui!

How BEAUTIFUL the cotton fields looked! In the middle of the day
it looked just like a night maiden showing off a dress adorned with
stars. The soft tufts looked lavish, soft, white to the eyes and
touch, spongy and warm like loving hands, laughing like brides on
their wedding day. The earth looked like it had grown old contentedly with gray hair, or that the quartz had transmuted its
flinty consistency into a glow nestled in the endless threads of
the skein.

Ol' Chuco knew a lot about cotton. In the mornings before
beginning to pick, he would stand looking at the tufts covered
with dew. As though his eyes had wheels, he would send them
roaming over the furrows. With a long harvest bag tied to his
waist, dragging along the ground, he cast a look that was half-
rancorous and half-defiant toward the sun; bending over, he began
pulling at the tufts, which little by little started to fill up the hungry maw of the snaking bag.

"You, pal, where are you from, huh? Are you from the States
or are you from south of the border?"

"I don't follow you."

"Hell, what kind of guy are you! I mean, are you from Mexico,
guy?"

"That's right, I'm from Mexico."

"Well, now. Well, now. What do you know about that, the
guy's a real square, sure enough. Right? Is this the first time they
got you to do the picking?"

"Yes, it's the first time for me to pick cotton."

"Well, watch your step, buddy. Look, here's how you strip
these babes."

The babes ol' Chuco was stripping clean were the cotton
bushes. He was a real sight, skinny and on the tiny side, moving
around with an agility so prodigious that it made you think of a
dancer or boxer or some feline who would synchronize his movements by combining his elasticity with tremendous energy. In just
a few seconds he could pluck dozens of cotton tufts, and he did
that hour after hour until he had the incredible quantity of 500
pounds in a single day.

We picked cotton in the fields of Marana, in Arizona. There ol' Chuco was the real champ, but there were others who dogged his heels. We would camp out in the fields themselves, in a hut that provided no protection from the wind, which made it roar like a sick animal. Ol' Chuco went about his business with a certain air of superiority, because, after all, he was the best. Later he found out from others that he had been the star in cutting watermelons in Yuma. In the harvesting of grapes, tomatoes, and eggplants he had also been number one. Ol' Chuco was all of 35 and, according to his own story, he had been in the fields since beginning his career at twelve. Twenty-three years breaking records! If the work in the farm fields had been classified as an Olympic sport, how many gold medals ol' Chuco would have won!

"Listen here, Chuco my friend. All that money you earn picking, do you spend it?"

"Well, not really. You know what? I help my mother out—there's a bunch of us kids. My dad, damn him, kicked the bucket. And as for what's left, I don't give a damn. You know how it is."

"Ah, my friend Chuco, how you like a good blast!"

"You know what, at night we go to the cathouse and dance with the girls. You know who the bastards are, so don't go squealing on me. Put'er there!"

That night we went to the dance. That devil Chuco turned into a dancing demon with a real cute chick. Too bad she already had a lover. He said to Chuco, "Come on, let's fight to the death over her."

"Come on, ol' Chuco, this is a foreign land, don't be a jerk."

"Nah, you know I don't shirk anything. I'm a guy you can count on. Only guys who're married get scared. I'm gonna take care of what my old lady gave birth to."

I carried what ol' Chuco's mother had given birth to on my back. His rival had left him all bruised where he wasn't bleeding. Ol' Chuco continued on his way to California and the grapes, and I stayed behind in Phoenix working construction.

Rolling stones find each other. Ten years later, just by chance, I bumped into Chuco in downtown Los Angeles, Aztlán. Boy, was he a mess! All wrinkled like a raisin, even littler and all bent over. I recognized him because he was making a couple of pedestrians mad. He had squatted down in the middle of the sidewalk

in a fetal position, with a straw hat plunked on his head. Ol'
Chuco was carrying on by himself. He was studying a lighted
panel in front of him that showed a Mexican sleeping sitting
down, his arms around his knees, leaning against a saguaro with
his hat down around his nose and wearing huaraches.

"Damned lazy people!"

"All they think of is booze and sleep!"

"Yes, drink and do something . . . mañana!"

"By the way, has someone called the cops?"

"Ol' Chuco, old friend. How are you?"

Chuco turned around. His aged face was lined with cares. He
smelled like cheap wine.

"You know what, pal? You see that pal there, leaning against
the cactus? These people, pal, say that he's lazy, that he doesn't
work, you know, but that guy's there, really, because he's all beat
and all sad. The fellow was the harvest champion, you know. He's
there because he's all tired out with no one to help him, not even
anyone to respect him, just like a shovel or a worn pick that's not
worth a damn anymore. . . . "

Up close I could see that tears were rolling down ol' Chuco's
cheeks. The others thought he was laughing, but I knew he was
really crying out of deep bitterness.

They braked loudly. Two burly guys made of steel got out,
looking like iguanodons. They picked ol' Chuco up by the neck
like he was an old piece of twine.

"Don't yank. You'll rip my clothes, stupid fucking police!"

They struck him and shoved him around mercilessly. His head
must have cracked from the shove they gave him.

Everybody was happy to see them carting the drunken Chicano off, real decent people, most of them wearing nice ties, the
sign of well-being and good jobs.

"So that pachuco was in a hurry to work."

"He was a real good worker and a real stoic, but the poor guy
is now old. But just take a look at how he can dance up a storm."

"Well, I was never impressed, if you want to know the truth,
although now that you've told me all this, I see him in a different light."

"He's really a great guy, I told you, but he's a pain when he
drinks. By the way, he's been sleeping it off for two hours now."

"Tell me more adventures about ol' Chuco, you can see they really entertain me."

"Well, it happened more or less during the first days I knew ol' Chuco. . . ."

THAT LECHEROUS INGRATE, Tony Baby, could never forget that when the tough business lady was alive, he'd had to work like a fool, hauling hotdogs around on a cart and moving mountains of bread. The old lady had strained her brain to come up with a kind of hotdog that would be in great demand in the area where her business was located. All she had to do was add chile and call them chile dogs, and the clients descended like locusts. What was certain was that her employees found it easier to call them hot chiles. Since her business began to grow, she soon saw the need to hire additional workers, but she was smart enough to get ones so needy she didn't have to pay them much. So, she gave her first job to a wetback. She was delighted with the wetback, paying him four dollars a day and a dozen "dogs." Tino was busy ten hours a day without stopping. He told the old lady that in Mexico whenever he got a job it wasn't even enough to buy peanuts. As the business grew, the old devil got herself more "wets" to the point of hiring them by the dozen. She liked to pretend she was charitable, a real Christian, since thanks to her those Mexicans were eating for the first time in their lives, to the point that their belly buttons would pop, and they knew what it was to wear shoes, even to put a few dollars aside or send them back home so that their families could eat something other than *nopalitos* and *quelites*. Once the voracious old dame began to count off the endless advantages the wetbacks had, hidden away in her hotdog factory, there was no stopping her. How excited she would get, extolling her own humanitarian qualities. At her side, her little Mexicans never had to risk snake bites or coyote bites from having to go to the bathroom squatting down out in the open where there was so much danger. By contrast, her business had indoor bathrooms, toilets gleaming from cleanliness, where it was a pleasure to sit down to read a magazine while you did number one or number two. The soft, fine paper cleaned your noble part without hurting it, not like in those uncivilized places where you have to use pointy rocks or grass that leaves you all broken out with a rash. How many times they would grab a cactus by mistake and, instead of cleaning themselves, end up hurting themselves with sharp spines. Oh! But she, the heart of Christianity, provided them with the benefits of civilization, even against their own habits. According to her, she gave them a job knowing full well that they were wetbacks, out of simple humanity. Who knows how, but when she listed her pious works, her face became more beatific than a sick calf. Full of emotion because she helped starving Mexicans, she even managed to squeeze a few tears out of her dry little eyes. Her contacts with fencemen and wetbacks were going well, until a setback changed things suddenly. She took a dislike to Choro, who was from Imuris in the state of Sonora, just because he knocked over a pot of chile beans. There was a wave of beans, and the old dame, who was just walking through, found herself in up to her ankles. She lost her footing and all of a sudden was splashing in beans up to her eyes. She sneezed violently and dirtied an entire wall with chile beans. That day the crafty businesswoman suffered the pangs of hell. Choro felt that the boss lady hated him and he lost no time in saying out loud what he thought, moreover saying it with less than holy words. Choro was of the opinion that, as a poor man, he could enjoy very simple things, admire the sunsets and sunrises. He could be made happy taking a walk, seeing flowers, seeing kids too, movies, and so many things. But the old gal had no other pleasure aside from contemplating dollar bills, and there is no doubt that Choro said, with a tone not free of a certain sarcasm, that the stupid old fuck only dreamed numbers, refusing to remember that the worms were going to get her just like everyone else. The old dame managed to overhear some of this and got all mad, promising to get even with the starving, thankless, and foul-mouthed greasers. While all of this was going on, all hands were constantly busy making chile dogs, as though feeding a single gut, fat and long and wrapped around the whole world.

This coming and going of hotdogs and enchilada dogs kept Tony Baby hopping and sweating like a pig. He took his outbursts of wickedness out on the cooks, whom he would hug with obscene intentions. The old lady had condemned him to wheeling hotdogs around in an enormous refrigerator in which a whole flock could fit. The refrigerator was kept in a storeroom next to the kitchen where the beautiful doggy meal came from, dripping with tomato and beans and a rare yellowish substance of dubious appearance called mustard. Tony Baby didn't utter a word, but with a single gesture he clearly announced his thoughts. It was a sort of half smile drawn back to his right ear, half burlesque and half disdainful, which betrayed his thoughts: that fuckin' old hag would die just to have the last laugh on the young chicks.

A little bit later, Choro himself, ex-salesman of quesadillas, began to organize a little strike against the old woman. The old dame found out about it, but pretended not to know. She stopped their salary for a month on the pretext that the illuminated sign she put out in front of the store had cost a lot of money, a sign that was none other than the aforementioned sleeping sombreroed Mexican. When the poor wetbacks least expected it, the Migra descended on them and carted them off without even time to pick up their pay. From that time forward, the men dressed in green would arrive sporadically, questioning the illegal workers, jealous guardians of the law. Nevertheless, they never bothered the old cunt of a businesswoman, despite the fact that on the border patrol list there were more than 200 names of Mexicans who had worked at Siesta Chile Dogs. By this time the woman was handling various chile dog and Mexican food stands. Death was not very amused by the financial pirouettes of the queen of the hot chiles. Just as she was deep into counting her finances, Lady Death came by with her scythe and took her heart away. That was when libidinous Tony Baby joined the ranks of the wealthy and set out to enjoy the many sleepless nights and sweat-filled days of the old tightwad. When Tony Baby came to realize that he couldn't seduce the girl of his choice just because he was rich nor could he buy true love, he became a dedicated frequenter of the border whorehouses, lost in the illusion that he was a rapist who couldn't be caught. Frustrated in his marriage to the beautiful and disdainful Talking Statue, Tony Baby reasserted the evil of his character and gave himself over to seeking among the whorehouses the victims of his desire to be a maniac.

OFTEN THE OLD YAQUI would entertain himself going over his memories, lost among the heavy traffic swirling around him. He was amused by the parade of gringos buying souvenirs. Some of them would come out of stores wearing serapes and charro hats,

while others sought out burros to have their pictures taken astride
their backs. Several walked around as family groups with a joking
and naughty tone, the young women showing off beautiful bodies
with short dresses. Everything swirled around him, dark faces,
shouts, laughter, voices speaking Spanish mixed with words in English, the squeal of tires responding to traffic lights ordering sudden stops, and the maddening song of car horns. Nevertheless,
often he would be deep in thought reconstructing memories, as
absorbed as a child trying to fix a watch. Dreamily he wove a
hammock ready to relive the smiles of an agreeable memory. He
fell into a drowsiness that erased the present while at the same
time running the film of a rarified past. As he dozed off, he was
able to see a very skinny and tall man, with a prominent Adam's
apple and half a dozen bees plastered on his face, holding on to
the hand of a little girl nine years old, plus seventy-three days,
wearing a shrill green percale dress. The little girl had on home-
made huaraches. The cut of her dress was just like her grandmother's, long and without decorations. The best story the chubby
little girl had heard was the one about many flavored ice cream.
Right after, two girls and a little old gringo woman filed by. He
couldn't see their faces, but half-asleep, he knew that the first
one, with dark bluish flesh, was wearing yellow pants and the second one red pants, her legs sporting a week's growth of hair. The
last thing he saw was the venerable old woman who was wearing
patterned shorts and, in parallel ancient columns, a bunch of
balls that looked like ankles.

Everyone who passed in front of the Yaqui turned to look at
him in response to his snoring, which sounded like a serenade of
pigs in heat calling for their females.

Among all his little childhood friends, the only one who remained in his memory, with his face radiant with goodness, was
Little Jesús from Bethlehem, the miracle-working Yaqui. From the
beginning Little Jesús had stood out in his mind, but instanta-
neously, without his being able to see him clearly. The light of the
sun did not serve as a backdrop to reflect recollections, and con-
sequently, as soon as the Yaqui closed his eyes with sleep, there he
was, standing out in his faithful memory, the sharp image of the
sublime little Yaqui, Little Jesús of Bethlehem.

HE DREAMED THAT he was standing at the door of Doña Mariquita's shack. Can Little Jesús come out and play with me? Doña María allowed him to play with her beloved son. He remembered very well the child's first miracle. Batepi Buitimea, Churea's little boy, had gotten covered with thorns from a bunch of chollas. Everybody knows, unless they're real stupid, that cholla needles slice into your feet just like they're cheese, and when you try to pull them out, they leave behind the sheath that covers them. If the flesh doesn't rot, the sheath doesn't come out. Not to mention biznaga thorns, these are long, hard as goat horns, and bent at the end into a hook. If they happen to get into your hide, you're done for when you try to remove them. How awful it hurts! Poor Batepito had stood stiff as a pole since the morning had given birth to the star in the midst of the whole range of reds, from pale San Josecito to the purple flower of the ocotillo. He had gone out to get an armload of mesquite wood so his mamá could fix the dry deer meat.

"When you return, my sweet, I'll give you some cooked pitaya, candy and a cup of batarete."

"He stood there for hours at the mercy of a sun that had turned into a stoned chameleon. In order to stifle his tears, his father reminded him: 'Only women cry, son, men don't, they only grin and bear it.' They called Cachipachi Güitimea to doctor him. The medicine man slathered him with well-known remedies that never fail. First of all, they peed on his little foot to loosen the needles. As this didn't work, a little Indian virgin in a state of grace also urinated on him, and another woman who was pregnant. Each time they pulled at the thorns, it stretched his skin and the little fellow was left on the verge of tears. Finally, they plastered his foot with fresh cow dung. Nothing worked. The medicine man explained: 'Well, just leave it that way, and when the bubble of puss forms, the thorn'll come out and the pain will stop.' That's when Chuyito arrived. He barely touched him, and so long, needles. The boy began to run he was so happy. Goodbye thorns and pain. So long, best wishes, and don't come back. Just like nothing had happened.

By the skin of his teeth, Little Jesús managed to be born in Bethlehem. They were in the mountains in Bacatete because the bloody dictator Díaz had given orders to make mincemeat of the lot of them. The bastard Torres was driving them, with orders not to mess around.

*They reached Bethlehem on the back of a burro. Poor Don Pepe
was all upset. The child was born almost immediately. Doña Mariquita, so brave and long-suffering, smiled with the sky in her arms. It
was a party full of good cheer. They say that he would touch the nopals
yellow with age and they would turn green. What plant did not flower
at his passing and what a singing of birds and frogs. No musical element
could refrain from saturating the air in his presence with the gentlest of
harmonies. They say that he was one of those beings who possess many
voices. There are those who heard him speak Nahuatl and Mayan at the
same time, his mother tongue being Yaqui. He spoke Spanish like Cer-
vantes himself. They also heard him speak in very mysterious lan-
guages, so strange that they did not seem to belong to the continent,
more like very ancient tongues. They say that up close he looked like he
walked like any other person, but that from a distance he seemed to be
floating. The sky has sidewalks for him.*

YOU HAVE NO IDEA, no sir! How can you possibly know? You can't
even imagine the wear and tear on a poor devil in order for him
to get to be a champion, picking cotton or whatever else. It's
enough to say that they risk their lives. Yes, yes, don't smile at
me, just believe me. They have to break their backs, and not just
that, their balls too. In those days when ol' Chuco got his crown,
there was a wetback called Pelele who kept close to him, dogging
his footsteps. That Pelele seemed to have a deer inside him, and
there was no one lighter on his feet. He was a bit bad tempered,
and if you said something to him while he was busy, he told you to
stop bugging him. There was also a long-legged black man who
hung around Chuco, creeping along like a panther. That bugger
would work his hands and laugh at the same time, like he had
cats tickling his ribs. But despite everything, they were all real
good, no denying it, and ol' Chuco hitched up with him. Yet, just
the same, on the days they competed, he acted just like a guerrilla, coming back in the afternoons all full of scratches and with
a long face showing utter exhaustion. The shells that protect the
tufts of cotton are hard and sharp, and they claw at the skin. He
would become feverish at night as a result of the tremendous effort
he had made, and he would fall into a deep sleep. How he snored!
From time to time, he would sit up raving who knows what, but
before the sun was up, there he'd be with his hands flying. They

proclaimed him champion because he picked 612 pounds in a single day. Can you imagine what it is to pick 612 pounds? No! How
can you have any idea? Like every good champion, he ended up
all done in, extenuated by the barbarous workout he had given
himself. His eyes were glassy for days, and he suffered fevers. To
celebrate his triumph, he got roaring drunk. The prize he received
for his deed was only the satisfaction of knowing he was the best.
Then he would show up at work and see out of the corner of his
eye someone looking at him with admiration, because there was
no question he felt himself to be a real Olympic prizewinner. He
even got to the point of thinking he provoked envy in those
around him, because there must be some reason why Pelele looked
at him mockingly. Pelele said that Chuco had won by mixing
rocks, clumps of dirt, and some unopened pods in with the cotton. When the weight man himself explained to Pelele that no,
Chuco had won good and clean, Pelele argued that ol' Chuco had
peed on the fiber to make it weigh more. The black, for his part,
said nothing, but he didn't smile at Chuco either. He would greet
him with a "Hello, champ!" and a burst of laughter full of bitterness. The true prize for ol' Chuco, his crown, was to hear the
whispers of the majority of his comrades and even his bosses, who
affirmed with emphasis: that Chuquito may be small in body, but
his spirit's got real balls! Others, less free with words, would only
comment: Chuco's sure got balls! Right? Harry, one of the gringo
owners of the field, the one who chewed tobacco as though he
were eating sugarcane, said as he spat a gob of chocolate-colored
tobacco on a rock, "A few more like this one and we wouldn't
have to invent machines!"

DESPITE THE SHOVELFULS of money they continued to put away and
the fear the Dávalos de Cocuch inspired, they were not fully accepted into the cream of high society. The man had learned more
or less how to express himself, but in many ways you could still see
what a hick he was. Everyone who has had a lot to do with horses
acquires certain habits and poses common to the animals—the
way you stand, the way you pick up sounds, your way of walking,
and an endless array of horsey details. You could see very clearly
that Don Mario de Cocuch's natural hinges had been altered. The
spread of his legs had grown wide enough to allow him to sleep

standing up. When he sneezed, his lips would vibrate with a sort
of loose and trembly sound. When he was with fancy people, early
in the morning, Mr. Cocuch's head would hang loosely and he
would doze with his eyes slightly closed. His conversation was reduced to barely moving his head and accompanying the movement with an affirmative rumble. He would then seem surrounded
by a swarm of mosquitoes. When he began to snore, Mrs. Cocuch
would embrace him feigning passion and pinch him on his flanks.
Without any comment and out of his own free will he had dis-
tanced himself from the high circles since the occasion when he
had gone overboard with the scotch at a special celebration. They
were particularly excited to attend a gathering of rich people honoring a German industrialist descended from kings. The German
was tall with a martial bearing and studied gestures like a movie
star. Don Mario committed an indiscretion, perhaps the result of
the German's voice, who was in reality cordial, even if he
sounded angry. What happened is that Mr. Cocuch patted him in
a friendly way, and under the sway of the drinks, told him with a
knowing smile: "Hell, man! You guys went just a bit too far there
with the Jews."

Mrs. Cocuch was the one who had natural elegance, but her
previous occupation as a full-time whore was betrayed in her habit
of chewing gum. Even though she was aware of how ridiculous it
was, the desire to chew got to be so great that she couldn't resist
it. She tried to hide it by chewing slowly, until she would have to
go into the bathroom for a few minutes to chomp on it furiously in
order to calm her nerves. She cuckolded her husband whenever
political or economic circumstances required it. She alarmed her
women friends when, busy trading secrets under the influence of
champagne and wine, she confessed to them that she was wild
over *nopalitos con chile* and affirmed that she would allow herself to
be poisoned by toasted maguey worms, as was the custom in the
capital. It didn't take long for the Cocuches to be ridiculed by
every callus-coated tongue-wagger in town. They were called everything in the book: nouveaux riches, uncouth, vulgar, ignorant,
parvenus; he was called a dirty satyr and she a whore. Old man
Cocuch, in turn, exploded in fetid terms, ticking off a gangrenous
list of society's peccadilloes. Bitterness required him to paint them
as queers and tramps, and in order to wound his detractors even
more, he affirmed that the majority of the young daughters of the

wealthy were not virgins because they no longer walked like fillies. Thus, the Dávalos de Cocuch, in order to separate themselves, became dedicated to touring the somber landscapes of misery, dreaming for other days, which they would not communicate to each other for anything in the world.

"HEY, GUY, do you think the work'll be over by summer? Nah, Chaleco! You know what, pal? With the money I've saved, I'm going to get hitched with a real cool chick."

"I sweat like it's poison coming out, and my shirt and pants rot real fast. Where does so much sweat come from, huh?"

"I saw this dame over at the cathouse, and this guy sure wowed her. Hey, let's grab a cup'a coffee."

"Naw, I don't dig coffee."

"Then let's eat. And you know what that chick said to me?"

"Cut the shit, kid, or you're going to get into trouble."

"I can't hack the winter, brother. I sure don't like it, with the frost you end up like an old rooster, buddy. You know, right? Are you gonna go do lettuce in Wilcox?"

"Well, that chick was looking at me and smiling. She sure thought I was cool. Let's go! Let's dance, come on. I'll be right back, fellows. I'm gonna go weigh this cotton and pick up my pay."

"Hey, to pay for the beer, right?"

"Sure."

"That guy's real drunk."

"Hah, buddy, that guy works for his parents. If he's got any money left over, he'll put up, like everybody else."

"That's great, pal. I don't have a mother. She died last year. I'd say to her: Calm down, little momma, I'll get you one of those houses like the gringos got, with a nice car, the whole bit. But you work your butt off, and no matter what, it always turns out the same way. You know what I mean."

"Here comes that guy. He's sure off his rocker."

"Yeh, no question about it."

"What does the old geezer who does the weighing have to say, guy? He didn't catch on you had rocks in your bag of cotton?"

"Nah, the guy's nuts. He gets all upset because of the green leaves, and he didn't catch on about the other load."

"He doesn't give you a break. How come Chicanos who work as foremen are worse than the bosses themselves?"

"Because the bastards're sellouts. It's worse in construction, pal. They try to do you in in just one day. These guys are real nuts and before you know it, they're talking to you in English."

"If I can save up a hundred bucks, I'm gonna go make time with that chick."

"This guy's all hot for the chick."

"Didn't you say she's treating you like a dog?"

"Like I was saying, I danced with her, cheek to cheek. See? She says she liked me from the moment she set eyes on me, but us guys who work back and forth in the fields on both sides are bad news."

"We all have to pay for a few bad ones, guy. Bunch of bastards that go from one crop to the next. Shit! They go after the chicks and then just leave them hot and hungry. You know what? These guys're something like professional fuckers, you know?"

"Yuma doesn't bother me, pal, even with all the heat that toasts you like a peanut. But the frost really stops up the pipes in my chest. A real drag. In the winter I go work in the canneries."

"Heh, Chuco! It's your turn to cook. Ok?"

"Shit! I cooked this morning. It's ol' Fairo's turn."

"Come on! I'll give you doughnuts and coffee with milk. That's real great!"

"Get out of here with your doughnuts, pal, let this guy put up the beans."

"You know what, good buddies? Better cut the gab and get to work. If we spend too much time talking, we won't earn a cent."

"You said it!"

"Get going!"

IN THAT VERY STRANGE frontier town, in appearances so happy but deep down so tragic, of all those who floated without moorings, the Indian Loreto was pained to see so many wetbacks teeming around with their faces of hunger, waiting to cross over into Gringoland. Like every peasant who reaches the city, they were timid in their behavior. They revealed so much desolation and appeared to be so hunger-stricken that they looked like a defeated army under Zapata, sentenced to look for food for their families in exile. Despite the terrible drama of their lives, they possessed the noble attitude of those who have caressed the earth like a mother. They had won the Revolution, only to be paid with hunger and fraud. During the periods of electoral farces, they were carted about in cattle trucks as though they were cows.

The paved roads stretched out across the country like fish-bones. The dusty old towns got a breather. The inhabitants sensed other fates. Hunger, the fuel of illusions, would no longer crash into the encircling hills, nor would it vanish in the immense esplanades that keep alive the feudal institutions, with the rust of the centuries clinging to their iron jaws. It is a desperate hunger which, jumping out of the chronicles, has taken to the highways leading north. These squalid men are not out to seek gold, traveling night and day. They are borne along by the vital demand of proteins. Hundreds of thousands cross the border with the U.S., and along the way their voices sow a sort of creeping vine of lamentation, like a rosary of blasphemy, like a ladder of questions without answers, voices born of the bowels of the earth. Men who have inhabited space, glued to the earth like the cacti and the corn, shoved along by the vital imperative of food, they all flow out onto the highways, combing the mountains with their bleeding footsteps. They are all on their way to the U.S. as though it were a Mecca for the hungry. Many die beneath the bridges, in washes or alongside the road, just like cattle or wild animals. They come to town like bandits at night and sleep on the outskirts. The townspeople protect their chickens and pigs against the voracity of the hungry passing through, who humiliate themselves by knocking on a door and asking for food, "because it's been days since I've had a mouthful." They file past the edge of the fields belonging to the heirs of the revolutionary leaders. They are on their way to the U.S. to seek food desperately. They are hungry, their children are hungry, their women are hungry, with a hunger of the ages, a rabid hunger, a hunger that aches beyond their own guts. . . . Back to their mother's womb! A hunger for a table with tortillas, with beans. The hunger to eat meat! Cheese! A hunger not to see their children with sunken eyes, nor the skeletal women with tits like dry wells. The hunger to eat something! So their guts will not howl like tortured dogs. Ah! That cry of hunger so blindingly acute, a hunger that digs graves, like a gravedigger who will never give up. Day after day of crossing the territory in order to cross the river or to jump the fence, coming finally to destroy their souls for a few dollars they exchange for sausage, bread, beans. The Migra! The border patrol arresting wetbacks, mistreating them, jailing them, because they break the law by working in an alien land. Ah! The wetbacks break the law by working in the U.S., but those who give jobs to the wetbacks do not. They have the freedom to employ them and to pay them whatever they want. They are not mistreated, fined, or jailed, as though they had a license to enslave. Slaves in an alien land, forgotten and banned in their own. Along those highways, eternal calvaries, many will survive their agony of thirst and hunger, watching the cars speed by in another time zone, only accidentally sharing the same space. Some drivers have seen them out of the corner of their eyes, but they have gone by indifferently because they know that, in the end, they are nothing other than shadows, phantoms, nonexistent beings.

Damn fever! It was making his brains boil all over again. The fevers left him dried out, but they had the effect on him of purging the voices of the invaders. Like bats, the bitter, foulmouthed words hung from his brain, the weeping and wailing of anguished beings. His head would heat up to the point of making his eyes bulge, as if they were corks for bottles of that fine liqueur the color of piss. And then the words would spill forth like souls charged by the wild-haired devil, like damned bloodsucking animals when they flee to their lairs muttering their rabid intentions. Things of beings in pain. Among all the foreign voices, clearly, those of the Indian Loreto himself, because he too was navigating like the most unfortunate in the bloody sea of suffering.

The person shot was a little kid who still had milk on his lips. With the coup de grace it looked like they had fastened a red bow on his forehead.

We come from every corner of the country, and we want to cross the border. Our families wait, dying of hunger. On foot, friend, following the highways. Yes, yes, many are left along the highway. No longer with any strength, you pick up any sickness whatsoever and are left behind stuck in the ground. The ground. How could the earth sustain us; they gave us the worst land, without water. You've got to believe me when I tell you that there even the hares carry a canteen around their necks, just imagine that. No, man, not even the least little bit. The brats of the Revolution and those with pull are the top dogs. And then we were set on by coyotes, friend, the ones who wear bow ties, talk about credits, politics, all that shit. Nothing but crap! But, see, you do it for the kids, this going and begging for beans from the damn gringos. Ay, friend! How hard it is to cross this desert on foot, you've got to turn into a cat, that's all I can say. We left eight lives behind there, pal, one after another, and we arrived with the only one left to us. Really nice cars would pass us along the highway. No, friend, no way they would stop. In the first place, they're afraid to see us in such dire straits, and moreover, they see us everyday, so many of us, that they no longer take pity on us, as though they were from one world and we from another. In the middle of our tribulation, friend, a kid died from thirst on us, with no one to give him a drop of water, poor fellow, and there he was making verses. You end up feeling such a stabbing pain. . . . I couldn't get it into my head, friend, how that youth was dying of thirst and saying such beautiful things, with his eyes as blue as lagoons of fresh water. And just as I'm telling you, as dried up as he was, he died with his face wet. Tears were coming from who knows where. . . . I can't even remember his name . . . hold on. . . . I be-lieve it was Lorenzo. . . . Yes, sir, we have more or less of an idea where we will pass. Look, friend, they are going to pay two hundred dollars and lead us along a road that passes behind San Isidro's lookout post. And we'll just have to pay our dues according to how the work goes. Shut your mouth, friend, they'll even collect from us there, be-cause it's just as I'm telling you, everybody's after us like vultures in order to eat us alive. . . .

Look, pal, just listen to me, don't be an ass. I was young like you, then. And in the wink of an eye, here I am, dried out like a harvest bug in winter. Just look at this face and these hands, they're wrinkled like the accordion of a blind street musician, but, ah friend, how they caressed them! I look after cars, see, and I also wash them. They pay me any old thing; I'm a refined man and I don't want anybody to give me a thing just to get by. Now I make six bits. Sometimes I make something, other times, not a dime, nothing. . . .

Now, brother, we're both Chicanos, right? Home? We live over here on this side. Don't you see, guy, the gringos took all this land away from the Chicanos. And now you see them working in the fields and all over the place, pal. It's tough going. School? Shit, pal! Oh, sure, they'll cart you off to fight in the war, and they're quick to kick the shit out of you. They won't give us rest periods because we're dark, see. Well,

you know how it is, so they can have people work free for them. In
school, they beat the hell out of you if you speak Chicano, you know.
What's a guy to do? Over here you're nothing but poor Chicanos and
over there they kick your ass. People'd better wise up, because if they
don't give us what's ours and start respecting us, we're gonna kick their
asses and the whole fucking bit. Look keen and your dough's green.
Take care of yourself, buddy, and I'll be seeing you around.

What a way to get by, for Christ's sake. Shit, you don't work, you
don't eat!

I'll wash your car, mister. Fifty cents, and I'll take care of it until
you get back. Okay, boss?

Yes, friend, I was a hurricane, and now I'm nothing but a bunch of
dry leaves the wind whirls through the mud.

Look, sir, I'm going to talk to you because you're old and I see you
like a father, and also because I'd like to have someone to unburden my
woes on. There's a lot of them, yes, sir, about four thousand by the last
count.

THE VOICES aborted by the streets, the sordid back alleys and
slums. So many voices wounded with human suffering were fleeing
the bitter planet to seek refuge in the caverns of the vast worlds of
the minds of sensitive individuals. Thus, the laments reached the
Yaqui Loreto, telling him common stories that move no one, no
matter how tragic they are, because they are repeated day in and
day out to a ferocious hammer beat that never ceases. Also the
voices of the whores, with their chilling suffering. But not those of
the opulent matrons that pursue their pleasure, but those of defenseless girls who cry for their father and mother, believing themselves lost in a horrible nightmare.

"YOUR HORSE, MARIO, is skinny but full of stamina. I assure you
that when they get tired in the vastness of these deserts, our
horses, as fat as they are, will be birdseed to the vultures."

"I'm not complaining, sir, 'to serve my country no matter what
the suffering' is my motto."

"Hey, man! How fine. I'll get a saddle and harness for you as
soon as we smash that madman Chayo's Indians. Imagine, taking up
arms against the government, alleging injustices, the enslavement
of Indians, bah!, little shit of a colonel. What do you think?"

"Peace and accord prevail throughout our sacred fatherland, and equality exists for every citizen. Colonel Chayo Cuamea is a rebel with strange ideas who deserves to be put down without compunction for the benefit of future generations."

"Hey, you're great. After this campaign, I'm going to recommend your promotion. You're full of pluck."

"Thank you, Captain, but there's one thing that bothers me. . . . "

"You're a humanitarian, and you're bothered by what we're going to have to do to the Yaqui Cuamea's people."

"No, sir, what bothers me is . . . this backbone."

"You've probably wrecked a vertebra."

"No, sir, I'm bothered by the backbone . . . of the horse."

"Ah, for Christ's sake, man! Look, as soon as we get to the bin, pick me out some tender ears of corn, roast them good and golden. I also want to grab me another plump hen, the fattest you can find. Fix it on the coals with chile peppers. Grab all the grease you can and then spread it all over the horse's backbone. You'll see how it gets better right away."

"Yes, sir, just as you say."

"And don't forget to take the breast to General Barroso. You can have the pope's nose."

"Ah, sir, don't even mention it to me, I don't like chicken."

"Colonel Chayo Cuamea . . . when we hang him, he'll dance our tune, by devil!"

"How MUCH MORE, pal, to the border? I'm giving out quicker than my feet are moving. This damn road is the very devil's back. Ah, pal! I've about had it."

"Shut up and keep moving. Don't be a fool, we're almost there. Have heart, we're almost to Mexicali. From there, we'll go on to Tijuana and then to the San Joaquín Valley or, at worst, we'll stay in the Imperial Valley."

"Look, pal, just look at my shoes. The soles are full of holes. The ground I'm walking on burns like a frying pan, and all I can see are lagoons everywhere, and my eyes hurt like they are boiling. Even my soul, pal, feels like it's being toasted."

"Act like you've got balls like a man, damn it. All I need is for you to start whining like a pregnant old lady. Shit!"

"No, pal, I can't go any farther, you're on your own now. Just don't tell anyone I crapped out, because God knows good and well that no one can go on with his feet a mass of bleeding sores."

"No, kid, what makes you think I can leave you here like this? You're my pal and I'll take care of you. If things get worse, they'll get worse for both of us together. Come on, hang in there and you'll see how we'll make it bit by bit."

"Just look at how my feet are bleeding. Hell, how can they bleed, they're nothing but scabs and clots! I don't have any strength left, pal, my hunger goes back before I was born, not to mention I'm thirsty enough to drink seas of water!"

"Well, what do you think, you bastard, that I've just come from a luxury hotel or that I've been sitting around swilling iced drinks? Huh? Get to your feet! I'll help you. We've got to get there at any price."

"No, pal, it's no use. We're not worth the bother. Why do they make fun of someone who's hungry? No! Let me die just like I was an old dog, because that's all we are. Look at the flames the sun's giving off. How the flames jump up from the ground, blowing and boring into the soul. Go on, leave me behind!"

"Look how screwed up you are! Have you forgotten you left your father dying without any medicine? Come on, man! And your kids and old lady are starving to death, eating dirt and weeds. Who's going to help them if you don't? Come on, tell me. No one is, no one. No one's going to suffer for them."

"Yes, yes, you're right. Come on, let's get going over the border to the U.S.! Aaay! It's okay now, I can make it. You can earn real money over there. Right, pal? Not just enough for the family to eat, but I can also buy them shoes. Aaaah. . . . And clothes too, right? Listen, you don't look so hot yourself."

"I'm sure you'll make it, but death's going to get me."

"If things go well for us, maybe we can even send the kids to school. Don't you think?"

"Well, that's the way things are, you've got to keep fighting, even if they kick your teeth in."

"Aren't your feet a mess?"

"Well, not as bad as yours, but my balls are bleeding red. My bladder's drier and more wrinkled than these sand dunes. Shit! I feel like I've got burning coals inside me."

"I'm sorry, brother."

"It's just that it's your first time. The first time I was also a mess, but a real swell guy gave me a hand. If some day a poor bastard needs your help, don't just leave him. That's the way it's got to be. Right?

"You're right."

"Look over there, man! Put your hands over your eyes, like a visor, so you can see. Can you see?"

"Something like a lot of dust, like smoke . . . , like. . . . "

"That's San Luis Río Colorado over there."

"We made! We made it! We really made it, brother . . . , hurray! . . . "

"Thank God."

"The first money I earn I'll send a little bit to them and then I'll buy myself some shoes with what's left, sweet mother."

"Come on, pal, don't give up. Don't fall on me again, man."

"The sand doesn't hurt as much now. It just feels hot . . . , we're almost there. Right? I'd also like to buy myself some socks, the kind that're soft. Aaaah, sweet Jesus."

"Come on, don't give out on me, take heart. I can't hear you. Here, let me get closer to you. What are you trying to say? Gerardo? Who's Gerardo? Ah! I'll ask him to look after your family, yes, will. Dear Lord, you're gone now, pal."

WHEN WE PASSED THEM, beyond Sonoita, he had his arm around the shoulders of his companion, holding him like a dead weight. He was barely touching the ground. They had the tender little faces of children, their hair was like dead grass, and their eyes and lips were like dry waterholes. They stank to high heaven like dogs that've been dead three days.

"Why don't you give them a ride? Poor devils."

"And what if they're dangerous and beat us up, which often happens? No, it's their problem."

"Well, today your turn, tomorrow mine."

"Bah! The problem is that you're a born sentimentalist. Be realistic. When we get to San Luis, we'll pick up something good and cold."

"I see them coming through here, friend. Want a smoke? Just like ants, my friend, they stream through all day long. No friend, there's no way it's going to rain. The animals are pawing the bare ground. So, they're off to work in Gringoland. They come by in groups of two, three, even five. I'm not kidding you, every now and then someone who's lost. Climb down, friend, and while the animal's resting we can grab some coffee. Loosen his cinch. No sir, fellow, you don't mess around with this heat. It's not just eggs you can fry on the rocks. If you're not careful, it'll even cook your balls. Listen, pal, those guys're just like orphans, just look at them, it's like they were foreigners in their own land."

WHO KNOWS how many fallen women there are. From everywhere. Don't you believe it, it's not so much out of shame. Well, yes, some because they like it, but the majority, no. No, after all. Poverty and human injustice. All of us were deceived as young girls. Well, you're born real poor and you grow up seeing things and wanting things. Not a prince exactly. A healthy, industrious young man, he doesn't even have to be attractive, just as long as he supports and respects you. From the time you're a young woman you want a home, maybe modest but at least clean. Well, look, we were all brought here by deceit, just to exploit us like animals. All that business about the long-suffering and self-sacrificing woman, the soldier's trusty helpmate, Mother's Day. Forget it, it's all a bunch of baloney. Millions of dollars, and all we get is syphilis and gonorrhea. Only enough to dress and feed us, depending on our figure and how pretty each one of us is. No, forget it, there's no chance to save anything. They're on top, sure. . . . We get here on top of bureaucrats, real important, not to mention all the ones who take payoffs. They all get fucked up, just like I did. Excuse my language, but they're nothing but criminals.

I lived down south in a small town, and one day a woman showed up, very friendly, very kind, selling clothes. She had her son with her, a well-behaved fellow, a darling kid. They came in a nice car, and the woman became friends with my family.

My parents said, "What nice people Doña Reginalda and her son are. They're so natural, what with all they have, and they're not stuck up at all. Just the opposite, they're very sweet." The woman began to carry on about me, how pretty I was, what a sweetheart, her daughter-in-law, which only makes you start getting grand ideas. But then I started thinking that the kid could be my good luck ticket. The woman offered to take me to the border, help me get a job, saying that I had made a good impression on her. Well, those of us born poor'll believe *anything. My parents gave me their blessing, and here I am. The lady went to Mexico City to fulfill a vow to the Virgin of Guadalupe at the basilica, and she left the place crying with emotion. They showed their claws back on the road. Before getting here, the young man had already taken advantage of me. He wasn't even the woman's son, but a vile criminal. The woman? Forget it, don't even mention her to me. When we got here she sold me like I was a chicken, and that pair of thugs split the money. The only thing the old bitch said to me was that I should dump my stupid ideas and get to work earning money. I bawled for a few days, but what can you expect, my dear sir; you're nothing but garbage they dump in a swollen river to be carried off by the dirty waters.*

All old women have the same complaint, some because they starve to death and others because they get killed.

Pay attention to what I'm saying, friend, and take a good look at yourself in this mirror. Life is like a bird who can't control its wings, thrashing around in an unfamiliar setting. When you least expect it, it gets you with its beak, and the dust it raises is carried off by the water or the wind. After a little while, they don't even remember having seen you.

LORETO, WITH HIS BITTER old man's vision of someone who knows the mechanisms of life, looked at everything without any sign of surprise. He sensed that he inhabited a suppurating gray dimension of gangrenous wounds. His world was dark, closed to the light of happiness. All the poor unfortunates who were dying of hunger constituted a precise framework for the enjoyment of human mercilessness, fittingly contrasted with the enormous privileges of wealth. While they, the dirt poor, cried out from the depths of their oblivion, others, bursting with health, amused themselves with sports and the bounties of art. Because they, the weak, were always half-naked and dirty, others, elegant, wallowed in luxury. Because wine and tidbits gave pleasure to a humanity that was surfeited, perverted in its egoism, the humiliated, in the cruelest of contrasts, were able to offer their painful vision so that the others could feel themselves to be the chosen. Life had fallen into this deplorable game, and their heirs took turns: some today and others tomorrow made happiness possible with a background in a gray dimension where malnourished children raised their thin cry in a single chorus like a thread that snaps; a dimension of pus, parasites, and tears.

There the dawn was unknown, except in the drawings of school children, who painted it with an open-faced sun surrounded by a chameleon crown, while the tent of clouds and smoke served as a sort of dirty sheet through which a few blind stars could be half seen like ashen coals.

THEY HAD WALKED the entire night before, and they continued forward ready to rest under the first shade . . . only their tired shadows dragging themselves along covered with the burning sand. Their eyes caught on the distance, hanging from some phantom of the forest or on one of the enchanting lakes that the sand simulated. Just plunge in their scorched bodies which longed to live, shouting "Water!" with every pore of their burning skin, wounded by dust and the sun. Their lips seemed to be pieces of coal dusted with ashes. The water was all gone. . . . Was the water all gone? It's all gone! Almost now . . . Just a little more . . . A little bit more. The infernal star went down, leaving alive the promises of returning more furiously. The men saw the absence of the celestial enemy like a truce. When the night caressed them with the tenderness of a black mother, they directed their eyes heavenward in prayer. They saw that the nocturnal backdrops were so old and deteriorated that an infinity of eyes shone watery through the holes in the dark cloth.

Lorenzo sat down on top of a dune. He contemplated the desert which spilled over the horizon. Goddess of naked creation, asleep in a dream of taut breasts awaiting the gluttony of roots that never arrive. . . . The anteroom of unexplored seas where nostalgic sirens die. A region populated by the voices of the dead, a city of the souls, ethereal presences chanting their canticles in secret dimensions. A mystery of absolute solitude. My God! The sky lighted by white doves that tremble with love. Luminous messengers of the soul.

The vegetable fields, the rocks, and the hillsides beaded with scraggly saguaros had been left behind, clumps of rocks like arsenals of gigantic warriors. Rivers without life that only know the dirty water of an occasional downpour, but retain the sound of the worn-out springs of bygone days. The presence of the water that travels from the sinister depths of the wells to the clumsy avidness of the pilgrim is left behind. Even farther behind remains the jungle with its sinful orgy of humid colors and the babble of illiterate parrots speaking in the dialect of the torrents, flying in bunches of springtime leaf storms. The towns were left behind, and in a lost corner of the world, their families waited, set upon by sieges of hunger. Farther ahead they would seek another jungle clotted with green leaves covered with dollar signs. . . . Now they trod the desert.

Lorenzo stood up to behold the desert. His poet's heart, anxious for the mystery that cannot be attained, contemplated on the barren plain the evidence that is hidden from our consciousness. Yet it sets itself down deeply, so deeply that only the powers of the soul sense it.

He saw the moon so close, so intimately nearby, that he opened his arms to caress it. He shouted at it impelled by a burning emotion: flickering light, alive, radiant—dead! Mercury for the deceived, a disk of howling, scales, rings, strands of sand hair. Whirl, deceitful moon, whirl! Symphony of symbols, whirl in your immense coffin!

They camped that night when they had no more footsteps left. Their feet swollen, their legs pink, their heads like a tank on the verge of boiling, and their testicles burning like a pair of hot coals. They felt they had reached the anteroom of something grandiose. Only silence and sand in an enormous solitude where there are no souls that pray. Along those mountains of sand, rudely disguised like harvested wheat: not even those bushes that cling like moles to the dried-out land could be seen in their creeping dispersion. Only a solitude and a vast surface wrinkled like the skin of a thousand-year-old lady who lies dead. They felt themselves overcome, humiliated in the face of a desert tolerating nothing. Nothing! Pedrito Sotolín prayed on his knees, with his hands joined together. But old man Ramagacha whispered to him: "Here the voices travel far because no one holds them back." Ramagacha, the old peasant with skin like the dusty soil, contemplated the distances with a sweet smile, "But there is no water here." Like a soap bubble the dreamy look on his face would pop, a face that knew how to erase all gestures. Perhaps it was off in some other land where the words withered. Ramagacha was one of

those individuals born looking like they're eighty years old. No
one could've guessed his age, and in fact he was around sixty years
old, not one of those run-of-the-mill ages that say "Only yesterday
it was New Year's Day." Ramagacha's years had been very long,
and the march of the hours continued to be slow, as slow as the
gait of a camel entering the plains of sand with his humps dry.
Ramagacha, with all his years on his back, was on his way to the
United States to earn dollars so he could support his two grand-
children, the only ones left of an entire genealogy swallowed up by
poverty. He trudged along obsessed with saving their lives with
protein, as though the continuity of his entire history were at
stake in the matter. He had joined the group when they met by
chance, joining forces to share their poverty. They came from the
south, in the opposite direction from their forebears, in a pilgrimage without priests or prophets, dragging along a history without
any merit for the one telling it, ordinary and repetitive in its tragedy. Nevertheless an episode from Ramagacha's life, a long time
after it happened, served as a reference point for a man who con-
versed with the group, slapping at the angry horseflies who sowed
welts and rashes by the hundreds on the sweaty skins.

They were holding a wake over a man who had died of heat-
stroke. They chatted animatedly about the victims of sunstroke. *If
you guys think it's hot here in May, you should go see what it's like in
the Imperial Valley, up there where the gringos are. Holy hell! That was
when I was a wetback. We were picking cantaloupes, and all of us were
pure Mexicans. When you pick cantaloupes, pal, you tie on a sack big
enough to hold a man, with straps that go over your shoulder and under
your arm, and then you throw it over your back so you can toss the
cantaloupes inside. It starts to pull on your neck as it gets full, pal, and
then you have to climb up a plank on a truck that's moving by real
slow. That's no kid stuff. If you'd like to know what the heat's like over
there in Yuma, well, you know, just go climb into an oven where they're
baking bread. The only difference is that they take the bread out after a
little bit, but there you've got to take it the whole day, and if you're not
careful even at night, because you can't tell me that the ashes aren't
dangerous too. Well, like I was saying. But give me a cigarette first so
I can go on. There was a poor old devil among the guys all fired up to
work like hell, just like a kid, so they wouldn't fire him, see? Poor
fellow! He collapsed in a heap, just like a sack of bones. We couldn't*

*even pry his hands open. . . . By the time they got him water he was
gasping. Of course he had a hip name, called himself Ramagacha, Bent
Branch. These guys get the weirdest ideas. And for what? I came back
a real mess, worse off than when I went. No, really, no doubt about it,
it was one of the worst sunstrokes ever. Don't tell me!*

VATE WAS THE ONE who always remembered Lorenzo Linares. And
why shouldn't he remember him, since they were such good
friends, and, moreover, it was like they had been born together!
Both of them were given to writing verses. Pedrito Sotolín was
also part of the same group traveling north. Of course it was a
different business that was carrying him to the border. Pedrito
would say as a joke, "What a gang of funny guys. There are now
more poets than there are locusts." Lorenzo was always laughing
happily, it came naturally to him. Not Vate. He was sad, always
veiled by a sadness that came from deep within him. But when he
spoke of the landscape, he sounded like a canary singing a serenade to the Creator. Don Ramagacha, who was made from the
clay of the land, looked like a plow breaking up the clods in the
cornfields even when he laughed. Doubled over with laughter,
Lorenzo told about the day his papá found him writing poetry and
said to him, "Well, truth is, the burro must have kicked you or
you've got a screw loose." Lorenzo shouldn't have died on the
road; the fact is their water ran out, but nevertheless the rest
made it to San Luis Río Colorado. Lorenzo got delayed and didn't
sleep the whole night. He was entranced by seeing that immensity
of wavy sand. And what is more, the moon was shining like a real
beauty! And that man who had never looked on the desert stared
and stared, and he even started to believe that he was at the bottom of an enchanted sea.

"Rest," Vate told him, and he answered:

"Look! This is what a canvas is to an artist, what a blank page
is to God, and what all the colors that would fit in this languid
immenseness are for the poet."

He ran around like a child, climbing the dunes and rolling off
them. His wounded feet were not hurt by the sand.

"Vate, doesn't the silence say anything to you?"

"We need what little energy we have left so much that I don't
want to awaken emotions, but . . . I see it, the moon and the

desert. The moon is a desert, and the desert is also a moon. Now I understand why the poet loves the moon, because the moon is like poetry: both shine with the light of others. As long as there's no one to read the verses, they're probably dead. If someone contemplates poetry with a radiant soul, it will shine with life just like that moon, animated by a luminous star. That's why you've fallen in love with the desert, Lorenzo. It's like poetry. It glows in the middle of its sober solitude when someone like you gazes upon it."

"Vate, what you've just said is beautiful."

"We have to rest for a few hours, Lorenzo Linares, brother. What you are seeing now as calm and white as a lamb will turn into a thirsty wolf tomorrow. . . . Come on, man, don't be a child. You've got to sleep to recover from so much wasted energy. We've got to get there."

"Sure, I'll be right there."

But Lorenzo forgot that he was conditioned to the time of his flesh and bones and became a part of the picture he was contemplating. He forgot the words and roamed over the dunes like a tender and loving breeze, touching the horizon in the distance, as though the sky were a ball of poetry contained within an ethereal blue made up of the holy gaze of beautiful eyes. He believed in his delirium that the moon, so beautiful, was becoming for the first time a tangible bride into whose ear he could speak beautiful things and who would cling tenderly to his arms. Suddenly, his mind felt the concept of God, and his lips flowered with a smile, while his eyes followed, fixed and spinning like planets.

Vate awoke in the morning raising his comrades with his shouting. They had collapsed like stones.

"Where's Lorenzo? Loreeenzo. Loreeenzooo. Loooreeenzooo."

"Come on!" Pedrito yelled from one of the dunes.

They could see him, standing stock-still like a saguaro. He didn't answer, and they went over to him. His gaze was lost in the expanse. Vate touched his forehead. Lorenzo was burning like a candle. It turned dark for Lorenzo at midday and he cried like a baby. No one has such an enormous grave. The entire desert! After burying him, Ramagacha crossed himself, murmuring, we are all dirt . . . dirt.

Pedrito, feeling Vate's sorrow, squeezed his arm and said to him, I will soon follow Lorenzo. I'm on my way to the border to exchange my life for a bastard's.

"You, Pedrito, do you hate?"

"I have weeds in my soul and a thorn stuck in my liver. Ah! If only you knew."

When they got to San Luis, the poet went on a real drinking spree. He didn't even know when he got to Califa. Pedrito and old Ramagacha had gotten there before him. The city with its roar of voices also swirled theirs around the way stations of sadness.

WELL, I BURIED MY BUDDY there in the desert. I had to wait for night-fall. I tried to during the day, but, damn it! The ground was so burning hot that it made me think about the head of a huge giant dying of fever, and then the ground was not hard at all. I didn't make a very large hole, just one large enough to keep the coyotes from eating him. Digging the hole was hard work at night too, but not bad enough to blister your hands. What I was mortally afraid of at night were the snakes. Sons of bitches! When I heard them hissing near by, rattling their rattlers, it felt like they were wrapped around my ears. What do you mean, are there snakes in the desert? I should know. If I didn't get bit it was because God is very powerful. I gathered together the scrub bush that clings to the desert floor like fleas, so that with the sand, dirt, branches, and hopping around I packed it down. I know his name was Manuel, Man-uel something or other. The guys called him Batepi. Millions of people are named Manuel. I met him in Empalme back when they were taking people on. I had the idea there were more of us, but Enrique Ramírez, Burro, said there were only ten thousand of us. And it was clear they weren't going to contract all of us, and more likely only those who could pay a bribe. Our fucking illusions were what had us there, good and tight. After a few hours, our hopes all gone, we told the whole business of standing around yakking to go to hell and decided to get to the other side as best we could. I finished the hole around dawn. I felt like shit. How'd I get to San Luis? Don't even ask. Who knows. A lot of people say that what we like is to have a good time and that we only leave the land because we're lazy. Well, there isn't a single town that isn't flat on its face because of the bosses and the politicians. As much as I love my land, as much as its burns in me, I know by virtue of my

own suffering that the more Indian the peasant is, the more he's condemned to slavery and oblivion. It's a good thing Batepi was squat, and
even at that I had to get him in on his side. I was in Empalme for three
weeks, there on the plain over by the railroad tracks. I had decided to
risk myself once again, hanging on to the idea of squeezing from life a
little bit of all it denied me. Because destiny was smiling on me with the
eyes of such a beautiful girl, it was all I could do to find some sort of
worthy future to offer her. Among all of us camped out in the open
there, a lot of sad things occurred. And why not, if we were the hungriest the country had to offer, and not just the country but the whole
world. I remember Moroyoqui, a little runt from down south who
joined up with us out of hunger. Among thousands of guys all jammed
together, everyday there were those who dropped from hunger; a case of
indigestion would have been strange indeed. It was in those days that
the candidate passed through. He gave beautiful little speeches in Mexicali and Guaymas, but when he and his entourage moved among us,
he stuck his head out of the bus and waved at us from a distance, very
quietlike. We just took our hats off, as serious as could be. There were
many thousands of us, and I'm sure he could smell the poverty. We
were grateful he didn't promise us anything. At least he didn't make
fun of our suffering by making promises. Moroyoqui was called Locust
because he was so skinny and he wore a little green hat that he'd picked
up God knows where. We were able to scrape some coins together that
came to around fifteen pesos so he could have something to eat. He put
some tacos beneath his nose, and with what was left over, he walked off
to where the whores were. In those days, they went for about ten pesos
if you bartered. Marlene said that when they were counting the coins
she'd earned, the Locust's eyes crossed and they never got them straight
again. One night I saw Manuel crying, caught off guard. He told me
about his sick father, about his wife and the starving kids. Nothing new,
since, for one reason or another, it was the same with all of us. I looked
around for something to make a cross for him. I couldn't even find a
crummy piece of wood. But I did find a pile of bones, I don't know
whether they were a dog's, a man's, or a cow's. But I was able to make
a cross. She looked so pretty with those flowery dresses. They were
beautiful! Always happy and cheerful. Why would she want me, I
thought. Seeing as how I was a poor bastard dying of hunger, so raggedy. I knew she loved me because she began to wear very poor dresses
when she would meet me. I spoke to her like a man. Wait for me, I'm

*off to make my fortune for you. Seeing tears in her eyes, I told her
again, if in two years you don't see me again, give me up for dead.
When I buried Manuel I began to cry, not for him, to tell the truth,
but to see the misery that comes to man and also because I saw myself
in his place. I know that in the storybooks, the poor young man goes
out to seek adventures, and he comes back rich and marries the daughter of the king. But now I also know that to be a Chicano or a wetback
is to be a slave and to live scorned. In the afternoon when the work is
done, I watch the sunsets, sad and luminous like the smiles of the poor
living in illusions. It's been a century since I left my village, and some-
day I'll return to cry for my dead.*

HE DIDN'T EVEN KNOW how many days he survived locked up in his
shack. Just by chance he found out it was Monday or Saturday.
What for? He couldn't even add the dead days to the calendar.
Besides, it wasn't worth the effort, let the days slip by into years,
let the wind carry them off, and let those who have joyous memories gather the dates. No, he had no use for a sampler of bitterness. He stretched his arm out and felt for the cans. The eternal
struggle, now that he didn't have anything to eat! He didn't even
know how many days he'd been locked up in his shack, cornered
like a sick dog. Between the fever that calcinated his worn-out
world and an occasional glance around him, he imagined that it
was Monday or Saturday. Something like a glancing, fleeting
thought, perhaps the custom of other days in which marking each
dawn with a precise date had some importance. His cloudy vision
of old age could not tell afternoons from mornings. When the
intervals between the fever spells gave him some moment of lucid-
ness, he was astonished to find himself prostrate. He thought suddenly that he had a gunshot wound or had been kicked by a colt.
It didn't take long for him to realize that his sickness lay with old
age, as though each year he lived was an injection of lead. His
hut seemed just like an old hat trampled by a herd of elephants.
He opened his eyes and saw the narrow walls, the ceiling so close
to the ground, the soap box on which he usually sat. The damn
humidity penetrated his bones. He felt the absence of heat and
food, and he sat down breathing heavily. His rebellious spirit
shouldered the thousand painful pounds of his body, and he
stood up dizzily. He took up his tools and headed for Revolution

Avenue. The first steps hurt. The damned physical defect made
him feel like a sparrow hawk whose wing has been yanked out by
the roots. He walked past the sand pit of the riverbed and got
ready to cross the railroad tracks. He turned around for a few seconds holding on to the back of his neck. He felt a pressure where
he had been struck by the glances that came from the holes in the
other lairs. He couldn't see anything, but the angry presence of
the damned floated in the air. It was Monday, and very early in
the morning, the old man walked along listening to the babble of
the morning world. The men were off about their jobs, in a bad
mood, half-asleep with the echoes of the buzzing chorus of the
taverns, leaving behind a jumble of cries from children and wives.
The nursing babies screamed for their breakfast, the older ones
were yelling that they were late for school, and the mothers were
shouting with such hysterical, sharp notes that, heard from a distance, you couldn't make out what they were saying. The volume
of their voices coincided curiously with the barking of the skinny
dogs. Loreto walked through the back streets, lost in dreams with
his eyes wide open. A sudden stimulus made him optimistic and
awoke in him a spark of ambition. It doesn't cost anything to
dream, and he could well dream about palaces, abundant meals,
piles of money that would, moreover, provide him with well-being
and, perhaps, even the affection that a long time ago had become
absent from his life. And naturally, once rich, he would deserve
respect. How he would be smiled upon! But the goals he forged
along his walk turned out to be more modest. He saw himself
reaching Constitution Street, where he usually set up his business.
Noting the strange fact that all the cars were covered with mud,
his sight faded away in an infinite line of cars smothered in all
sorts of gunk. He saw many kids and others as poor off as he was
trying to clean them, except that it was an impossible task because all the owners were waiting for him, only for him, and he
clearly heard the words of the drivers affirming with anguish, "If
this car isn't washed by Don Loreto, the worthy Yaqui, no one, I
mean no one, will touch it. There is no one in this city, in the
whole world, who does it better." His dream didn't stop there.
Rather, the greedy Indian contemplated the problem of the uniform, not being able to conceive of himself without a distinctive
suit. Dressed in white? No. You'd be able to see the spots too

much, just like a fat cook, and worse, he ran the risk of being
confused with a baker. He smiled remembering that when he was
a child he asked his father if the bakers had been born of a mother
or if they came from an egg. Aside from the fact that some queers
choose to dress in white, like brides, and walk the streets wiggling
their butts like ducks. Let's set aside the business of the outfit,
except that the fact was that under no circumstances, especially
with so much success, could he continue to wear his usual clothes.
His ancient shoes looked like loaves of egg bread. Since they were
all unsewn and you could see his toes, his feet gave the impression
of a fancy-pants toad out serenading, singing to his lady toad with
captivating eyes. Not to mention his pants, full of holes and
patches. They were so stiff from oil and dirt that once . . . Ah,
damn pants! A red ant crawled up the pants leg, one of those ants
that can make the strongest of men cry. First it bit him on the
butt and then all over the place. He cried out so much and
jumped higher than when he was a kid. Some ladies who were
going by were greatly amused by Loreto's dance. And he, who was
always so polite and gentlemanly, was so mad that he called them
old bitches.

He couldn't kill the traitorous insect because the cloth would
not bend. If it came out it was because he danced around on one
foot like the Tapatío fandango. He really needed another shirt!
The one he was wearing had been blue with red checks, and now
it was more of a chocolate color. His clothes were full of so many
holes that once a bratty kid, already a fourteen-year-old bum,
made fun of him saying, "The cold isn't going to affect you, old
man, because it comes in one hole and goes out the other." The
poor guy hadn't had a hat for a long time. Since he was a
dreamer, he wished for one like the Texans wore, with little stars
on top. . . . He came to from his simple dreams as he walked
through the side streets where the most defenseless prostitutes
lived. Since their best years were over, the bad life had turned
them into two-legged monsters. They had been around so much
that they'd gone down in value and were available for commerce
with the poorest workers and the blacks who came over from California to raise hell. Poor little whores, he thought, the wicked
have gone and now you can rest. The unfortunate women would
probably be dreaming the heavy dream of booze, their breasts all

bruised and their sex almost on the verge of bleeding. A few dollars scattered around to pay for their clothes, which the men who hold them in their sad prison provide for them on credit. He imagined them in their cells with the walls covered with the images of saints, with even some statues of saints standing on their dressing tables. Poor kids, Loreto thought, they're afraid of loosing their soul and what is certain is that the devil can have them for the same reason. After that came the brothels for the middle-class people. They looked like ships, what with so many sailors. And then came the ones frequented by the local aristocrats, foreigners with dollars, and some poor jerk who abandoned his family in poverty in order to act the playboy. These looked like ostentatious palaces. Loreto remembered that, fifteen years ago, he spent fifteen dollars of his savings one day in the arms of one of the cheapest chippies of the lot. Of course, the whore had neither teeth nor waistline. Fine, but that was back when he was a young man sixty-five years old.

Midday came, and all his attempts were in vain. All of the cars were shiny clean and their owners said no, moving their heads like elephants. He sat down on the curb, a symbol of sadness, and was hungry. He was to the point of spending the last of his energy and faith, when the picture changed.

GOD DRESSES THE LILIES very finely and makes the birds happy every morning. Fortunate is the man made in His image.

The city awoke with an invasion of shoeless children, defenseless old people, and all those who are forced to seek their survival with despair. They went in search of a happy mortal who might want to be a millionaire. They ran through the downtown streets in search of the bossman. They would jump in front of him, pull at his arm, his jacket, and beg at him with persuasive voices.

"Win a million, sir."

"No! I'm not interested."

"Half a million, sir."

"I just said no, and I'll repeat it a hundred times. No!"

"Come on, sir, a quarter of a million for you. So I can have a meal, don't be mean. Yes?"

"Give me a share, then. Damn it. You guys are real pests."

When the day was already well along, they would go over to where the whores were sunning themselves with their legs spread apart and their faces vinegary, and there they passed out millions right and left. They tangled with the pedestrians on the sidewalk, offering them riches.

"Here are pesos by the millions, sir."

"Mister, mister. Look, money, money."

They wandered among the cars when the traffic slowed with congestion, shouting in the windows.

"Get rich, sir, buy a lottery ticket from me."

Doña Candelita got up early to sell shares of lottery tickets. She wasn't sure exactly how old she was. She just knew that by the time the new century was born she was already a young lady who danced and had a boyfriend. When Porfirio Díaz was overthrown, she'd already given birth to her first child. One morning she related the happy news that she knew she had a boyfriend because he squeezed her hand when they danced. Not like today, where in broad daylight in the middle of the street youngsters from the best families fall all over each other kissing each other's ears and going kissy kissy as if they were in heat. In those days, no sir, you danced far apart, either the polka or the waltz. "Ah! What business." She was answered by a young Indian woman who sold lottery shares. "Just go see the spiders fight." The old woman got angry, and answered the young woman back, that in her day people had shame and covered their bodies. She ended up telling her accusingly that now everybody goes around with their rears hanging out. Another woman selling shares, wearing a miniskirt, blind in one eye, and the other all runny, chimed in that in the old days they didn't show their feet because they were all crooked and covered with bunions from wearing shoes that were too small, or they didn't even have enough money to buy shoes. Doña Candelita told the young woman that the skirt she was wearing was so short she could see her underpants. "Of course. That way they'll look." She slapped her, furious. "Well, I've got something to show, not like you, you old hag." Candelita had to move off to another corner with her tickets because the competition was getting out of hand there. Before moving off, she shouted to the one who had something to show. "What you're showing, you tramp,

are underpants full of yellow stains. You probably think it's gold
embroidery, but it's pure pee soup."

Doña Candelita extended the folds of the lottery shares for all
the tourists and pedestrians, making sad eyes at them and speaking in a thin pleading voice. Buy some shares from me, sir, come
on. I don't have a crumb to eat. Nothing. They looked at her as
though asking for an accounting. "Well, just what are you doing
here in the world, old woman? You should be good and dead."
Doña Candelita returned to her hovel. An adobe room without
plastering, but with cockroaches and rats, a symphony of crickets,
in addition to other bugs that usually won't show their faces. She
took a piece of hard bread out of a hole, dunked it in a glass of
water and begin to gnaw at it with her gums. A sort of bloodish
liquid oozed down her wrinkles from her tiny eyes sunk in the
smog of the years. Doña Candelita got crafty the next day. That
was it, she wasn't going to die of hunger. That day she sold all the
shares she set out to. She put a soccer ball she found down the
back of her dress, and the clients stopped to look at the hunch-
back. A spark of greed ordered them to buy from the old hunch-
back. Some could not resist it, and they touched her hump. The
little old lady smiled condescendingly. Her rivals choked with
rage.

Listen, Cloudy, look at the crafty old bitch. She's really selling
those shares.

And Cartucho saw her. Damn it, she's so old she knows more
than the devil's own grandmother.

THE JOURNEY IS A LONG ONE, *brother, you have to make a beeline,*
even though so much walking ruins your feet. Because, pal, the road
seems like it's never going to end. Sometimes you feel like turning back
halfway there, but then you remember that you left your family in
God's hands, hoping you'll send them dollars, while their stomachs
growl. You won't lack for water in Sinaloa, friend, but Sonora'll screw
you! It'd be a good idea for you to act smart, because the only thing
you can do in the desert is put rocks in your mouth and play with them
so they'll bring out the saliva. What you'll not have enough of on the
road for sure is food. But that shouldn't surprise you, right?, because
from the time you were born your stomach's been more of a decoration.
Now, if you want some advice, you'd better pay close attention to me,

and don't go saying later that the one who told you was crazy. Don't ever ask somebody who's rich for food: they don't see someone who's poor as someone in need, but as a runaway slave who's committed the crime of deserting. I'm half-obliged to tell you that you are not to go near homes where you can't see a lot of poverty either. Can't you see they'll come out and insult you? They'll call you a bum, a jerk, and they'll turn the dogs loose on you as a joke. No, pal, I don't care whether or not you believe me, but the only ones who'll help you kill your hunger are the poor themselves. You approach their shacks with shame, as though you know what they might be able to give you, which they need for their kids so much. The poor little kids look like skin and bone piñatas, naked and potbellied, starving from before they came out of their mother. They know you're there when the dogs attack you, although they're nothing more than barking and bones, so skinny they look like stringed instruments. They jump all over you barking as though they wanted to eat you, because they're starving to death too. Despite their own misfortune those people see you with your sunken face and your wild eyes, and they give you bean burritos and water and conversation, pal. You walk and walk, urged on by the idea that the gringos are gods or something like that and that there is no poverty on earth. I've just returned from over there, brother, and if I don't discourage you it's because I don't want you to go believing that I want to do you a bad turn, no, pal. You're better off finding out for yourself. All I can recommend to you is not to go getting any grand ideas, pal. Better you not get hurt too much. Now, if you insist, I'll tell you the real truth. You know good and well that there's a lot of money here, but it's all in the hands of a few hypocrites. Anyway, those rich types, why beat around the bush, are the ones who cause poverty, pal. You laugh, because I'm not telling you anything new. Well, just hold on. You think you're going to rake the money in with a broom, but there're a lot of poor people. And just so you'll know, the majority of the ones who eat well do so in order to withstand the workdays. Ah, my friend, they're heavy ones, and the people work harder than a dumb animal. And what is more, you, like me, are real dark, and over there that's worse than a crime. But, you know something, maybe God will help you and you'll do just fine. It's hard to believe it, fellow, until you go and find out for yourself. So, go on, don't let anyone tell you different. I don't want you to say later that all I do is talk and never say anything but lies.

THE DAY WAS ALREADY into its second half when the Yaqui Loreto received payment from some foreigners whose eyes were a sea of goodness. They gave him two dollars and their thanks with so much respect that you could see from a mile that they were generous of heart. He felt his soul caressed by a gentle breeze. He walked along balancing himself like a penguin until he reached Don Chanito's stand, where he treated himself to a taco which cost him fifteen American cents. When the "chief" handed him his change, he dropped a coin, and it rolled away. La Malquerida picked it up and kindly handed it back to him. The Indian looked at her sweetly by way of reward. The eyes of the poor whore filled with tears. La Malquerida was sitting alone on a corner. You could tell by the bags under her eyes that she had been on a real drinking binge. The truth is that the night before she had created one of her terrible scandals. Valente, the Vaseline Man, had come up to her with his irresistible act. He feigned tenderness and spoke to her about commitment, about getting her out of that life of hell, buying her a house, and building a happy future and leaving the past behind. He got her halfway confused and for a second the embers started to glow in her again. But when she realized Vaseline Man was up to his usual perverse tricks as a pimp and that all he wanted to do was to make her work for him, she broke a bottle and gashed his face, leaving him with a harelip. Valente did not go to the authorities because he was a criminal himself dealing in drugs. His lip was left hanging by a thread, and he had tried to tape it back into place. He had to resign himself to being harelipped for the rest of his life, and his only choice was to grow a mustache like the Kaiser's, and, even then, he was left looking like a dog who's always in some scrape or another. Once the incident was over, the cantina owner, who pimped for the women, began harassing them—get the clients to drink, get yourself a client more often, you here, you there, hitting them and insulting them. He looked angrily at Malquerida out of the corner of his eye in his usual abusive way. In addition to being in charge of that bad business because it went with his character, he was more of a coward than a cornered hare.

Loreto carried his food over to where he usually sat, a cement wall facing the street in a small vacant lot. His food consisted of a loaf of French bread larger than his hand. It was about a foot long with the ends narrowing out into little tits. He looked quizzically at the ends of the loaf of bread, which was split down the middle. He saw three pieces of roast beef and five small slices of avocado; *ahuacatl*, he murmured, feeling the ancient voices of Nahuatl stir in his blood. On top of the dark green slices of avocado there were three bright slices of tomato stuck to the bread crumbs, pieces of fresh-cut onion, and a medium size chile, a jalapeño, stuck in the middle of the bread. He tasted the food with his eyes half-closed, remembering his home, the guerrillas in Bacatete, and the rattlers adorning the legs of the Yaqui *pascola* dancers beating a steady din. He only ate half. He dozed for a few minutes, just enough for his subconscious to raise its periscope. His friend who came from the same town crossed through his mind as always when his heart felt heavy.

I, my friend, knew Jesús of Bethlehem in person. Maybe you don't believe me, but it's true. What a beautiful Yaqui! Belén—Bethlehem— is one of the eight Yaqui towns. That Chuy was a great medicine man, you'd better believe it. People in the town used to laugh at him because he was the son of Don Pepe, the one who made pots. But over in Vicam and Potam he accomplished marvelous cures, you might almost say miracles. Over there toward La Sangre, over by Las Polvaredas, he's called Uncle Chuy. He didn't charge, and would take whatever they wanted to give him.

They say that old man Espinoza wanted to follow him, hearing him talk about spiritual wealth, and the old man said: "That's the way it should be." So he rode up on his fancy Arabian horse, prancing around. Uncle Chuy, who had never seen him, told him: "Well, just go dig up all your bags full of pesos and give them, along with all your herds of cows, to the poor, and then follow me. There is neither darkness nor death in my way." Old man Espinoza almost had a heart attack, and being tighter than a tick, turned around and fled. He even made a speech: "Give away everything it took me so long to put together to a band of jerks just so they can keep lying around and fucking their women—no way, man, I'll kick ass first, and the devil can have my bones. And you should've seen how those people flocked around Jesús of Bethlehem, my friend. It was a sight to see. They came from all over the place, some of them lame, others blind, and lots that were already more in the next world than in this one. And he'd just stand there looking at them, lost deep in thought. Ah! But his eyes were love itself, with lots and lots of heart. What a beautiful little Yaqui! Look, friend, I'm not lying to you, and I swear to God Our Father who is in heaven that all he had to do was to touch your clothes with just his hand and your sickness would vanish.

I knew him, friend. He used to come and rest with my neighbors. You probably remember Malena and Tita, Lazarón's sisters, that fool who used to ride wild bulls without a cinch. There was a rumor that Malena was half-crazy and that she was a friend of the devil's. Tita was real quiet. Well, one day, Malena was going down the street, looking for trouble, and she runs into Chuy. You won't believe what happened right then and there: all of a sudden, Malena became someone else, just like overnight, just from listening to that beautiful man say: "Cleanse your soul by repenting well, and don't turn your back on anyone, my children. Because eternal life is for those who are not ashamed to beg for forgiveness. I love you all very, very much, and I want you to be happy, despite all the tears you have shed, no matter what it costs me . . . for the sacrifice . . . "

The government was afraid he'd get the Indians all riled up. How the poor loved him, and how they still venerate his memory. Even the gabachos are getting caught up in it. No, don't harm him, he's nothing but a poor innocent. But Chencho Torres said, "That man's got to be killed no matter what." Well, they weren't content just to shoot him. Just look at the injustice and the vileness of man: they tied him up tight against a saguaro with huge thorns. And as he was dying, he prayed for his executioners, "Forgive them, sweet God, for they know very well what they are doing." No one can forget Jesús of Bethlehem. Many have tried to deny him because he was a Yaqui. Others venerate him for his profound humanity, and many adore him for his miracles. And that's not counting the clever ones who trade on his name.

LORETO ACHED on the inside, without admitting it, for having resented, on the verge of hate, the impoverished children who had argued with him over his shitty little job. He felt a heaviness in his chest, like something rotting painlessly, taking your breath away and making you suffer more than physical pain. He saw the children as if in a dream, not sad and rickety, but rather cheerful and enthusiastic. They were washing a beautiful car, and they were doing it with so much skill and energy that the silver the car was made of glowed with marvelous glints. He saw the surprise on

Chalito's face, the one whose coffin had a lining of white silk, very pretty. The inside of Chalito's coffin was gorgeous. It was cushioned with pure white silk, and the child shone like a little gem in a fancy case. Someone very gently placed a bouquet of flowers in his crossed little hands, daisies or carnations.

Chalito hovered, suspended in air just like a hummingbird, beating his wings so fast he seemed transparent, or he was borne aloft in an air balloon. Then he saw him standing there, his arms outstretched to receive the prize. He only saw the owner of the jewel, strolling around with class. He wore shiny new shoes, an elegant suit, a green vest with a chain hanging from it and a tie that looked like a rosebush. Suddenly he saw the face, it was his, it was him. Loreto! He drew handfuls of money from his pockets with which he filled the hands of the kids. They looked on him with the fresh eyes of children which are like fresh, unused film. He heard the warble of swallows, and the children rushed off. Very happy.

A slimy net of words had been woven around those present, with the alcoholic mist given off by whitish and slinking words. The words floated over the thick smoke like newborn bugs. The sensitive hearing of each individual reached them in unison, and they shook with a sticky vibration. The setting was saturated with the nauseating buzz of dozens of drunks, who shouted as they drew bunches of viscous stupidities from the depths of the pools, dripping ironies with the shuddering of sharp-edged bursts of laughter and the hammering of the loud and fragmented conversation.

"If they don't give up, we'll have to bomb their country and turn it into a parking lot."

"Sorry, I'm Spanish, but I never learned to speak my grandfather's language."

"Is that right?"

"You better believe it."

"In the whole world, there are lots that're strong, but we're the strongest. Go on, friend, just feel this bulge."

"Shit! Georgie, you have the biceps of a champion weightlifter."

"And it's for real, no kidding. When I expand the muscles in my arm, I rip the sleeves of my shirt, no matter how large they are."

"Your old lady must love that."

"If you don't believe me, let's give it a try."

"No, go show the devil."

"I'm the strongest! The strongest! The . . . "

"Shut up, pothead!"

"Who shouted that, who was it? Whoever said that is a motherfucker!"

"That's right, we've get some mother fucking going on here. But who's more to blame? Those who come with their money to corrupt us or ourselves? They come with enough to pay someone to debauch his own daughters; to pay for divorces by the carload; to throw away money gambling, drinking, shooting drugs, whoring, and anything else you can imagine. Then when they go too far, they toss them in jail for being pigs, and when they get out, they go around babbling all over the place that the border is the sinkhole of the world. Those jerks don't realize that it's them and their shitty money that spoils everything. Isn't that right, pal?"

"Well, I guess so, but we're the ones that string them along. Just tell me this, pal. Isn't it wrong to go around on your knees, mister here and mister there, make yourself comfortable. No, pal, why deny it, we're in on it too."

"There's the key, see. It's the damn money that ruins everything. Sure, we're to blame, don't you see? What's the color of gold? Don't tell me it's yellow. No sir, it's the same color as shit. No one's to blame, because we're all covered with gold."

"Well, not completely. Not enough to have another drink, buddy."

"Ah! What a mess."

"This one makes eight. Do you remember that little dark-haired girl, the one you saw me with in The Butterfly?"

"Yes, if I remember, she was real cute."

"Well, I also had her."

"Casanova's going to be jealous of you."

"Just look at me. I'm not rich. Take a good look. I'm not even handsome. I'm going out now with a blonde who's real cool. Sunday I'm taking her dancing to Mascarrote's Place."

"Don Juan'd run errands for you."

"I'm going to call her. I'll be right back."

"Just a minute, friend, don't forget your buddy's a conqueror too."

"Right. He's a nut whose shadow doesn't even stick with him. I put up with his shit because he buys the beer."

"There's a lot like him. Here he comes. Damn! He looks like Frankenstein when he was little."

"Take it easy, fellows, take it easy. Don't bang the table. The barmaid'll be right over. Chulis, take this pitcher over to those guys raising hell."

"I sure as hell won't. They pinch my butt every time I go over there."

"So what."

"You go, then. Shit, that's all I need."

"Don't cry, pal. Take it easy."

"I'm a bastard, a real S.O.B. I bought booze with all the money I had to buy groceries for my family. I've been on a toot since yesterday and the house is bare. There aren't even any beans. . . . What's going to happen to my lovely family?"

"I'm afraid of my old lady. She's going to bite me, and I haven't been vaccinated."

"Don't cry, pal, just calm down. Anyway . . ."

"In any case, now that the lie has been invented, there's always an excuse. Here's to you!"

"Ah! To my famous buddy."

"Come on, let's have some order."

"Smash him in the face for talking too much."

"Either go outside and fight or I'll call the cops."

"Forget it, they've already left. Let'em kill each other in the streets."

"Cut it out, you've already wrecked everything."

"You don't give a damn. You don't care, go mind your own business, or I'll kick ass."

"If you kill him, I'm a witness."

"I'm real moocho, meycho. God damn, go to hell, you bastard!"

"Look at the state they left him in, man. The Happy Day gets all the trash."

"Aaah! Brother, all I see is red. What's going on—it looks like I smashed into the train."

"You can't see because your face's all covered with blood. I'll just have to clean it with these rags I use to wash cars. . . . The water's not very clean, but . . . "

"Ah, hell! It's ice cold. It's running down my back."

"There. Take care of those cuts. You look like a ripe pitahaya fruit."

"Damn bastard. He took advantage of the fact that I was drunk. I've been hitting the grape for a week. Come on, have a drink, guy."

"No, kid, I don't drink."

"What's bothering you, pal?"

"I live from my job washing cars. I also have a job watching the tourists' cars."

"Well, you're sure an old man, mister. Listen, why don't you insist they give you your retirement pay . . . ? Don't look so glum, pal. . . . You stand there looking at me as though to say, what do I want with pensions . . . ? Don't let them rob you, old man, you gotta keep a sharp eye out."

"Why'd you slam into that guy so hard?"

"Because he's sold out. You know what? That guy's a fucking Chicano. 'Hey buddy, take it easy. Hit me, will ya?' The guy says he doesn't understand. 'A light, then.' He doesn't know Spanish. 'A match, jerk.' The guy answers, 'Don't bother me, I don't speak Mexican.' And so I yell at him, 'You're a coconut, a sell-out, brown on the outside but white on the inside.' The guy came at me like a truck. Look how he left me."

"Just because you called him a coconut he got mad?"

"Right. He's one of those Chicanos who set up shop and then act like an Anglo. You know? They're called coconuts because they're brown on the outside and white on the inside like Anglos. Get it? They're also called brown Anglos, and they're real ashamed of who they are."

"Poor devils! It must be hard for them, without any personal pride."

"Hey old man, you're real bright. I hadn't looked at it in those terms."

"Whenever I'm busy washing cars or watching them in front of places, I always see you drinking and fighting with someone. How come? What's your problem?"

"You're right, fellow, I get upset over every little thing. It's just that I'm always riled up about something. I just can't explain it, buddy. Us Chicanos were born without words, and people have forgotten their language. In whitey's schools they put us apart like we were morons for not speaking English. If we do talk, it's because we invent words, and then only when we're drunk, because if we don't drink, pal, we'd be better off just to shut up for being so ashamed of not being able to speak. You lose your illusions quick, pal."

"But you're only about forty."

"Well, you can see I can't work. Over in the States, if you don't work hard, they kick you out, and they get guys who're like horses. That's the way it is, you know. If you work pruning or whatever, you've got water to drink at the end of the rows. You've got to be at it ten or twelve hours to make it, and since you start out as a kid, you're washed up fast, and you can't work like an animal. Since you're always bending over, you wreck your back and the sun drills you so that the S.O.B. bosses kick you out. They take on new guys once they see you're washed up, get it?"

"Why don't you guys go to the law? You live in a supercivilized country."

"Come on, pal! Laws're never on the side of the Chicano, not even the eight-hour workday. Since you don't know English, you can't file a complaint. The guys got it set up that way to make you a slave. You don't think so? But when it's time for elections, they go and tell you that they're your comrades, that they're going to help you out. And then as soon as they win the elections, you know what? They wipe their butts with their fucking promises. And some of the dogs even ban strikes."

"It's the same everywhere."

"Tell me about it, guy."

"Life is real tough. Maybe I could've been rich and powerful over there at another time. But human suffering really gets to me. You've got to have a lot of dignity and not lose your pride or humiliate yourself. It doesn't matter how hungry you get. . . . "

"You know what, pal? I'm going to shove off and grab myself a drink in some other bar."

"But man, it's just as bad elsewhere."

"That's the way I do it, so give me five, mister, and thanks."

"My pleasure, young fellow. I'm the carwasher, Loreto Maldonado."

Good Chuco strolled off into a concave world, leaning to one side like a cocktail mixer. The buildings went flat, and the streets stood up like paved walls. The signs of the city fell like gobs of spit, with the stubbornness of their messages splashing around in the fountains, latching onto people's necks with the insistence of eye-clawing harpies. Revolution Avenue was filled with night revelers. The feverish hymn of the rock-and-rollers drowned out the dawn song of the cocks. The lights reflected against the smog served as a rotten curtain covering the view of the gloriously star-studded sky.

Old man Loreto Maldonado, drowning in his thoughts, struggled against a cloudy past, like a swimmer trying to navigate against the current of a rushing river.

VATE TOOK TO DRINKING. In the cosmic vastness of his internal world of poetry, his mind became a falling star dragging along a tail of orphan words. Although he knew well by memory a letter that was by now in tatters, he reread it out of pure obsession.

Vate: take good care of my husband, since you're like a brother to him. Take good care of him, Vate, because I'm waiting for him here along with his children. Vate: Lorenzo is like a little boy. He has a transparent soul, and he likes to play with the colors and music of pretty words. You who understand him so well, because you're a poet just like him, take good care of him, Vate, so he won't die in those strange lands. We need him alive. He sometimes forgets he's got a body and wants to be pure spirit. Vate: tell him to come back, not to go, that even if we're down-and-out poor, we'll get by. Tell him not to go abroad, to stay here in our town instead. But . . . he won't pay any attention to you, and he says that he'll use the money he earns to make his children doctors and lawyers, that he won't let any more of our children die for lack of medicine and the ghost of hunger will never return. . . . Vate, take good care of my man, Lorenzo Linares. May God be with you and watch over you. . . .

Loreto woke up to the rude screech of two cars at a red traffic light. Two guys were hurling insults at each other, each from his own taxi.

"Your mother-in-law drives better, you fucker. Go take some lessons!"

"Show me how to have kids and raise them. Asshole!"

When the light turned green, the traffic started to move again, and the loudmouths disappeared.

A strong odor of dead horse made him roll over on his right side. Seated next to him was a hippie talking to himself. His eyes were glassy, and he was about twenty years old. His appearance and dress made him look like Christ. The Yaqui sank his gaze into the hippie's eyes. The latter emerged from his incoherence and began to speak with the lucidity of a Spanish university professor. The hippie told him, with a voice full of deep hurt, that in his country there was a holocaust going on against the young, with so much cruelty that the blood of those being sacrificed could fill riverbeds. The Yaqui slipped into the distance as he listened to the hippie, who was going on about how they had legalized mass murder of the unborn, only because they had no voice to defend themselves in the courts. And that the survivors were turning to drugs in order not to have to witness their sinister destiny, that the tragic presentments were unleashing barbarous instincts. And that on the one hand the children and on the other their parents were turning to orgies and bacchanals. Two heavy tears rolled down the hippie's cheeks. Suddenly he burst out laughing with a vacant look and started to mutter words in his own language. Then both were lost, separated by the space of centuries, even though their bodies were next to each other.

SEÑORA DÁVALOS DE COCUCH ordered her servant to let in the neighborhood delegation that was going to ask her for help for Chalito's burial. The delegation consisted of Chepa and a woman nicknamed Honey Bunch. Doña Cocuch had addressed them about the charitable matter. Her sacrifice in the name of noble causes had her up three nights a week playing canasta with the other ladies who were members of the club over which she presided, the Daughters of Samaria.

"Ah, Señora de Cocuch, Chalito has died. A little angel, ma'am, and since we're neighbors, we said, Señora de Cocuch, such a sweet soul of God, will help us out."

The other old lady shrewdly seconded her.

"If there were no little souls of God, what would happen to the poor? It's just like my friend Chepa says, only Señora Cocuch is going to be moved by us. And so, here we are, with heavy hearts, to ask you for a favor, Señora Cocuruchi."

Señora Dávalos de Cocuch signed a check for a coffin. The smile that shone on her face was the very flower garden of goodness. Señor Cocuch came in at that moment. The old ladies took in his hawk-like gaze and fled out the door.

"Little woman, little woman, you'll never be anything but the very personification of goodness. Your heart is the most precious of jewels, but you don't learn, my treasure. Have you already forgotten when the shitty Indian refused your good intention?"

She looked at him with candor, and both of them burst out laughing and hugged each other.

Each knew his own affairs. He, with finances, saving up, assured earthly glory; while she, administering things of the spirit, won heavenly, eternal glory. That pair of sharpies knew how to be among the chosen. For ever and ever.

Don Mario Cocuch's method for triumphing in everything had turned out to be infallible. It consisted of being servile with the more powerful to the extent of dragging himself slobbering and kissing the feet of his superiors with no mind to how his wife was helping out in her own fashion. . . . Ah! But with the humble, it was something else again. With the weak he became cruel, despotic, squashing them without compassion. He enjoyed their wounds, and yet nobody could deny the evidence of his enormous progress. He was very wealthy and held a seat in congress. . . .

THERE WHERE THE UNITY of the green is broken by sky-blue, the pale earth, like a dead beloved, strikes with its mirror pregnant with the sun anyone who contemplates the solitude of the immense surface. Beyond, in the distance, illusion plays with the blue of deeply limpid waters that fuel the desire to feel the soft caressing breeze between space and the sands. The desert! The body of the desiccated sea, a wasteland holding the mysteries of the mind, sordid refuge of heroic reptiles, frustrated holymen who curse defiantly with vertical gazes. Before crossing its thresholds of fire, we knew it was a toy, with the romantic ardor of someone who harbors in his illusion an airy ship that will leap any obstacle. Couldn't even fool us. Already in Sonora it revealed to us its manner, as we violated its land with each footstep. Bushes and squalid trees told us with their isolation that they struggled to death with the damned desert, scrawny mesquites that looked like undernourished shadows, ironweeds as hard as the greedy earth that bore them. Beyond, the gobernadora plants clutched the ground with their bunches of vare-jones covered with little green leaves that looked like flies. Beyond the rivers that sign their names on empty riverbeds. You were smiling, Lorenzo my friend, without knowing it. You, old Bent Branch, like a burned out trunk, wanted to flower again in other lands, walking deep in thought with ashen steps. And you, the one they made fun of, with your wings of hate, you could well cross the same hell in search of revenge. Before crossing its doorstep, we became acquainted with the haughty heroism of the cacti. Like unbending warriors, dying gloriously on their own soil, struggling with an implacable enemy that drinks the juice of each plant, sickly but erect in their pride, they defy the enemy, their bodies lined with sharp arms. Armies of prickly cholla bushes that do not distinguish between adversaries when their projectiles cast themselves out to wound the intruder. A campground of sibiris cacti with arms that enclose the flesh, drawing forth a red sweat when they plunge in their sharp nails. Barrel cacti armed with daggers, looking just like pregnant camp followers who lie down to give birth on the road. Patches of fierce beavertail cacti, their tails upturned. Mounds of saguaro cacti! Watchmen guarding with swords of steel, philosophers of elevated thoughts, their hearts tender to the friend. How valiant the cacti are! With only the arms entrusted to them by nature, they surround the enemy to impede his advance, enclosing him within their confines with the suicidal will of one who always goes the full limit, against the immense power of the desert for whom the sun is the commandant and the air currents are the captains.

Deseeert! We will march against your sterile womb, you hangman of the green growths of the fields. Covered with thorns we will go forth masked as cacti, and just like them we will guard the water in our bowels in order to fool the voraciousness of your urges. We will tread holes in your sands, indifferent to the pain to our feet, which will blister and bleed on your soil carpeted with tiny coals, ignoring your flaming breath that toasts the soul and evaporates the eyes, darkening our faces. Our journey will stake itself out on top of your dunes, leaving behind a cemetery of exhausted dromedaries and the reclining bulk of beheaded elephants. We will come to your center, cursed desert, anointed by the spirit of the ancient gods of our race. And there, filled with rage, we will drive into your unmoving heart the torn flag of the wetbacks. Who *are you, desert? You have stolen the beauty of the seas, aspiring to the majesty of its movements. Who are you? A monster of otherworldly refuges, lost in the chaos of the primeval times. Altar Desert . . . Are you perhaps the promised land of the hungry who have no country? Ah! Now I know who you are. You're the immense tomb of the banished and of the empire of the Indians. Yuma Desert! Onomatopoeia of the underworld. Yuma, flame, weeping, wailing, Yuma, flame, tower of fire, no mooore . . . Ah . . .*

LENCHO GARCÍA Y DEL VALLE, the father of the poor little dead Chalito, did not express himself like most people. He didn't talk like the common people, like the down-and-out and low-class people talk. Lencho had taught himself with pretentious and ready-made sentences. His clichés were not extracts from great literature, but sentences repeated by generations of politicians and ass-licking journalists, blind in their imaginations. In the depth of his murky poverty and his vices, there lived a small-time burgher and an ambitious political hack. Lencho used the devices of his rhetoric to get good and drunk, because he liked liquor more than food. Lencho did not work, judging manual work to be beneath his talent. . . . Vile jobs, he would say, or with a smirk he would assert, "Only the stupid do hard work." He transformed his wife, Beatriz, into a rabbit, and just about every year he had her having another baby. He already had ten kids, the oldest nine years old. There were two sets of twins. He cackled in his drunkenness and said that he used a shotgun.

Lencho García y del Valle was tall and thin. His complexion looked a lot like a kangaroo's, although his face, more because of triangular bags under his eyes, looked a lot like that of a vampire. Despite his tacky clothes, he insisted on wearing a tie, and he had two, one blue and the other striped. In his drunken bouts he would do the stupidest things, and he was the height of simple-mindedness, to the extent of dancing into the air without any concern over whether the jukebox was playing a mambo or a zapateado.

The García y del Valle family survived thanks to the efforts of the women, who washed clothes and made tortillas to sell. Of the ten kids, four were girls. Of the others, two worked the streets shining shoes, and by last count three were busy washing cars.

The littlest still nursed. Of the girls, two were so small that only the others helped their mother. The poor little girls already did the work of mothers, taking care of their younger brothers, and when they had time off, they devoted themselves to playing with their sickly dolls. The yelling of the gang of kids and the shouts of the mother gave the idea that the house was about to fly through the air with an explosion of frogs. Beatriz, the politician's wife, spent her life always on edge, her belly always way out for all the neighbors to see. The intervals of her birthing were spent in bed fasting, dopey from malnutrition and what she'd had to go through.

Lencho García y del Valle had already exhausted all his tricks to take money away from the larger kids. The ones who shined shoes walked up and down the street carrying their shoeshine boxes on their backs, and after a while their bodies were bent over double as though they had carried not a shoeshine box, but the coffin of someone dead.

Their mother was making tortillas one afternoon over a fire, which muttered threateningly with the whirls of flames that leapt from the half-broken grill that the kids had carted up from the garbage dump. Every time she took an already cooked tortilla off, a bunch of hands rushed against her with the shriek of hungry birds. The woman yelled shrilly. "Get out of here! You're driving me crazy." She slapped and pinched right and left, but in the end the disk of dough was yanked away and devoured in a flash. Chalito slept in a corner, snoring as loud as a worn out sixty-year-old man. On one occasion, Amadito grabbed a tortilla from Juan Pedro, the "elder bully." He ran to take it back from him, tripped over one of the little girls and fell near the fire, singeing his hair. The woman ran shrieking to help him. She went on with her work, and as she worked the tortillas, she wiped the tears with her arm, sobbing. When she tossed a tortilla on the grill, she took a moment to push the hair back from her face and blow her nose loudly. The dough ran out, but the hunger of the children seemed to have increased. She saved two of the last three tortillas for Lencho García y del Valle, and she shared the one left for her with the two little girls, who were so hungry that you could look right through their souls. Like witches' magic the yelling and the running around stopped. Just like they'd been put under a spell, they all were as still as real statues. Sleep overtook them one by one, caressed by their mother's eyes and from time to time by the sound the woman made with her snivelling. That's how they were when the man of the house strode in. He had a newspaper in his left hand and looked elated. His half-opened mouth bore the smell of many taverns. A stench rose from his feet that assaulted the nostrils. Turning the hut into a theater, he improvised a scene and opened his arms reciting, "They've torn the mask off the unknown! The Institutional Revolutionary Party has named its candidate! Prosperity and social justice! Land and Liberty! Amnesty for political prisoners! Barbecue! Government jobs! Get ready for it, woman, a new house, a car! Citizens! I . . . " The man collapsed like a sack of potatoes, and the poverty of the place was enveloped in the madness of his drunken torpor.

At night and already asleep, the children's voices clamored. "Shine your shoes, mister? Only a nickel. Come on, mister, can I do'em, huh?" They turned all their earnings over to their mother, avoiding their father. He hung around the others who'd begun to pick up pennies. Lencho not only did not contribute to supporting his family, but he made things worse by stealing from them anything he could to feed his vices. That afternoon, Lencho came home: two small rooms with a dirt floor and a crib for a roof. He did not frown over the three little kids, nor did he yell at them angrily as he usually did. With his arms wide open and a wide smile, he went over to them. His large, thin-lipped mouth was a wide horizontal stripe.

"Sons of my descent, you are already contributors, by your fertile and creative efforts, to the greatness of the country we all share."

The children looked at each other and smiled with surprised innocence. His wife stopped doing her laundry and pushed her hair back from her forehead with a look of disgust, knowing where the future president was headed, and she rushed over to tend to the little one who was screaming like a stuck pig because he was hungry. Lencho took advantage of the moment to hit his five sons up with the pretext that they should give him a "contribution" for a party for Buzz Saw's birthday. Buzz Saw was the nickname for Amadito, who was four years old, and his name came from his pointy, spaced teeth. The child quickly sucked the woman's teat dry and went on with his screaming. She was just in time to see Lencho put his blue tie on with a gesture of triumph.

"No, Lencho, no, for the love of God. Those ten dollars are for pencils and notebooks for when school starts."

"Woman, I already told you, the great future of the country. The people do not live by bread alone. I'm on my way to pick up a shipment of American chickens, so we can celebrate together the birthday of our little rosebud, ill-named Buzz Saw, with a banquet. Don't forget, woman, as far as the petroleum is concerned, not one step backwards."

The woman began to shriek with rage and emotion while the children seconded her with one voice, chicken, chicken, chicken. Lencho walked out with a haughty air. He did not look at the ground, and the corners of his lips were wrinkled like those of a horse that'd been pulling on the reins.

Lencho lost himself in the hustle and the colors of the city. It was daytime and happy laughter held sway, along with the sounds of yelling voices. Even purple seemed a happy color, even if it is the color of those who have been strangled or bitten by a poisonous snake. This was because the sun, all vigor and fire, clung to the bones, warm and tender, making everything glow with carnivalesque flashes.

An old woman with crooked eyes, who carried in her hand a play phone she'd bought for her grandson suffering from polio, stopped in the middle of the pavement to look at the sun. The angry traffic parted around her. Don Lencho del Valle was among the very few who heard what the old woman said. "What a cute sun! It doesn't even look like the tubercular sun we used to have in the olden days, always spitting out icy clouds." Lencho regaled the old woman with a bud from his bouquet of simplemindedness. "Have some civic mercy, ma'am, be patriotic and move along." The old woman only saw the back of a scarecrow wearing very short pants, and she wondered, "What did that puddlejumper mean?"

Lencho walked along on the lookout for people who looked important. He would bow slightly to them and as a greeting he would bring his right hand up to his eyes and then let it fall in a declamatory fashion. For the humble folk he showed a disdainful indifference. "The shapeless masses," he would mutter, putting his nose up in the air. Three blocks before he crossed the border, across from the corner where the hawker shouts through a funnel used as a horn, "Good shoes, attractive and inexpensive," Lencho heard a remark from Monón López, a man with a wild mat of hair and no job. Monón spent his time with his band of followers making comments to pretty women and insulting those who were ugly, "What zoo did that monkey escape from? . . . " Del Valle answered mentally, pretending he hadn't heard. "Ah, the unwashed masses! How lacking in agriculture you all are." Set to cross over to the United States, Lencho ran into an immigration official who seemed to have been born, precisely, for that oh-so-serious and inquisitive position. He checked his passport and asked him dozens of questions. Where he was from, what he did, where he'd been born, if they'd stolen his marbles when he was a child, if he believed in God, if he'd been born butt first, this, that, and the other thing. When the interrogation was over, Lencho let loose with something from his repertory. "We are countries joined by strong bonds of friendship, our disposed consciousnesses springing from the fountains of peace, liberty, and justice. Let us march forward with our hands linked along the paths of the centuries, forever sovereign." As when he always burbled a string of babblings, Lencho sighed with emotion, just like the politicians do when they run on with their stupidities and put the hungry populace to sleep. The official watched him walk away and frowned trying to understand what he had heard. Five minutes later he shook his head with a barely perceptible smile. The embryonic senator reached Gringoland walking with the same meticulous care as the natives, respecting the traffic lights religiously, admiring the order and neatness of his "cousins." Before entering the supermarket where he would buy the chickens, he contemplated a truly strange scene. For several minutes a middle-aged man, a transparent blond, shouted at the top of his lungs with a Bible in his hand, twisting every which way, falling to the pavement, and then bounding up like an acrobat. He began to shout even louder and the veins in his neck were swollen to their fullest, his color changing from yellow to cherry red. He was foaming at the mouth and every thirty seconds he mentioned hell or its president, the devil.

Lencho went right away into the supermarket, bought ten pounds of chicken, ordering it to be cut into pieces. They wrapped it in white paper and Lencho set out back home with his precious cargo. Since the clever fellow still had a few dollars left, he went into a bar along the way and asked for a whiskey on the rocks. He realized that the money would not last long that way and left. Whenever he drank whiskey, he would speak English without realizing it, just like any old bum. The act of buying the chickens turned out to be unusual, quite strange in the mental mechanism of his drinking sprees. He went into one of his watering holes with the package of meat. What Lencho García y del Valle did there is worthy of being called one of the greatest of his stupidities. He asked first off for a *parida*, which consists of a beer and a glass of tequila. If his tongue was naturally loose, with the drink, it suddenly became a valley of vipers. He looked at the bartender and the customers with an air of superiority, glancing meaningfully toward the package of chicken meat that he had placed in front of him on the bar, in plain sight of everybody. He insisted on staring at the package so that they would ask him what was inside. Since no one guessed, he started his ravings.

"The Revolution dismounted, sirs, so the children could eat. We in the supreme hour have drunk in the "waifful" springs. I proclaim that a youth that does not eat chicken will grow up crooked, because chicken, my fellow citizens, will give future generations wings. I bring accusations against any father who does not bring abundant meat of the volatile bird home to his children. May the fatherland sue him!"

Despite the fact that Lencho was known even to the dogs, he attracted the curiosity of the people. The simpleminded man punched a hole in the paper so a wing would show. He looked around him with a defiant smile, shouting like a vegetable monger: "This is what we eat in my home, sirs, and I'm very sorry if your families are undernourished with just beans." He tore the paper even more and took out two drumsticks, a breast, and the liver. He laughed as he said, "And the unmentionable interests even affirm the chronic suffering of the masses of the conglomerate. Fatherland, Masiosare, Mexican, your byword is to vote!"

By the time the bartender and his clients realized what was happening, Lencho had already flung the ten pounds of chicken pieces along the bar and was babbling feverishly. As he spoke, he made sure no one touched the meat. The brawl was not long in coming. Lencho set to fighting with a seedy old man, insisting that he had hidden a chicken neck under his hat. Since the old man was already all creaky, his sad reflexes, without being able to avoid it, saw a blow to his head and some jabs coming. When Lencho knocked his greasy hat off, you could see the neck caught in the few white hairs he still had left on his head.

The bartender turned around and, taking aim, landed such a tremendous kick to Lencho's butt that he fell and then tried to crawl away on all fours. The bartender was able to land another blow, as though from a mule in heat, to the same spot. Lencho fell to his knees crying for them to allow him to gather up the food his family was waiting for so anxiously.

In the confusion, the hungry old man emerged wiping the drivels of blood from his nose on his shirtsleeves. Since he was bald, blood had dried on his pate, and he looked like he'd been wounded with an ax.

"Gather your fucking food together, and get out and don't come back, you stupid asshole, pronto!" The package in which he'd brought the chicken was in shreds. Lencho quickly took his shirt off in order to use it to wrap the chicken, and he rapidly began to gather up pieces of meat from all over the place, with his blue tie dangling around his neck like a cowbell. Down on his hands and feet, half-naked and sobbing, he looked like a monster from outer space. Some of the pieces had fallen into the ashtrays and he found others on the floor. A drumstick was sticking out of a spittoon, and a breast had a heel mark stamped on it. He gathered together about seven pounds and stopped looking for the rest because he could see the menacing bartender out of the corner of his eye, and he knew how terribly painful his foot was. He made a package out of what he'd been able to get together and ran quickly to the door. He felt he was safe now, and he shouted back at them at the top of his lungs: "Now there's a real man in charge, assholes; we're on our way up and forward, sons of bitches." Everybody commented to the bartender on Lencho's incredible madness when, rotten luck, the bartender felt the impact to his right eye.

A chicken breast! A few minutes later it was all swollen, and he was seeing streaks of red.

That night Lencho García y del Valle's children had a real banquet. The table was set with a beat-up tray containing the pieces of chicken set out for the children. They took care of it with great care, knowing through bitter experience that such a lucky event would not repeat itself in many years. They ate making infernal noises. Only Chalito remained lost in a strange silence, barely touching the food. His mother had dressed him in clean, unironed clothes, and she had put a bag of rags over his chest so he wouldn't cough. The baby cried out in the other room, and the mother went to feed it. Lencho held her around her shoulders and nibbled her ears. Above the shouts of the kids, the cries of the set-upon female could be heard. At first they were feeble and then there were bursts of laughter and the heavy breathing of a duet, intertwined with yelps. While the baby howled away in his bed, the couple rolled around on the floor, making the child that would replace Chalito, who at that very moment was burning with the fiery breath of death. The next morning at three on the dot, Chalito spoke for the last time, asking if the world was trembling. When they went to bury Chalito, Lencho went crazy with grief and drunkenness. His weeping and yelling made him seem like a stuck bull. His mouth gave out a parade of the most incredible stupidities. He shouted that he was living in a society where only cheats prosper, where the pretty sayings of the two-faced only conceal sad realities, and where the commerce of whores is free and open. Lencho shouted at the top of his lungs that the judges sold for gold like the prostitutes. People looked with pity on the drunk who had gone mad from yelling so much. He ended up embracing Chalito's tomb and swearing, as though that would bring his son back to life, that in the future he would abhor the slimy vice of alcohol. He confided to him, sobbing and shaking, that he would be a working father filled with tenderness, that he would never, never let them lack clothes or food. The drunk collapsed on the grave, covering himself with the mud and dust that mixed with his tears and the slobbering that went with his sobs. That same afternoon, in his delirious unconsciousness he promised the dead little boy that he would take him to Disneyland, and there was a moment, before he fell into the slumber of the drunk, in which he laughingly called out to his absent son. "Abelardo, my son, come, I have something to tell you." Many people who knew Lencho García y del Valle affirm that he never touched a drop again and that he became sad and taciturn. He worked at whatever he could and did menial jobs. But others affirm that after his oath he drank little because he was in jail, mainly because he had gone over to the opposition party and went around with his new credo shouting such things that they lost no time in locking him up.

I FELL ON THE PLAINS that divide the border like someone falling into a no-man's-land. In the desert, virgin in the absence of any will toward the creative, my words threaded their way among the dust storms. The sky became tinged with a black wind that cloaked the dunes with layers of pale sand. I turned to see my tightly spaced steps, and they had already disappeared. Any innovation was answered by nothingness with its dead bell towers. And I was God writing pages in the wind so that my words would fly away. In the mysterious loneliness I sought the traces of His look. I only knew it, like an unspeaking child, intuiting fire in order to form worlds, planets, galaxies, with its little hands, urging on the life with which the clay animates itself, with water the color of the dawn. I wanted Him to say something to me. Now I know that He creates life and that I invent the language with which one speaks. Nevertheless, I lose myself in the tangle of vocabulary and the words that still are not born of thought and that make one's heart ache. I lost myself among the sand drifts of the Sonoran desert, seeking Him so that He might teach me the language of silence. I sought Him so that He might tell me what He asked the stars, feeling my heart so alone on that surface so full of sand and in that sky so full of lights. I was overwhelmed with feeling, and I cried to see in the desert the dreamed-of fatherland that would take me in its bosom, like a mother who loves and watches over all of her children equally. No more would my soul be wounded by the thorns of scorn and indifference. In the future I would be a true citizen requesting and receiving justice. I was overtaken by illusion, and I saw in Yuma the cosmic solitude of the Sonoran desert, the Republic that we wetbacks would inhabit, Indians sunk in misfortune and enslaved Chicanos. Ours would be the "Republic of Despised Mexicans." Our houses would emerge from the dunes that rise up to look like tombs, and the nomadic race, its feet wounded by centuries of pilgrimages, would finally have a roof crowned by good fortune. From the immensity of the sterile sand, bread would be born like grace. The lakes that magic paints from a distance, as though they had only been lighted by the centuries, would suddenly take on the life that would return them to the reality of the movement that animates the fountains and the rivers. Scourged by the tenebrous winds that roast with the cruelty of pyres, the voices of the deceitful would flee, bearing with them tribunes of hypocrites who betray the trust of both their children and their forebears. I was overtaken by imagination, and I saw in my pilgrimage many Indian peoples reduced by the torture of hunger and the humiliation of plunder, traveling backwards along the ancient roads in search of their remote origin. They ended up downcast, ceremonious in their gait and with the ritual gestures of beings who know the depths of human secrets. They came to seek life and the worthy embrace of the graveyards. I was overtaken by the enthusiasm of dreaming with my eyes open, and I saw that through the wide doors of the unploughed lands there entered multitudes of Chicano brothers who made paths and roads to peace and tranquility from the immense sandy plains. Their backs were bent and there was bitterness on their faces and the infinite weariness of slaves. They embrace their Indian forebears, and together they all cry in silence, burying those who have been killed, who are so many that no one can ever count them. I began to drown in feeling, and I cried over that warped wasteland with its outcroppings. Sand and moon dripped from their clothes, and driven by the thirst of the winds, the exodus of wetbacks dragged its feet because of the greed of the powerful. And behind them, the life of their families was conditioned to the adventure that they would experience in a strange land. I was hurt by the despair of feeling that utopia is ever a burning coal in consciousnesses tortured by the denial of sublime aspirations, and I fell to my knees begging for mercy.

"WHAT'S GOING ON, MAN! How ya doing? You sure look great."

"Well, here I am, brother coyote, like the devil with St. Michael."

"Damn! You're sure skinny. If you're not careful, the vultures are going to fly away with you. Did they put the basket of tortillas where you couldn't get at them?"

"Yeh, the burros are all skin and bones."

"What happened? Did they have you in jail?"

"No, but the fucking gringos have just laid a stiff penalty on me. What happened is I went to work on the other side, over in California. I lasted three months."

"No, man. Really?"

"Damn shits, they want to do you in in one day. Just look at me, they left me sucked dry. And the worst part is the INS got me. They rounded up about 250 of us in Tucson and locked us up in a little room barely big enough for us, in the middle of July, so you get the idea. I had saved up $312. That got lifted from me in the lockup, who the hell knows by who. If they dumped me over here by California, it was because I told them I'm from Matamoros. The ones from over there say they're from over here, and they drop them where they're from. That way we get the best of them. But sometimes they even dump you over in Veracruz. Some of them are real neat guys, but others are assholes, and that's being kind."

"How many times have they picked you up?"

"This makes four times."

"Shitheads, because they have no idea what to do with you. You enter by breaking the law, and they've got to get you out by force. The gringos saw that they can't keep up with the numbers that need to be detained."

"The fact is that it's their own fault. We wouldn't go if they didn't give us work. Why bother? They punish us, and the ones who give us jobs get off scot-free because they have someone to do their harvest for lousy pay."

"You planning on crossing over again?"

"Probably."

"Then, if they like the bad life, they can go fuck themselves."

"But it's tough over here without anything to eat."

"No, man, you can make a living over here too, there's always a way. Go find one."

"I've got a great idea, but it's not selling the kind of junk you push."

"Come on, fellow, maybe that ball you've got on top of your neck is good for something."

"I'm going to see if I can get in as an apostle. Maybe I'd like to be St. Peter."

"Yeh, they really left you daffy."

"No, I've got a good lead. I'll tell you about it later. See you around."

"Don't be afraid of me. *I'm an ugly old man, but I love kids a lot. What's your name, little fellow?"*

"Chalito, sir."

"How old are you?"

"Seven."

"Have you earned a lot of money today shining shoes?"

"No, sir, barely four pesos. I get tired, and the sun bothers me."

"The sun isn't bad. Poor kid, you work hard. Yes, don't look at me that way. It's got to light the day, and since it gets tired too, at night it tells its wife, the moon, about it. Do you know her, Chalito? She's white, with splotches all over her face, and he tells her, you shine while I sleep. She answers, I'm real scared. So you won't be afraid, my beloved moon, an army of stars will guard you."

"And when you can't see the moon, where does she go? Come on, let's see."

"Humm, well, she goes home to make love to her husband, the sun, so the lagoons will tremble with toads and the fields will turn green, green and beautiful, and the storks will land bearing children."

"Hah, hah, hah, what funny tales you have to tell, sir, hah, hah, hah."

"Chalito, look at how much money I made today washing cars. My pockets are full of money, thousands of pesos. Take them, as much as you want!"

"What a nice man you are, Mr. Loreto! How good you are. . . . How . . . good. . . .

Part Two

So God's hereabouts. I never thought I'd meet Him in person, much less here on the border. Well, yes, I have my illusions about meeting Him, but there in His glory, if it's His pleasure to remember this sinner. Did you say that you can see Him every day? Listen, tell me about it. He's that guy over there? Well, I'm going to catch up with Him and have a chat.

"Excuuuuse me, sir. Wait up, Don Jesús. Damn, what I least expected, to discover Him here in California. But He didn't get away here among all these people. Listen, my friend, yes, you. Did you happen to see which way an Indian went? He was about this tall, real big, kind of fat, with eyes like stones, but real lively."

"The one called Little Jesús of Bethlehem? He went in the market there. You'll have a hell of a time finding him. When he's sold his pieces of paper he goes and has himself a drink."

"Well that takes care of that, what with so many old women selling vegetables and this swarm of flies from the devil and nobody bothering to bathe him."

"Lemon water, baaarley water, saaaage water!"

"Come on, if you don't buy, you can't squeeze the merchandise."

"Listen, friend . . . "

"What's up, fellow, what's the matter?"

"Give me a quarter and I'll tell you where the guy is you're looking for, and I'll let you have one of Little Jesús' papers for twenty cents."

"Here you are. Let me have the paper so I can see what it says."

Dios EN CHANÍA. *Dios en choco. Hehui.*

I have seen many burros, but there are burros that are more burros than the burros themselves.

The universe is asymmetrical and has no end; it's round instead.

Time does not exist. It is perennial space.

In the stars and in all matter there is only temporary temporality.

Mind-space. Body-star. Soul-universe.

Humanity . . . Ah, there's your son, woman. . . . Ah, there's your mother. . . . Ah, there's your cross, humanity.

Jesús of Bethlehem, Sonora. Yaqui Nation. Republic of Mexico.

"My God! Who is that strange man who talks both like a clown and a wiseman? I want to meet him."

"Boss, try a hat on, look how pretty they are. Come on, boss man, I'll let you have it cheap."

"Don't be a pest. I'm in a hurry."

"Peanuts here, sir. Buy some from me, so I can be blessed."

"Buy yourself a jacket, chief."

"Open up or I'll drag you out."

"Now we've really blown it."

"Move over, sir, he's carrying ice for the ice cones."

"Let's see when the hell I can get out from under this crowd. I can see the Good Samaritan Tavern over there. I'm sure the Messiah is over there having a cold beer. The sun outside is so strong that I can't see a damn thing in here. I think that's him over there at that table in the corner.

Now that I can make things out better in this heavy darkness, I can see that Jesús is not very old, even though he's not roasted in the first burst of flame. As far as I can see, he's about 33. He's tall and full bodied, and you can see he's good at eating and the wine's never very far away. Hot damn! But he's a pure Yaqui for sure. No wonder he's so quick witted.

"*Sir . . .* "

"*What do you want?*"

"*I believe in you, Jesús of Bethlehem.*"

"*You're lying!*"

"*Let me stay by your side. I want to be a fisher of men.*"

"*Stupid is what you are, you're really a dumb one. I don't need you. I work on my own.*"

"*Are you the Christ?*"

"*I am Jesús, because that's the name they baptized me with. I'm from Bethlehem because that's where I was born, in the Yaqui nation. Sit down, but you pay for the beer.*"

"*I know that you go from town to town curing the sick and forgiving sins in the name of God the Father.*"

"*And what's it to you!*"

"*I want to be your shadow, sir, to help you save souls.*"

"*You would deny me the first time there was any danger. You want to follow me because you think this mission is a gringo movie in glorious*

Technicolor. But it isn't. You have to traverse the deserts, suffer the snow out in the open, put up with being stoned and whipped, share filthy jail cells with carnivorous rats, fight against a hunger so bad that you feel like it's eating at your innards. Saving people is like dying over and over again, rising to your feet under the weight of a cadaver, spit upon even by those who you thought were the faithful. Just because today you see me enjoying myself with this delicious foam, you can't think that my life is all fun."

"I've always thought that I wanted to become something. . . . Something, that's why, sir. . . . "

"Shut up! Don't call me sir. I was born Jesús of Bethlehem, in Sonora, just like any other guy down on his luck. But stupid people have turned me into a miracle worker on their own. Certainly, my name and the name of my hometown are just like those of that blessed man I beg to cure the sores of my sins."

"Why have you gone so far as to claim you're God?"

"Because they've convinced me. I was only twelve years old when the warlocks of my town proclaimed my word to be wisdom. What I did then was to dance the pascola and to talk about things having to do with the faith and to eat huacavaque. And when I grew up, I had to go along. Those with neurasthenia trembled before me, but they calmed down the minute I touched them. I got scared and tried to run, but my parents wouldn't let me because it wasn't to their advantage. How could they if the minute I became divine their stomachs began to shine. The little old holy women turned me into a walking altar. Old sluts without any business would bow before me a thousand times, looking like they were oh so sweet but really vipers. I swear to you that for a moment I accepted the sacrifice and thought about pure being with all the faith the tormented can muster."

"Are you drunk already, Jesús?"

"Bah! I'm just getting mellow."

"Whenever anybody's mentioned your name, I know you've sown good, planted faith, and that your memory is venerated."

"You're young and you don't know how to distinguish hate from feigned goodness. Some say my name with tenderness and their tongue is rotten from cursing me in silence."

"Curse you? When all you've done is lavish love."

"I was twenty-two when I left my hometown with the goal of changing my name, very anxious to get married to a good girl, because my blood was already becoming like what a volcano spews out. I couldn't sleep I was so hot. It was in those days that I crossed the Bacatete range. I spent four days and four nights contemplating the rocks down a ravine, the trees, the animals in the hills, the sky, the riverbeds, and everything that I am and what I do not know. I knew then that I'm an old tree, very old, and you can't imagine the sap that flowed within me. In my arms, on my shoulders, in my hair, a symphony of birds lived. I felt myself happy, very happy, in spite of how those were the days when the sun hurled its columns of fire at the earth. The nights were cool to me because I went about naked like an animal. You see, I would begin to sing out of happiness, and my voice would go out from the throat of the canyons to fly among the valleys. Have you ever felt yourself to be a raging river? How marvelous it feels! You come down from the heights, roaring like a bull, carrying along with you the dry, useless branches, bringing the greenery to life, and you carry along in your current the seeds for those same trees withered by the years to be born again, just like you were a stream of life. It doesn't take long for you to feel like a tree yourself at the same time you're a riverbed. You also feel like a deer when you see them running like they were flying with those horns that in reality are dismembered wings. I sat down to think, wanting to know about the rocks and the sky, when all of a sudden I began to feel myself full of thorns, and why not, since I was made of juicy pulp, full of sap and chlorophyll. If you want to feel something really, really beautiful, pretend you are a prickly pear. When I got up from that spot much later, I felt very, very much like getting married, like having a woman that would be like a valley where my seed would bloom. Don't think that it was just my idea. It was something very, very strong that came from within me, but also from without. And so I emerged from my meditations ready to have a woman no matter what. I wouldn't be lying to you if I said that I was overtaken by a single fit of trembling, and I trotted off—better yet, I took off in a dead run—to look for a woman because I'd gotten the itch. I'll tell you, I could feel them all swollen. I reached a far-off town, certain that I would begin a new life. I entered riding a burro that I had stolen along the way. There was a fiesta going on. The arches over the streets had a legend that said "Welcome, Jesús of Bethlehem." To make the story short, that very week I fucked the mayor's wife and his three daughters. Hah, hah, hah, hah."

"Damned impostor! You're nothing but a clown!"

"Hah, hah, whuh, whuh, hah, hah."

"Stop your laughing, you devil, you're making the earth tremble! Impostor!"

Impostor! . . . Are you crying? Your cheeks are streaming with tears, false redeemer. . . . I can see . . . a lot of pain in your face. What a strange man this one is. His upper lip hangs there for a few seconds, limp on top of the lower one, as if all his cleverness were already overcome, and you can even see foam at the corners of his mouth. Then, in an instant, his eyes start to shine so bright that it's as though he were burning on the inside from knowing so much. Just a moment ago he was shaking from laughter just like a leafy tree as though he were capable of going crazy. All his damned sensuality and craftiness overflowed his belly with jumping grasshoppers, and burlesque maliciousness flowed from every pore of his rakish face. Then suddenly I can see in his face full of the suffering of humanity all the anguish and tears accumulated throughout the centuries and the whole tragedy of the tormented Indian. The way he looks at this moment, he could be nailed to the cross, wounded on his side, contemplating the vastness of space. My God! He's blowing his nose so hard, worse than Joshua in his best days as a feller of walls.

The people turned me into a redeemer, for I was a poor sinner so full of passions. I swear to you that in my sad farce I have known suffering and I have cried alongside the poor. How many times did they come trembling, crying for my help! Bread, Lord! To the health of the one who comes for your blessing. Justice, Lord! I blessed them and ran to hide myself, to cry with powerlessness and to beg for forgiveness from my Lord! Pardon me, Lord, for bearing your blessed name, for having been born in a town with the same name as the glorious town in which you were born! I am not guilty, I am not to blame. . . . Serve me another glass, son, before it turns warm.

"I don't understand you. Who are you, strange man?"

"Just an ordinary human being. Do you think I am not tormented by the horror of my sin? In order to pay for my sin, I will be accompanied by my crosses wherever my steps bear me. . . . "

"Crosses?"

"Look at my shirt. Do you see my back full of scars? Just take a look at my chest and abdomen covered with the signs of torture. These scars on my back are from when they tore me to shreds with thorn-covered branches in one of those towns that exist all over the place. I shouted for anyone who had bread to share it with the hungry, for

anyone who was dying from the cold to receive from his brother who
had clothes a piece of his blanket. What most bothered the rich was that
I yelled that the worker must be paid what is just, otherwise prayers
would not suffice to get the exploiters out of hell itself. As in most of
those towns, in all, not just those in the Sonoran Valley, there are three
or four rich men, and the rest are hungry and live enslaved. There was
always a Judas to denounce me. These do not need to pretend and are
to be found in abundance. The rich, who are the law, ordered Procopio,
a chief who remembered he had a pool filled with blood for his pleasure,
to punish me. They whipped me with thorn-covered branches of green
mesquite. They were going to hang me, but as a storm with lightning
came up very suddenly, the cowards thought that I had supernatural
powers and let me go. In the capital, they kicked me until they thought
I was dead because I went through all the streets announcing that the
politicians are aborted fetuses of the devil, and that no one like that
would enter the kingdom because they were so brazen and covered with
the eight deadly sins."

"Aren't there seven?"

"Politics makes eight. You have no idea how many towns have per-
secuted me for talking about redemption. I have known more than 100
jails. And you should know that it is hard to play the part of a saint,
because the business dealings in this commerce of the spirit are so strong
that those who already have their position will not allow any competition. It's good for you to know that there are pharisees and real Judases
in every town who are in possession of the laws of God and of this
world. I have only been false because I was born with the tragic destiny
of redeemer without having been sent by the Supreme One."

"But what about the miracles? There are those who say that they
owe their lives and their health to you."

"Ah, right! The sordid dragged themselves to me, after so much
sinning their twisted souls actually caused them physical pain. Adulter-
ous women who mixed their sins with their prayers. Blood thirsty and
powerful men who dripped pus from their stinking consciences. I recognized them just by looking at their startled eyes, because they had already lost all hope of being forgiven. They knew very well in their
hearts that it doesn't matter how much money they pay out, they'll be
burned anyway. I would stare at them and ask: Do you believe in the
name of Jesús? Are you prepared to sin never again? Just at the suggestion of the precious name, they would break down in tears. Almost all

of them were susceptible to the sufferings of remorse. One day they would awake very sick with liver trouble, and the next day they would have heart trouble, migraines, back pains. They would even invent illnesses. When they were cured by suggestion, their physical pains would disappear and they would go forth to preach my divine powers without realizing that all they'd done was stumble on their own faith. I was the most surprised to see how some of them were cured, although I also saw the pernicious, determined to rot away."

"Blessed be God."

"The frustrated would complain about the pain in their chest and their migraines. Those bastards were the tomb of some great moribund affection. They had loved with such strength that they had not resigned themselves to casting out the beloved who had abandoned them or whom they had abandoned in a moment of blindness. And since they bore him within, shrouded in anxiety and rancor, he rotted away on them and poisoned their flesh little by little."

"Then, Jesús, you don't just cure souls, you're also a medical doctor?"

"Well, listen to me well. Even though I'm a clown, I'm more of a doctor than many creeps who lost a lot of sleep studying at the university. Just think, I bet you know some of those dopes."

"Sir, let me refill your glass."

"Better you serve me nothing. I can see you've never had more than sweet atole to drink. Look, tip your glass this way, otherwise it fills up with foam, and more than beer, what you drink looks like burro piss."

"Well, pardon me."

"If you're going to talk to me about beer, talk to me about beer that's good and cold. I don't give a shit which brand. But don't go saying that the beer is warm, because that would really be the end of our friendship. There's a lot of dumb-ass people who grab the beer mugs with both hands. And what do you expect? They warm the beer up in two seconds flat, and then drink it like it was soup. I suggest you pick the glass up with two fingers, take a big draught, and then leave it in peace on the table. Don't worry about your glass being taken away, and as far as I know it doesn't have feet."

"And were you able to cure the ones who were frustrated?"

"The majority, yes."

"Also by suggestion, Jesús from Bethlehem?"

"In order to help their suggestion, I prescribed vomitives and ene-
mas, and I assure you that none of them had bad insides. Since the fact
is that those who suffer from the soul don't take care of their body, I
would get them with their bellies good and full. They would unload so
much junk that even their corrupt ideas would pop out like the cork
from a bottle of sparkling cider."

"Then, sir, you've provided salvation and are on the way to puri-
fying your soul. Let me follow your steps and lavish good fortune."

"Don't be an ass and order another pitcher—my bladder's just
starting to unwind. If you think being a redeemer means being filled
with chocolate and cookies, answering the stupidities of the powerful
and dumb old ladies, trading on the name of the Lord, you sure are
wrong. And don't think that it also means driving a new car like those
gringos who carry fancy Bibles around. . . . Hummm! No, look, it's
best you understand that anyone who plays the part of redeemer pays
the consequences sooner or later. No person who is unjust realizes that
he is unjust, no way. Leave that for others. It's enough to tell you that
a lot of bastards cry like babies when they hear the word of Our Lord,
praying and all that stuff, but don't ask them for charity and justice for
the hungry, because then they will call you a Communist and an enemy
of God. How does that strike you? They'll turn you into a rabid dog
and beat the shit out of you. No, they won't beat you! But if you insist
and if you have enough guts to defend the poor and give them counsel,
they probably will. So then, come follow me, we'll see if you can give as
good as you talk. And if you split, you won't be the first who's all talk."

"Damn! Come on, you shitheads. The police are on their way
over here."

"Ay, sweet mama, those heartless hangmen are coming, thirsty
for blood. Blessed Jesus! What can I do, little mama, I can't move
from this spot. That's Trompas, accompanied by two mean dogs.
Trompas is the one who's paid to kill students in Mexico City. He
came to the border with his tail between his legs because a careless photographer took his picture at the same time he was getting
a student during one of the many bloodbaths. Now he's a police
lieutenant. He broadcast to the whole world how many time she'd
gotten drunk, and took real pride in having everyone call him
The Falcon. But everyone calls him Trompas, Elephant Face, because his mouth looks more like a dangling appendix. He's a little
squirt with mad monkey eyes. But . . . Who's that guiding

them? . . . It looks like it's the same old stool pigeon. It must be the same rat fink as always, the traitor Bullas el Chilacayote. They won't be long in arriving, and they're looking for him. My God! What a look on his face. . . . Jesús . . . you don't look like you're afraid, only that you're calm . . . and filled with infinite goodness. His face is glowing. He's so ugly, but now he looks as handsome as a river that flows so clear that you can see sand and bright stones on the bottom and the green world of the plants covered with clear water. What a strange man! I knew him as a coyote, but now I see him looking sad and smiling with a resignation that is so great that I don't know in reality if it's Him."

"*Come and seek me. Come near, Prieto, and try to cover me. Let's see, pal, earn your fifty cents and point out the one called the Redeemer.*"

"*It'll be the one I hug, chief.*"

"*Master . . .* "

"*Chilacayote, will you sell me for two bits?*"

"*Is that you, Jesús of Bethlehem?*"

"*If you say so.*"

"*Is that you, the same one who goes to the plazas, the marketplaces, the streets, denouncing the government at the top of your voice and shouting against the police and the mayor of this town, against honorable people, stirring up the common folk and spurring the Indians to revolt?*"

"*All I've said is that blessed are those who are hungry for justice, because they will be filled.*"

"*Take this, shitface, maybe you'll learn!*"

"*Chief, you broke his whole jaw when you hit him with the rifle butt.*"

"*So what? You, Squinty, give him a kick in the balls.*"

"*Ayyyyyyyyyyyyyyyyy, ayyyyyyyyyyyyy!*"

"*You, Jackal, kick him in the mouth so he'll learn.*"

"*Unnnnnnnnnnnnnnnh, unnnnnnnnnnnnh!*"

"*Carry him off to jail! Tie him up and whip him if he starts to fall asleep.*"

"*Chief, this one walked with Jesús.*"

"*Aha, so you're one of Jesús' followers.*"

"*No! No, sir! Look, I sat down next to that Yaqui because there were no free seats. I don't even know him.*"

"As far as I know you're an ally of this agitator creep, a word that makes me throw up. Just enough to beat the shit out of you! You don't know how much I want to beat the hell out of you, just in case."

"But boss, I was just sitting there next to that damned impostor, and we didn't even say anything to each other. I even made a bad impression, and he thought I was a moocher."

"Get going, then, and watch yourself."

"My God!" How painful it is to be a redeemer. I'd be better off tomorrow to slip through the fence over to Gringoland and pick cotton, over there by Peoria, Arizona. I'd rather be a cotton picker than a gatherer of the down-and-out.

LORETO, THE NOSTALGIC YAQUI, lived for a few minutes the dream of an episode in his life, a dream that was more intense than actual fact. The young hippie who remained to one side watched over the sleep of the ancient man with great seriousness, as though that Indian were an important piece in something he needed to identify.

"Chayo Cuamea, brother! Colonel, sir."

"Loreto, my pal!"

"I said you can count on my brother Loreto. Now these guys'll see what happens to traitors. You, buddy, are my second in command with the same rank as when we were with Cachetón. Colonel! Review the troops, then."

There wasn't even a hundred of them. Loreto saw them in his dream, perhaps as he had thought about them in that faraway day: a group of silent Indians alongside skeletal horses. He walked over to touch them."

"Cuamea, buddy, these soldiers . . . They're made of stone! "

Rosario Cuamea, the man who deflowered death, laughed out loud. His expression changed suddenly. It was no longer laughter, but tears. He looked hard at his buddy Chayo, who looked just like him, but tears were streaming from his eyes. How strange! When he was alive, Colonel Chayo never cried, at least not in front of anyone. But dreams are rather capricious like that.

"Yes, Loreto, pal, they're probably made of stone, but that way they can't be shot, nor do they bleed. And if someone hits them, ah, my friend, how their hand'll hurt."

"Come take a look over here, these two are my sons, José Jesús and Jesús María."

The two little Indians' eyes were half closed, like oblique slits, and their cheeks were like clenched fists. The other Indians also looked humiliated, their hair down over their forehead. If you looked at the eyes of the horses, they were sad and as black as diamond mirrors, with an immense bitterness in the bottom of those eyes as though all the trees had lost their leaves forever. The Yaqui Loreto was so anxious to return to his land that he sought out its ancient landscapes in his mind. Only he couldn't make out the mountains or the trees. He discerned a desert with dark shades that disappeared against a black backdrop.

Cuamea, buddy . . . What about my godson, Chayito, where's he?

Perhaps Loreto's dreams had already been corrupted by the influence of television, vomiting out its filthy stories. But the fact of the matter is that suddenly the image of the petrified Indians vanished, to be replaced by the vision of his godson Chayito. He was hanging from a gigantic and very strange, dried-up tree, and he did not look like a run-of-the-mill hanged man, not at all. He was dressed up like the fanciest dude on a holiday, and he swayed back and forth like a heartbeat.

"My buddy Loreto!"

"My pal Cuamea! Where are you?"

"We're being attacked."

"Who's attacking?"

"The live forces, who else."

"But the people, buddy . . . the people . . . the Indians . . . "

What he could see in the background was not just a few petrified men but thousands, millions. He turned to look at his buddy Chayo, but he was also made of stone, with a grin that ran from ear to ear. No. Instead he was crying out loud like he was in agony. He remembered suddenly Cuamea's crafty deed when the latter seduced Death. He imagined her furious, her bones cracking in fits of rage, beating herself by clacking one bone against another, hysterical because the gutsy Yaqui had stolen her virginity. Ah, Colonel Chayo Cuamea. But he got his way. Strange dreams, the Indian Loreto's. Despite the drowsiness into which he'd fallen, he was awakened by voices that he could not understand. Loreto

heard the stubborn horn of a very fancy car. He started to walk
over, thinking that it was a client, despite how very clean the car
looked. He wasn't the one they were honking for, but rather the
hippie who had been sitting alongside him. The latter didn't realize it, and continued to look indifferent, pretending he wasn't paying any attention. A man about fifty years old got out.

"*Come here, son. Let's go home.*"

"*I don't feel like it. Leave me alone.*"

The man's eyes were the color of water and his look had the
hardness of steel. An old woman, crying, stuck her head out of
the window of the car.

"*Dear Bobby, don't break your poor mother's heart.*"

A huge dog with pumpkin eyes and hair combed like that of a
real person was sitting on the seat next to the woman. The dog
wore a richly bejeweled wristwatch on one of its front paws.

"*Bobby, let's go home.*"

The hippie angrily stood up and spit at the man.

"*Get out of here and leave me alone. As far as I'm concerned, you
can go straight to hell.*"

The man returned to the car. Those who were behind him
were honking noisily at him to move on. They pulled away. The
old woman's whining was joined by the barking of the dog.

The Foxye family lived across the border in the neighboring
town of Green Land. He had important business interests in real
estate and had managed to accumulate a huge fortune. Bobby was
their only son.

In earlier days the couple worked around the clock trying to
put their projects on a good footing, saving every penny in total
abstinence from anything that meant spending a cent on having
fun. They even ate poorly in order to save money. The precepts of
religion were a great help to them in their economic goals, since
they were forbidden to drink or smoke or do anything that meant
spending money without income. But that did not keep them from
accumulating wealth, even wealth based on the suffering of
others.

In their the desire to save money, they would manage to con-
vince themselves they were not stingy, but rather a very moderate
couple who lived in accord with norms of prudence and who were
very much opposed to the ugly sin of gluttony. He pondered the

virtues of the lentil bean with considerable erudition, declaring such seeds to be the ideal food. Thus, days would go by in which they would alleviate hunger with steaming pots in which a few dozen lentil beans floated. In the end, they grew tired of the large quantities of iron that the lentil beans contained and chose instead any old consommé made from bones stripped of all meat and skin, bones that even starving dogs would have turned their noses up at disdainfully. On another occasion they became vegetarians, allowing themselves to be swayed by one of the many heroes of the young, and they stuffed themselves with spinach. They washed their own clothes on the pretext of getting physical exercise and getting the blood circulating. In order to save the cost of electricity, they only turned the lights on in the room where they were. When they drove their car, they cut the motor on the down grade. And the height of avarice was that both of them wore the same underwear so much that they became shreds of cloth hanging from the elastic band, like Hawaiian skirts.

Bobby's birth altered the tasks of the couple. His crying took a lot of time away from planning their business operations. Since they were so stingy, they refused to pay a babysitter. Seven months after he was born, whenever Bobby cried at the top of his lungs, the two of them would look at each other as if saying, what dopes we were! It's a curse for misers to have children. Proof of how much it hurt them to have to support Bobby was the decision the two made together. They decided that Mr. Foxye would be fixed. Mr. Foxye went to a doctor who performed an operation that took about fifteen minutes and that would prevent him from having children for the rest of his life. With great skill and precise instruments he got fixed faster than a wink. Despite having been left a castrato, the doctor assured him that he would be able to continue having sex and that maybe even his sex life would be more intense, something that left Mr. Foxye indifferent since his first love lay with accumulating gold. According to him he had no time and energy to waste on frivolities; that was for unemployed bums and not for him because he was so careful. From then on, Mr. Foxye was like the geldings and the eunuchs. When Bobby turned seven, the Foxyes had already amassed their first million, and the gears of their business dealings were so well in place that their capital grew unchecked and new millions were not long in coming. About then they allowed themselves the luxury of hiring a nanny to take charge of the child. The reaction of the wealthy pair turned out to be paradoxical. They went after the million dollars in order to feel themselves secure and, when they had the million dollars, they suddenly saw themselves isolated, upset, cursed by an immense solitude and with no real friends. All they had were enormous material interests. She became active in high-class clubs, while he became sullen, immersing himself even more in his sea of numbers. Both seemed to be prematurely old by the time they were about to turn forty. Being a millionaire prompted Mr. Foxye to increase the song and dance about his family tree, and every time he was introduced, he would go on and on about his glorious origins and his great-great grandparents who had descended from a ship with a springtime name. It seemed to him superfluous to clarify that they came to America because they were dirt poor in their place of origin. According to him, they had come off the boat surrounded by the glow of the divine mission to Christianize the Indians, so much so that the Indians received the angelical hosts like brothers they had not seen in a long time and shared with them whatever they had, beginning with the turkeys. They ate together and praised God for having entrusted the destiny of a blessed nation into their hands. Mr. Foxye ended his lovely story by adding that his people had shown their gratefulness to the Lord for His great gift by not sinning or drinking spirits or smoking tobacco, and by doing much less of what they called fornication. All human evil was contained by these three sins, according to the millionaire. If he knew about any others, he glossed over them. The few times that he happened to have his son Bobby near him, he told him the same story. He told him so many times that the child could see in his mind's eye his forebears getting off the boat with the enormous wings of a bald eagle. An enigmatic smile would appear in Bobby's eyes and on his mouth, fixed by the image of the women with their vaporous clothes and the blush of innocence on their cheeks, the men tall and proud with the sententious dignity of the prophet. The woman began to want another child with fervor, and the desire for another son clutched at her obsessively—nature finally asserted itself over her. Her maternal instincts awakened with a fire that she was unable to extinguish, but both of them had been accomplices in the decision in favor of sterilization. The hapless Mr. Foxye guessed what was going on, and as a consequence he felt like King Midas. His wife frequented high social circles and was involved in charity benefits. But this was more for the purpose of flirting, since she wanted urgently to find a real man, someone who would put out that raging fire that had her on the edge of hysteria. The woman tried to drown her tears at night, but her husband, who had discerned the reason for her crying and in order to mask his frigidity, offered to buy her whatever she wanted in order to make her happy. The woman calmly answered that she didn't even know what she had. From his tenth birthday on, the child was raised in boarding schools. Despite the fact that these boarding schools could not offer the warmth of the home, he preferred it to his parents'. When he visited them, all he heard about was business. They swam furiously in an enormous sea of numbers. When they took a break, they would watch television and, without exchanging a word, laugh uproariously at the comedians who filled the screen with pratfalls and pies in the face. They never talked to him, except about trivial matters.

When the episode of the dramatic rupture took place, Bobby had already celebrated his twenty-second birthday. The dog had been bought when he was tiny. The wealthy woman came to love it with the love of a mother. She prepared a bedroom for it, and daily she lavished him with snow-white sheets and delicious steaks. As happens with rich women, the little dog with the watery eyes, tender look, and the behavior of a spoiled child captivated her immediately, touching on her most intimate maternal heartstrings. She baptized it with the name Angel. The man didn't like what was going on, but since he saw that his wife had calmed down, he accepted the consequences. Angel grew by leaps and bounds, and on his hind legs he was as tall as an average-sized man. Nevertheless, he howled with the demand that the putative mother concede to the habit of putting him to sleep in her lap every night, singing him bedtime songs and giving him a bottle. The veterinarian who took care of him was in seventh heaven with such a wealthy client who came by twice a week. He said with enthusiasm that it was the prettiest dog he had ever seen. He was the one who took charge of providing her with bottles with special nipples so she could give the dog warm milk. The jubilant old woman paid back the praise with unusual displays. The dog became a little like a human as the result of living in such comfort, and he would grunt when he wanted to take a leak. The last straw was when the eccentric millionaire put a television in front of the lucky hound's bed. The only thing the dog lacked was to be able to read books and discuss stupid politics like the lying bosses. Things backfired on the clever Mr. Foxye. He had himself fixed so he wouldn't have another child and thus save money and time, and the dog ended up costing him more than if he'd had a dozen kids. It didn't take the spoiled Angel long to jump up on Mr. Foxye's legs and lick his face. Although influenced by his wife, the truth was that he felt little passion for the dog, although a little affection. And he was sincerely grateful to him, because thanks to the animal he no longer had much in the way of marital obligations in that area where his capacity had diminished so notably. In the first place, because he had had himself sterilized, and secondly because he had a tremendous appetite for chickens. And, moreover, he had himself shaved in a barbershop. Of course, it was Mr. Foxye himself who suggested that they brush Angel's teeth with a sweet-smelling toothpaste, because his breath smelled like beans. The dog was not content to express his affection with just growls, but rather he liked to stick his slobbery tongue out and, quick as a wink, lick Mr. Foxye's face with marked effusion. When the Foxyes took a trip to Alaska to visit friends, Angel was not allowed to accompany them due to the commercial airline's regulations. The sensitive woman left instructions to have him call her every day at four in the afternoon. Honey-filled words mixed with sobs and barks from the lonely dog crossed the ice from Alaska to Green Land. The four-legged animal became a little human, but also the Foxyes became doglike. Their personalities already betrayed a marked canine accent. In reality Angel was not a pretty dog. Too large and fat, he moved clumsily. His ears were each the size of catcher's mits, and his snout was bigger than that of a lazy politician. The affectionate woman decided to take him to the beauty parlor, and there they managed to change his appearance by giving him a wig. Long hair and a cut toupée over his forehead! Finally, although they would never have admitted it, they found in Angel the son they had wanted.

This was the way the strange rich couple lived, and fortune, like an avalanche, continued to snowball. Bobby had not been home for three years, but he wrote them constantly. They'd had to increase his monthly allowance significantly, and he attended the most prestigious universities. He spent the summers studying in Europe and promised to turn into a brilliant lawyer. The couple was surprised that Bobby had not visited. The student was evasive about the reason and made up thousands of pretexts, while his parents feared something abnormal in such a prolonged absence. The rich man confronted his son and told him to come home immediately, promising to increase the allowance for his studies even more and alleging that it was necessary to take care of some document shaving to do with money to be invested in his name. Once in touch, they agreed on the day and hour that Bobby would come home. But he was late for the date and didn't show up until a Thursday afternoon. The patient thriftsavers lived in a three-bedroom house in a section of the city where a thousand identical houses had been built out of prefabricated materials. The old woman spied Bobby and recognized the outline of his body, but since it was growing dark she could not make out his features. She was looking out the window waiting for Angel, who had gone out to go to the bathroom. She started yelling, here's Bobby! She was all excited about the arrival of her missing son. Old man Foxye told his wife that he would put his extensive business dealings in the hands of his son. His youth and his education would be powerful levers for making the capital produce more. They congratulated each other on the occasion, happy to have a son. They were overcome by such an intense emotion that they decided to retire from business and to travel and enjoy life, because finally their son would be more clever than they at handling finances. The man's tongue got away from him, and he affirmed, "We'll even take little Angel with us, no way will we leave him behind." The woman reacted contentedly, because just to mention the beloved dog was to touch her heart. But at the same time she was anxious to embrace the child she had never had enough time to cuddle when he was an infant. When the doorbell rang, the two jumped up automatically, filled with emotion. When Bobby came into the house, the two stifled a cry of surprise. The young man was wearing a

strange suit of clothes, full of holes and covered with dust. It
looked more like clothes that were falling apart after having been
worn for many months by a car mechanic, one of those who get
covered daily from head to foot with oil, or a mason who spends a
busy life among clouds of cement. His pants were so worn out that
they required patches from top to bottom. The seat was decorated
with a red patch in the shape of a heart, and in front there were
others in the form of sunflowers. The knees had appliqués in the
shape of stars, and the sweat and grime gave his shirt the exotic
appearance of an undefined color. His pants were held up with a
length of pig rope, and he was barefoot. His feet were so grimy
that they looked like a lizard's nest. You could barely see him hidden behind the long and matted hair, which had become in addition a colony of voracious parasites. His beard was grown out, and
it was impossible to see how the young Foxye could ever eat.
There was a funny little toupée over his forehead! He filled the
room with a penetrating stench. He gave off such an odor that a
skunk would have been embarrassed to discover the fetid inferior-
ity of his own odor. Mr. Foxye's eyes went white. How was the
nightmare he was beholding possible? His son! How lucky that his
glorious forebears could not see him, those ladies who were all
delicateness and modesty, and those gentlemen who were so neat
and honorable, predestined by the Lord to found a paradise in the
land of Aztlán. The scion of the Foxyes behaved incoherently. Try
as they might to say something to him, the words turned into a
sticky mass between his teeth. His eyelids would droop suddenly
over eyes that seemed like cracked glass. He fell asleep on the
sofa. Before the anguished silence of the Foxyes, their son snored
like a pack of invisible lions. The upset old folks set in motion all
their mental resources that might serve to deceive them. That he
was probably tired, that he was probably sick, that this and that.
What was certain is that they couldn't sleep, and they were visited by a bitter presentiment that they could not clearly define.
Angel came in barking, jumping around and nipping playfully, as
was his habit. When he performed for them one of the most celebrated tricks of his repertory, standing on his hind legs and fold-
ing his front ones as though he were human, the Foxyes saw his
face sticking out from behind the toupée and they looked at each
other with concern. The next day they confronted the young stu-

dent, all set to clear up his behavior. In an extensive harangue, the old man spoke to him of his plans.

"Son, it is my wish that you take the reins of my businesses immediately. I will give you the appropriate training. As a lawyer, you'll do a better job than we can. . . . "

The boy looked at his progenitors and then dropped the roof on them.

"I haven't been a student for more than two years, Father, and I'm not interested in being a lawyer and even less in handling business affairs. I only want to live, love, and not bother anyone."

The old man's face got as red as a glowing poppy. He slapped him.

"You've been stealing my trust, exploiting me through deceit."

The prodigal son replied without any sign of feeling. "Haven't you gotten rich by deceiving the whole world? You have deceived yourself, believing that by amassing money you would make yourself happy. Are you happy by any chance?"

The old man collapsed in his armchair, covering his face. His wife jumped up, screaming at the rebel.

"Everything's been for you! Our money, our affection, everything, everything! . . . "

Bobby, like every clown and like any movie fan who's spent years seeing crap in the movies and on television, assumed a dramatic pose and, showing his profile, answered in a declamatory tone:

"You told me many times, full of comforting emotions, that your forefathers had come and embraced the Indians like good Christians. But you never told me that they then killed them to steal their possessions. The money you made for me, how did you make it? By foreclosing on the homes of poor laborers, capitalizing on the sweat and tears of blacks and Mexicans. Affection? You speak of affection when not even you, Mother, were ever able to caress me. The kisses you denied me when I was a child you've now given, full of love, to this filthy dog you're holding in your arms."

The old woman gave a terrible yell with all the resonance of a howl and threw herself into the arms of her husband. The young man left the room. The millionaire couple called the family doctor, believing the frustrated lawyer to be stark raving mad. When the doctor had been appraised of the case, he asked to examine his personal effects, and it didn't take long for him to find the evidence he suspected: Bobby was a drug addict. Phrases like "But how," "It's not possible," and "Why" poured out. The doctor answered:

"This is not an isolated case, but a national epidemic, as grave as any of the plagues that have been the scourge of humanity."

Old man Foxye, like a true hypocrite who spurns his share of guilt by dumping it on someone else, commented:

"Our laws ought to be stricter. We've got to close the borders. The criminals who sell drugs are poisoning our youth."

To which the doctor answered realistically:

"Let's not be silly. The root of this problem derives from the conduct of parents and the system that governs society. In their drive to power, people overlook their own children."

The doctor advised them to seek treatment for the young Foxye. They soon discovered that the sick young man had disappeared. With the help of a private detective, they found their descendant in Mexican territory, seated at the side of the Yaqui Loreto.

IT WAS ONE of those days in which the lives of old people are filled with unaccustomed vigor, and they go forth to show their smiles, as though these were the last green leaves of a tree ready to wither away. For Loreto it was a very pretty day. He had enough to eat for several days and he felt strong enough to stroll through the streets, to see the flowering plants, to enjoy the joy of the young, to contemplate the children who are the dawn of another generation. The rickety Indian sought to reflect his momentary contentment in the face of other old folk who manifested their glorious sunset in nostalgic gestures, illuminated by flashes of gold. It had been a perfect day, but as luck would have it, while walking along Madero Street, he turned into an alleyway and bumped head-on into a spectacle that suddenly filled him with indignation. The fat man people called Kite was squatting down before an enormous tray filled with all kinds of food: tamales, tacos, beans, tortillas, pastry. He was shoveling everything down with both hands. Indignation showed on the face of the Yaqui. Kite felt his look and raised his eyes. The Yaqui saw the smile of a child on the round face of the stubborn man. It was the first time he had been up close to Kite, and he observed that his hair was almost completely white, despite the fact that the man was still a long way away from being old. Something strange emanated from that abject being, something inexplicable that held the Yaqui in his gaze, quite in spite of his disgust. The bum finished up his copious snack and then lay down on a half-rotten mattress that he had tied to his pack. Before falling into a lethargic sleep, he stared hard at Loreto. The Yaqui shuddered when he saw so much sadness painted on the face of one man. Tears continued to roll down the face of the beggar as he snored with the sound of someone dying. A fat little old lady appeared at that moment, her face overflowing with goodness and fatigue. She picked up the platter on which the man, whose feet looked like those of a turtle, had eaten, and noting the presence of Loreto, she smiled at him and said: "He comes every afternoon to eat, and I save up the leftovers from my customers for him. I have a restaurant, sir, where very humble workers eat, but the food they leave is clean, as is this tray on which I serve it to him. I offered him a corner of that small house for him to sleep in, but he refused. But every now and then, he holes up right there. Some days he doesn't show up. If you want, sir, I can bring you something to eat. Although I'm poor, God helps me with my little business." Loreto answered, trying his best to smile and make his voice sound sweet. "Thank you, ma'am, but I cannot accept handouts. I am an honorable man." The woman smiled with a measure of bitterness, and looking over toward the man sleeping, she spoke with an accent meant to excuse him. "You have no idea, sir, of how little I am returning to him of all that we owe him. He gave us moments of great pleasure. My husband, may he rest in peace, adored him, and he made a lot of people besides us happy, particularly the children. How they loved him! He sowed laughter where there was anxiety, and wherever he went, he left behind a breath of pleasantness. What a great artist he was! Didn't you know him? He made money by the buckets, and he would give it away as fast as he received it, without even enough time for the coins to get warm in his hand. Even before he went completely mad, he suffered attacks where he would cry

like a child, thinking that he was going to die. He was a great
actor, sir, and when he fell on hard times, everybody forgot him,
even those he had helped. But I haven't. . . . "

A spontaneous smile broke out on the Indian's dark face,
which he gave the sentimental little old lady as a kind of goodbye.
He walked away, feeling in his heart a profound commiseration for
that mysterious being who turned to public charity in order to
survive, just like dogs who have no master.

"MAN, HOW EARLY you are and in the middle of the week. Huh?
And here you are in the Happy Day."

"Well, what do you expect? This day's been a waste. I was
walking about aimlessly, and my footsteps brought me here."

"Well, you can bet I'm dying to know what has happened to
our friend Good Chuco. We haven't seen him around here for
several months. I miss him, despite how feisty he is. Excuse me for
not having asked what you'd like to drink."

"The same as always, the same as always . . . beer."

"You look heavyhearted, more pensive than on other occasions. Don't tell me something serious has happened to
Good . . . "

"Well, . . . maybe not something serious, precisely. Everything
is so relative."

"Tell me, while there are still only a few clients. But I hope
he's not dead; he isn't, is he?"

"No, no. He wasn't much interested in dying. He's in jail
serving a four-year sentence."

"Really? But was the poor devil's crime all that serious?"

"I don't know. . . . Frankly, it wasn't so bad."

"Did he hurt someone?"

"He stole something."

"But how?"

"He's not a habitual thief. He stole four bottles of wine from a
liquor store, egged on, no doubt, by the same wine he'd drunk
several days before."

"It looks like he got a year per bottle. Who handed down such
a harsh sentence?"

"Rudolph H. Smith . . . Look, I'm going to tell you everything I know about that incident with all the details. It's really got

me upset, and it's always good to get it off your chest by telling someone about it. It's like getting rid of something that's rotting at you from the inside."

"Tell me, and so you can see I'm interested in the story, the beer's on me. Here, let me get you another one."

"Thanks. Here's to your health! It tastes great. You know Good Chuco more or less. In any event, I'll start by telling you about Rudolph Smith. It's important to know him, because he's one of those types cast from a mold. Rudolph H. Smith is around fifty, but in his gestures and behavior, he looks like he's about one hundred. He serves as a judge because he's honorable above all else, and besides, he's a very good Christian. There's no chance, my friend, that you'd catch Mr. Smith at rowdy parties or involved in ignoble adventures. He looks like he was born to judge the crimes of his brethren. Here among us, even when he sits down to eat, you'll see him rigid. When he opens his mouth to take a bite, there is so much ritual and dignity in his gesture that he looks like he's about to pronounce a sentence."

"Excuse me for interrupting, but it really moves me to hear about honest judges. As far as I'm concerned, see, it doesn't matter how wise and pretty a constitution is if it happens to be wielded by corrupt judges. Excuse the comparison, but it's like a silver boat sailing in a sea of shit."

"Most certainly."

"Tell me more about this little gem."

"Mr. Smith was not the spawn of millionaire parents exactly, but they made ends meet. There was nothing Rudolph H. Smith wanted that he didn't get. He's had everything in abundance. When he needed scholarships for his studies, all he had to do was open his mouth to get what he wanted."

"Imagine that."

"Rudolph H. Smith has always dressed neatly with notable elegance and never, not even once, has he had to go a day without eating. Naturally, he's convinced that this situation is perfectly normal and that he deserves everything. As a bachelor he had some very discrete adventures with women, but since he's been married he's been a model of fidelity."

"Look, let me take advantage of you lighting your cigarette to tell you that those goody-goody types are half-impotent and take advantage of that fact to cloak themselves in purity. It's like Lucifer showing his horns. Go on, go on, please."

"Rudolph H. Smith, honorable judge at all costs, developed, nevertheless, a certain allergy to the presence of dark-skinned persons. For him, it was more than natural to believe that not to be white constitutes, in a certain sense, a crime that must somehow be punished."

"Well, if you look closely, there are legions of racist pigs like him."

"You can say that again! And that's not all. Rudolph H. Smith made a cult of cleanliness to such a degree that after bathing, he doused himself with liquids that kill all germs, a real phobia against microbes. It's enough to tell you that he hated, like it was the most abominable crime, anything that looked like poverty and dirt."

"There's no doubt that cleanliness is pretty, but to go from there to having your body smelling like soap and water and your soul a shit hole is quite a distance, don't you think so?"

"You're about to see how. Those details in addition to the perseverance of Mr. Smith in reading the Bible make him think he's a judge with credentials straight from the Eternal Father."

"You make me want to ask you not to go on, because I've pretty much got the idea already. There are things, friend, that make you want to throw up. But I'm interested in knowing how Good Chuco got mixed up with Rudolph H. Smith. But, tell me, how do you know so much about that man?"

"Look, I'm going to be frank with you. A little bird's told me all this. Later, we found out about Good Chuco. He was in jail, and things got ugly because he broke a window to help himself to some bottles."

"The poor devil must have really been drunk."

"I went to see him and took a pack of cigarettes. You should have seen how he almost went crazy he was so happy."

"PAL, WHAT A good buddy you are. Only real good friends are going to go see their brothers in jail. Let's see those cigarettes. What a guy, what a guy, you also brought me some matches. You're sure a swell friend."

"Ah, Good Chuco! You went too far this time, damn it!"

"*You know what, brother, I sure made a mess of it. Hell! But I was so hung over that I couldn't see a thing. You know what? That guy in the liquor store refused to give me credit. Can you imagine, after I spent so much money there. The Mexicans are good customers for his liquor. I asked for a bottle on the cuff, and he got mad. People buying his beer and wine have made him very rich. No way, after we spent so much there, and the damn guy saw how sick out of my mind I was from lack of booze; he refused to help me out. Damn! So I just went and broke his glass. Well, the asshole went right to the police. You know, buddy, the police treat us Mexicans like we were mad dogs. Hell! Looks like they're going to go hard on me. Next week I've got to go to court. Come catch the show, pal.*"

"*Who's going to defend you, Good Chuco?*"

"*A guy assigned by the court, a nice guy. He's Anglo, but they say he can talk Chicano.*"

"*Well, then he'll serve as your interpreter, Chuquito.*"

"*He looks kind of dumb. As far as I'm concerned, all he can do is suck his thumb.*"

"The conversation's great, but those customers are calling me. I'll be right back."

"Go on. Meanwhile, I'll go take a leak."

(*Damn drunks. They come in herds like cows to the water trough. Those shits soak up the beer like sand pits, especially the gringos. It looks like they're on a short leash at home and when they're let go, they act like hell on wheels.*)

"What happened! I thought you went to the bathroom."

"I was taking a look at the writing on the wall. It's hard to put up with such stupid people."

"Yes. They're a pack of foulmouthed jerks. They write one obscene thing after another on the walls. But don't let me catch anyone doing it, because I'll kick the shit out of him for being so crude."

"And you'd be doing everyone a favor."

"Let me get you another beer, okay?"

"No, no, this one's fine, thanks."

"Go on with the story, because I'd like to hear it."

"Well, as I was saying . . . "

"Damn! More've just come in."

"Well, I've got to go anyway. I'll tell you later."

"Yes, please don't stop coming. I'd like to imagine Good
Chuco standing in front of Rudolph H. Smith."

"Well, you'll see that it's worth knowing what happened that
day in the holy halls of justice. I promise to tell you in detail. It
makes my skin crawl just to remember it."

"Come back, man. Don't forget."

"See you later."

"So long."

MR. SMITH'S HOUSEHOLD awoke that Tuesday in July floating in a
space of holiness, despite the fact that beyond the house's thick
walls the sun had already pushed the thermometers up to around a
hundred degrees, set on bursting them. But it wouldn't go beyond
the attempt, since in recent days it probably hadn't gotten up to
120 degrees. Seated at the table with a succulent breakfast before
him—juice, bacon and eggs, hotcakes—Rudolph H. Smith asked
his wife, Gloria, to turn the air conditioner down low, because he
felt chilly. Rudolph Jr., a young man, twenty years old, commented that during the night he had had to cover himself with a
heavy blanket because he had awakened dreaming of a winter
landscape. He had dreamed in black and white. Right in the middle of a city populated with cars enchanted by the snow, he wandered about naked, his teeth chattering out telegrams. The older
persons laughed with amusement. Rudolph Jr., enjoying his success, added something more. He reported that he had wanted to
urinate during his dream and that, just as the stream had started,
a delicate arc of ice formed in space. His parents smiled wanly, but
the young man choked on a strip of bacon because he was rocking
back and forth so much with laughter. His mother commented
that the summers in the Imperial Valley are uneconomical because
electric energy costs so much more. The elder Smith smiled condescendingly and then he offered a short bit of oratory. "No, it's
not uneconomical at all, quite the contrary. The summers increase
the wealth of our beloved country by many millions of dollars:
oranges, grapes, watermelons, cantaloupes, cotton, and so on
burst forth in fabulous quantities from this land that is so extraor-
dinarily fertile. And, moreover, they provide bread for thousands
and thousands of workers. What would become of our Chicanos if

they did not have the relief of these labors, which, thanks to the divine grace of our Lord God, enables them to survive. Despite the great consumption of electrical energy, this land is blessed. Thus, we live in a paradise. The honorable judge Rudolph H. Smith carved a hotcake in crescents, divided it into pieces, and ate them parsimoniously. With supreme delicacy he wiped his lips with the napkin and prepared to drink his coffee. Gloria and young Rudolph contemplated him with adoring eyes. Rudolph H. Smith had spoken to them the night before about the terrible dilemma in which he had been put by a young female university student, very pretty, white like innocence itself and blonde like blessed bread. The girl was from an excellent family, but through the tragic twists of life she had fallen into error. It turned out that the inexpert youth, having been seduced by one of several young men who labored under the illusion of being stallions, had given birth to a little girl. Desperate to the point of madness because of such an inopportune occurrence, because of her aristocratic family, her position, her future—in short, beside herself—she had strangled her little daughter to death with a pair of her nylon panties. Rudolph H. Smith related to them emotionally the tremendous inner struggle that he was experiencing within himself to go the humane route and accept from the psychiatrists and her wealthy parents that the girl was out of her mind when she committed the crime. When he clarified that the sick child had been sent to a mental institution to recover, the Smith family felt a bouquet of angelical laughter on the ceiling of their house. The young Rudolph half closed his eyes in a prayer for the just man, and Mrs. Smith let a round tear fall on the table that sounded like a silver coin. She had always loved him with the same admiration that one professes for heroes or saints, rather than out of passion. She was convinced that her consort was illuminated by divine grace. Young Rudolph followed the gestures of his progenitor, and imitated him even in his manner of walking. He was studying law and, without a doubt, would also be a distinguished professional. He was tall and husky, thanks, his father said, to healthful and abundant food. His wife added that the care of the doctor, vitamins, and exercise, had turned him into a true athlete. In any case, thanks to his high grades at the university, he had been spared the army. Rudolph H. Smith made ready to leave for the

office. He kissed his wife's and son's foreheads and then stood still
in a speculative position with his index finger in the air. Oh, yes!
She had to tell Ramón Ponce, the Chicano gardener, to cut the
bushes neat and even and to cut the grass that grew around the
curbs good and close with the shears. Right away, he added: "Tell
him to do a good job, because there are a lot of people out of work
willing to take any job." Gloria took care of Chavela Moreno. The
Chicana maid straightened up the five bedrooms and dusted rev-
erentially the dozens of books held by bookcases in the living
room and other rooms of the house. They were all very expensive
books, with ample references to the constitution and to its respec-
tive laws. The boy left in his sports car to go to class, and Mrs.
Smith occupied herself with the business of her charitable ladies
club. No sooner did Rudolph H. Smith set foot outside his house
than he felt the onslaught of the heat, and covering his eyes he
exclaimed: "My God! What an inclement heat." It was still but
the sun was already beating down like a burning ember sitting on
the earth, with the Imperial Valley a chicken roasting on the ro-
tisserie. Good grief! He quickly got into his Buick and started the
car. He quickly put the air conditioner on and got ready to pull
out, but not without first glancing at the façade of his house built
in the "Mexican style": kiln-baked red adobe walls, high parapets,
a large arch for an entrance, in addition to various smaller arches
over the windows which, of course, were covered with gratings. In
the middle of the patio there was a pure white fountain in whose
depths little red fish swam around. Various sculptures scattered
around the place showed off their nakedness, imitations of Roman
mythological goddesses, although rather gaunt and bony with feet
larger than usual.

Since in reality the case was a routine one, the spectators were
limited to some eight people. Seated in the third row were three
characters wearing ties. They wore suits wrinkled from three days
of sweat, particularly at the armpits, which showed salty moons.
The faces of the trio showed neither suffering nor happiness. No
one knew why they were there precisely on that day. All anyone
knew was that they were quiet, that they smiled reluctantly, and
that their hair came down almost to their tailbones. In the second
row there was an expectant old woman, wearing a blood-red dress,
with a yellow melon hat set on top of a heroic wig. When some-

one murmured that she was a journalist from the local newspaper, the three characters who were in front turned around to look at her, and they found out that the woman had eyelids that were so small they only covered half her eyes. In the same row, with three seats in between, there was another very perfumed woman. In any case, she had been pretty when she was a girl. Seated in front of her, at one end of the row, was a young blonde woman whose eyes were blue stars and whose body was full of grace. At the other end, two men of Mexican descent were seated in fraternal company. One looked like a Creole and was white and angular. Although he insisted that he had a bigwig uncle, he was only a law clerk and fed himself on crumbs that he carried around in a knapsack. He professed great enmity toward giants and nasty magicians. The other Chicano was a tall and heavyset type, prematurely gray. The legendary Yaqui shone forth. He represented the stereotype of ignorance, making fun of the ostriches dressed like peacocks and writing books no one read.

Rudolph H. Smith made his entrance and seated himself at his raised bench. When the cloud began to dissipate, his august face could be seen, so majestic and haughty, turned up before the eyes that contemplated him. A theatrical air weighed heavy in the atmosphere. Those present showed their impatience by shifting a little in their seats. Rudolph H. Smith cleared his throat and immediately covered his mouth as though he had committed a sin. The lawyer and interpreter stood in front of him, behind a guard leading Good Chuco. The guard was a mixture of beast and saint, with long, powerful arms, a prominent chin, and the soft eyes of a faithful dog. For a few seconds a certain religious feeling was reflected in Good Chuco. Nevertheless, he had not entered a church, but rather a courtroom. He passed his eyes over the public and made out the two Chicanos.

"*Great to see you, fellows!*"

"*How ya doing, Chuquito?*"

"*Hanging in . . . screwed up and punched out, buddy. These fucking guys make fun of me here.*"

Rudolph H. Smith banged his gavel twice. Then he was able to train his look on the pachuco. His face turned red from indignation and he made a grimace of profound hate. His eyes grew small and his mouth puckered up like the rear end of a chicken.

Good Chuco in turn looked up. A tremendous physical exhaustion could be seen in his dark face, burned and wrinkled by thirty-some hellish summers, along with the toils of liquor, the fear of a cornered Indian, and yellow rage.

"*Jorge Curiel, alias Good Chuco, you have broken the laws that govern this society of free men in which you live and wherein each citizen has the same rights and privileges. Do you acknowledge your guilt?*"

"*What the hell's with this stupid old geezer, with his stupid monkey face?*"

"*I'm asking you if you're guilty.*"

"*Tell the crazy old man to go fuck his mother.*"

"*Behave. I'm your defense lawyer.*"

"*You know something, friend, you're a real cabrón, too.*"

"*Oh, no, come on! . . . He's the law.*"

"*Hell! His kind wipe their asses with the law. The law for these guys is like a whore's underwear, on and off as it suits them.*"

"*What does the accused answer?*"

"*Your honor, Mr. Smith, liquor has driven this man crazy.*"

"*I want to know what the guy's saying.*"

"*I told him you're crazy.*"

"*Your fucking grandmother's the one who's crazy, stupid shit; I'll beat the hell out of you.*"

"*I order you to tell me in English what this man is saying.*"

"*I cannot, your honor, Mr. Smith. Please don't ask me to.*"

"*I demand it this very minute.*"

"*He says that the judges deal with the law like it was a whore's pair of underpants.*"

"*What?*"

"*He says that you in particular, your honor, are a motherfucker. And the accused asserts that you are a fag and says that . . .*"

"*I order you to shut up. Shut up! Get that scum of society out of here, illiterate, shameless caveman. . . .*"

"*Let me go, shit faces! Sons of bitches, motherfuckers. You can stick your laws up your ass! All judges can go fuck their mothers! Let go of me, jack-off! The entire police force can go fuck their pigs of mothers! Ay! Dumb fucking monkey, that's enough. Ay, Aaaaay!*"

IT WAS ALREADY LATE on Saturday, and the city was coming to life with quite an accelerated pulse. The floating population had arrived in full force, and the sidewalks were filled with tourists good and ready to have fun. The street was a long line of cars that looked like trains with thousands of hysterical horns. The local residents sniffed around the visitors looking for a way to get a few dollars out of them. They peeled the greenbacks off them little by little like they were heads of lettuce, selling them this and that, placing them here and there, thanks to the dozens of pimps wearing red-jacketed uniforms for the occasion. Kite stood in the middle of the street cloaked in sheets of paper. The wind was not blowing. He was shouting and waving his hands. "Come in, ladies and gentlemen, and see the Great Tolito in action, the greatest comedian of all time." A policeman shoved him along because he had caused the traffic to stop. Pieces of paper lay in the street, curled up like serpents. Kite was crying at the top of his voice, but no one could hear him because of the noise of the horns and the bombardment of insults that the drivers hurled at him. The nightclubs spewed out groups of humans from one door to the other, in a tireless coming and going.

"Here, mister, here. Oh, yes! Yes, yes, sure, they're gorgeous. Behind the glass you can see them being combed. Only twenty bucks. Oh, no! No, they're very clean."

"Here, mister, here is the floor show for you. No clothes, mister, buck naked."

"Come on, mister, come on. Thirteen years old, little girls, mister, come on."

The whores crisscrossed the streets on their way out of the beauty parlors, ready to go into action in the dives.

"I'm thirsty, honey, buy me a drink."

"Here's a token, here's a token."

"Wanna go to my room?"

"La Campana is busy with a client. She'll be right out."

"Estrellita, here are the clothes."

"I can't open the door, I'm busy fucking."

"Give me the key, I've got a client."

"Give me the money first, honey, so I can pay for the room."

"Knock on that chicken's door. She's been tied up in a knot with that red Gringo for more than an hour."

"Get the clients who are coming in to have a drink."

"Let me have those five dollars, you fucker, I'm the one stole them from the gringo. They're mine."

"Not on your life."

"Just because I'm a whore you think you can walk all over me. Give me the fiver, I earned it."

"She's the one in the floor show who just gave birth."

"Yeh, that's what you say. Look, when the sailors start to bite at you, squirt your tit in their eyes. That really sends them running."

Two mysterious men entered the brothel called The Pill, dressed like gangsters in a movie. A chippy called Borola whispered to the manager.

"Those guys are not here to drink or anything like it. . . . "

"Get rid of them."

"They refuse to go."

The manager walked over with the face of a fighting dog.

"There's no room here for idle eyes. If you don't buy, you don't stay. Get going, come on, right now."

"No way," answered one of the men, as he flashed his badge. The manager's throat snapped shut like the bolt on a Mauser and he turned into a cuddly kitty.

"A thousand pardons, sirs. At your orders, gentlemen, pleased to be of service."

"Get Rosenda Pérez Sotolín, alias La Malquerida, for us."

"She's the dark one there, with the long hair. Yes, sir, she's a real looker, very pretty. Careful, she's a difficult one."

"Well, madam, we've been looking for you."

"If you look for me, you find me. Now what?"

"Are you Rosenda Pérez Sotolín?"

"That's me, yes, sir."

"Do you know Pedro Pérez Sotolín?"

"He's . . . my brother."

"Come with us."

La Malquerida appeared before the authorities. Her crying had made her makeup run. Her beautiful eyes glowed in the midst of her tragedy, in spite of everything, with the beauty of innocence. She had just identified the body of her brother Pedro, who had been shot to death.

"Calm down and answer our questions."

Her hair was a mess, but she looked on with the majesty of a wounded lioness.

"Your brother stabbed Don Mario Miller de Cocuch to death as he was leaving his home. His name and the location where you're employed were written on a piece of paper found on him. You are being investigated as an accomplice. What was the relationship you and your brother had with Don Mario M. de Cocuch? If you want any leniency in your case, answer, we're waiting."

"What's the difference between one prison and another?"

"Speak, please."

"Do you really want to hear my story?"

"Not your story. Only the part that has to do with Mr. Cocuch."

"I grew up in a town on the coast."

"Be brief, ma'am."

"Don't interrupt me, or I'll shut up and not answer your questions. I was a humble typist with my soul full of very pretty dreams, because the mirror never lies. Since I was good and honest, I deserved the best in the world. But one day, to my misfortune, Doña Reginalda and Carlos arrived. That damned hyena overwhelmed me with her talk and made me believe that here on the border I would have a job as a cashier in a restaurant, with good money and her friendship to boot. I came along following a clear sky. I wanted a brilliant future for my family, so humble and long-suffering. Carlos tried to seduce me on the way to the border. Crafty pair! They pretended they were mother and son. I hit the coward. Doña Reginalda chased him off with harsh words in front of me, just so I wouldn't be suspicious. Once here, she had me enter a palace by the back door, saying it was her house. The bedroom had bars on the windows. She locked me in there, and the bitch sold me to this whorehouse. They paid good money for me, seeing as how I was still a virgin."

"You're going too far, ma'am. . . . "

La Malquerida's voice had gone hoarse.

"First off, they sold me to an old libertine. The old geezer charged in like a beast in heat. Slobbering all over the place, he scared the hell out of me, even if he didn't have the strength to rape me. He looked like a dead man just risen from the grave. I half killed him scratching and hitting him. But then they sold me to a crazy gringo named Tony Baby. I desperately clutched at the

bars on the window of the odious prison trying to defend myself
and I saw two policemen. 'Help me, help!' I cried out. One of
them answered back, 'Shut up, you lousy slut, or we'll toss you in
jail.' Tony Baby charged me like a rabid dog and tore my clothes
to shreds. I defended myself as best I could, but the son of a bitch
struck me so hard that not even my mother would have recognized
me what with the blood all over me. He yanked me about by the
hair. I called for help and justice at the top of my voice so much
that my lungs hurt. But who helps out a poor girl with no money
or political influence? Like a tiger, he broke my membrane, tear-
ing me apart body and soul. My soul too!"

La Malquerida started to sob convulsively with bitterness. The
representatives of justice looked at each other.

"We don't see the connection, ma'am. . . . "

"My brother arrived yesterday. Who was responsible? He asked
me who the bastard was who stole our honor. Because back in my
town, you should know, a woman is not ruined without someone
paying for it. My brother was raving mad. He assured me at the
top of his lungs that he would live only to avenge me, that he
would drag the bodies of those responsible for my perdition and
the dishonor of our family through the streets. 'Who were they?'
he shouted at me full of fury. 'Don't hide the names of the bastards.' 'There were two of them,' I answered, 'Doña Reginalda and
Carlos. She was the heartless hypocrite who sold me.' 'Doña
Reginalda! Who bought you? Tell me, right now, come on, out
with it.' My brother roared. I was choking and unable to say the
name of such a slimy individual. He shouted at me again, 'Who
bought you as though you were just a piece of merchandise?' I told
him, the owner of this whorehouse. Don Mario Miller de
Cocuch! . . . He couldn't even avenge himself of the others."

La Malquerida was taken off to her cell, hysterical and shouting like a madwoman.

"There's no justice for the poor! No justice, whatsoever, no
justice for the poor. Only for those who have money. Damn you,
damn you!"

The poor prostitute's screams, mixed with agonizing hurt, were
followed by the glassy stares of those present, who either avoided
each other or collided with the sharp edge of self-accusation. The
barriers protecting the cynicism that hardens the spirit fell during
just a moment of carelessness. The silence was overlaid by the

vain echoes of demagoguery and its ridiculous oratory: "The Mexican woman is self-effacing and faithful," "she is a camp follower always at the side of her Juan," "the foundation of the home," "the procreator of future generations," "blah, blah, blah." In the same barrage of seconds the sneering laughter of the thieves echoed, lined with gold, satisfied, masters of a power similar to that of cruel kings, the pampered children of justice.

THE NEWSPAPERS were sold out in a wink, like pumpkin tarts just out of the oven. On the first page there was an article of the following sort on the scandalous crime of the day.

PROMINENT CITIZEN VICTIM OF IMMORAL MAN

YESTERDAY MORNING, when Mr. Mario Miller de Cocuch, a well-known businessman, left for his daily rounds, he was assaulted suddenly by a criminal who, without saying a word, driven only by his evil sub-human instincts, attacked Mr. M. de Cocuch with a knife, after which he fled. The zealous guardians of order were informed, and they set out after him, ordering him to stop. The members of the police force were obliged to shoot after the fleeing man, who collapsed mortally wounded as the result of the impact of one of the shots fired by the brave sentinels of the law. The murderer, who paid for his crime and his evil deed with his life, went by the name of Pedro Pérez Sotolín. According to documents in his possession, it became clear that the aforementioned was from the country, one of the many adventurers who, with notable anti-patriotic disdain, abandon the tilling of the land to lend their services to the foreign interests of our neighboring country. Mr. Mario Miller de Cocuch was attended in his last moments by fifteen eminent doctors, whose determined efforts were frustrated by the designs of the Supreme Being, who took the soul of such a distinguished gentleman. Only one of the knife blows was mortal, since the others did no damage to vital organs.

Mario Miller de Cocuch, a distinguished gentleman of the political and commercial world, is grieved for by his most beloved wife, the honorable Doña Reginalda Dávalos de Cocuch.

THE MADMAN they called Kite crossed the street like a phantom. One of the paper streamers he was dragging behind him caught around the neck of a North American. The man said "God damn *it" and yanked it away from the beggar, who was holding thirty-three corn tortillas the rats had nibbled.*

The cars bunched together in the streets, snaked along anxiously like hungry worms, honking their horns and sounding something like the shouting of hysterical old women. Along the front of the buildings the neon lights feverishly jabbed out the names of the dives, brothels, and all kinds of shops. The place was crawling with sailors over from San Diego, anxious to kill in an orgy the terror they felt over the fearsome cannons that would consume tons and tons of their doomed flesh. Thousands of eyes reddened by alcohol and lust reflected their confusion in the windows. With the impulse of braying beasts they entered the places touting spectacles of miserable women; women obliged to stoop to the most denigrating acts so the gold would flow like puss in the consciousnesses of the perverse owners of the dens of wickedness where money and shit run together.

The brothels in this lost area allow us to derive the satisfaction of a stupid life and a future without glory. Drowning, we have rowed across a stinking lagoon of alcohol, fearful of the encounter. . . . Streams of music, rivers of tequila, precipices of immodest laughter, mires of dirty words, all the shame floating in this atmosphere clouded over by gasoline. That woman dancing on the dance floor surrounded by walls of cynical eyes looks like a hydropic frog. She dances and if anyone becomes distracted, she puts her fingers in her mouth after rubbing them over her sex. She's the floor show star of this cursed whorehouse. The other show that's a big success can be seen in the nightclub on the corner: the "artist" asks the public for a shoe, and if they give her one, right then and there she pees in it and puts it on. How much wickedness just to satisfy this evil crowd and local maniacs and the interminable perversion of the immaculate descendants of the Mayflower? What each person tries most to hide shows forth spontaneously in this mist. . . . Suddenly, he is at my side! You . . . Damn you! We quickly looked at each other and then took a step backwards. With great fury he said to me, "Aren't you the philosopher? The infallible, the one with talent." Swallowing my pride, I looked at him. He had hit bottom. A poet, the glory of literature. Then and there our rivalry ended, both of us covered with slime. We embraced each other crying and we drank a toast to our defeat.

An old teacher, all heart and sweetness. With all the fervor of Saint Isidore, he had sown the good seed in our tender minds. A stimulus that would not grow, that would fade away, diminished, but one that would subsist like a thirsty plant. When his impoverished knowledge was only able to give us a handful of letters from the alphabet, beating out our spelling with his own stuttering. He was also undernourished. He would lift our spirits every day by telling us: "You, you'll be a poet; you, a philosopher; you, my dear, a very famous artist . . . "

He grabbed my arm and said to me desperately: Tell me about something from when you were a child, something beautiful. I saw his terrified spirit in the shadows of disillusionment, wavering on the edge of a deep precipice. He tried to turn back, terrified by the nothingness of the abyss. He sought some pleasant recollection in his mind that would hold him like an umbilical cord. He could not find it in the aridity of his life and pleaded for a crumb, like an old man with bleached-out eyes. The voices in waves propelled cynicism, pain, happiness, and hate in grotesque masquerades. The voices broke and sank into drains of indifference. I spoke to him of my childhood, and I swear to you that I was sincere at that time, because I too was dying!

We were living in the desert. Dry land, as greedy as a mother without teats, under a sky that was like a magnifying glass, at the foot of slopes so rocky that from a distance they looked like they were covered with petrified turtles. My younger brothers and I had a little friend we adored, a little stream. It rolled down in a curve to where we lived from a hillside that at night turned into a mountain. Its pebbles were toys that we loved so much. We played with it every day, caressing its dream until one day the miracle of the rain would awaken it. Then, lively, naughty, noisy, it would run like we did, joyfully. When we caught sight of the rain, we would run to meet it. It's looking for us! Would you like to play with us, little stream? Yes, yes, let's go play! You know something? The water is like a magician or a fairy godmother. It's colorless, takes on the color of things, tastes like life, and brings forth the voice of nature in everything it touches. As it rushed downhill, we would hear the scrub brush and the branches drinking eagerly, thirstily. It would conjure up the whistling of the large and calcinated stones. When the current spread out, the little stones, half out of the water, would sing together a sweet song of babies dressed in white. We would run to meet it. And in order to get down to where it was flat, we would wait at a two-meter waterfall that took the water over an enormous crag, which slapped strongly like a dry tongue and then noisily continued to drink. We continued to run. In front of our house we

*would quickly improvise a dam with branches and sand. The stream
hidden beneath the leaves made its way to us—foamed chocolate. It
stopped suddenly, and we laughed happily. We wanted to stop it even
more, and it got away from us playfully between our legs, spraying our
faces. Then it went off, becoming lost in the distance, only to disappear
in the afternoon. My mother called us in and dressed us in clean
clothes. We sat down in front of the window to watch it, absorbed and
with our eyes glowing, without the slightest attempt to explain to ourselves the deep happiness that welled up in us.*

*He laughed and laughed as he shook me. Thank you, brother! Only
poetry is truth. We wove a whole skein of recollections of what could
have been. It was in the cursed dawn when I shouted at him, I don't
know why, you're lying! Neither poetry nor poets exist, and everything
is a masquerade so we can't see human tragedy. Only the slobs who
ignore suffering and crime, those who toady to power, sing to the flowers with the eloquence of beggars, show no embarrassment as they pay
homage to the powerful, and they repay flashiness and riches with a
prostituted art. Fools!*

"No! No . . . no."

*I went in. The brawl had already begun. The raucous noise of the
scuffle scattered the notes of a hotshot orchestra, all of them with their
hair looking like Little Red Riding Hood, dressed in effeminate clothes
that fit them so tightly that the seams of their pants deeply parted the
cheeks of their buttocks. Their yelping and the notes of their music rode
over the smoke of the cigarettes. The dance floor was filled with dancing
monkeys with a strange human appearance, men and women rotating
their butts as though they had a burning coal stuck in them and the
dance floor were a pool of water where they could put it out. It didn't
take long for me to find her. She handed the bartender the key and a
dollar for the rent of the room. She gave me the remaining four.*

*A young gringo smiling and chewing gum at the same time said
goodbye to her. His eyes were the color of dirty slate and his sandy hair
was all mussed up. I went on outside because I didn't like to see her
working. She and I were joined by a cord woven of lust and passion.
Old man Lalo sure had it right: one hair of a woman pulls stronger
than a train, and two tits pull harder than two carts. I ran into Rosa on
the way out. She looked like an old clown whose lungs have gone bad,
and she spat at me with a few oaths. Her name was the only thing
pretty about her, and it wasn't hers, but one they'd pinned on her just*

because they felt like it. When I reached the street, I heard a kid screaming. When I got closer, I saw he was about fourteen years old. Lord! It turned out he was eighteen, and continuing to sob, he said that one day the gringos would carry him off. An old man with a bad leg had held him in his arms as he cooed at him tenderly. "Come on," he said to me. "Just listen to this kid so you have an idea of how rotten life is." I had already downed a couple of shots of booze. I don't know why I got so mad and I screamed at them: Both of you can go straight to hell.

Perhaps I'm afraid of him and want to run into him, more out of fear for my recollections than for his presence, as if in those final years without any direction I had lived without a shadow and had suddenly discovered the one from my childhood. He seeks me out because he needs me to pardon him, and I flee from him because I need my vengeance. Just so I won't run into him I have a drink in each brothel, walking among this crowd of stinking insects that have shed so many masks today, including the one of beatitude, in order to show off their liberated bestiality. Some of them are ridiculing themselves as they vilify another race, while the others let their consciences rot for a few dollars. Dollars! Dollars to plaster all the buildings inside and out, dollars to cover the surfaces, the streets, the floors. Dollars to roof over all the buildings. A hurricane of dollars like a windstorm of dry lettuce leaves. Dollars to buy authorities on the take. Dollars to yank poor stupid girls from their miserable villages and turn them into whores. Dollars to blast the footsteps of the wetbacks. Dollars to order drugs. Carloads of dollars to trade for marijuana, marijuana in order to forget the war . . . supply and demand . . . dollars, dollars, dollars. Who's got drugs for saaaale?! Here I see them colliding with each other, those who have been corrupted and walk about in disgrace and the miserable ones who spit down from the vantage point of their opulence. Executioners and victims in the same swamp like dirty and strange beings who sink and resurface, slither along, live and die in the slime. How many times while she is inside do I wander along these cursed streets drinking in the alcohol of the very atmosphere, breathing in the fetidness of the crowd, sick and tired of the songs that scream out failure with stupid posturings of masculinity. I hate them all, and I feel that I am myself being consumed by evil. There in that canyon at the top of the hills the day laborers live, and that's where the shoe shine kids sleep, the very ones who disappear around midnight crushed and wounded by fatigue and *revulsion. That's where the day laborers live, the men who don't make enough to eat, who can't live with what they earn. They feed on rancor, and life molds them with the same patience with which the sea expands the coral reefs, so that one day they will grow wings like rabid and thirsty vampires. . . . Alma! Pardon me, Alma, I will take you away from this damn, cursed heap, and I will build you a white house. "Give me a drink, bartender. Look, I've got dollars." I will cover you with dignity, I will make you so happy you'll want to die. I will wipe the suffering away from your face with my soft hands. Your suffering as a whore, as a frustrated wife, as an outcast woman, your suffering with a gonorrheal sex, your breasts gnawed by the immoral persecution of evil. Alma, I love you above all this sea of shit.*

KITE STRODE BY, looking down all the cross streets with a startled face. He was alone and looked a mess. He sat down quietly, but the streamers continued to play with the wind. The old Yaqui had never seen him so quiet, and he felt pity for the parasite, and an outburst of compassion made him come nearer the beggar. He looked like a wounded animal. "Are you hungry?" Loreto asked. Kite smiled very sweetly and shook his head. "I'm not hungry any more. . . . I'd like to know if you know Raulito Molina, my son. . . . Sir, is it true that death is a lie? Is it true that it's just make-believe?" Loreto thought: "This man has never stopped being a child." Kite burst out in tears and wiped his eyes with his clenched fists. His tears were not crystalline, and the earth poured itself out through his eyes. I'll get you a cup of soup. Not a single word would come out of Kite's open mouth again. Men wearing nice clothes asked various questions, why he was called Kite and where he was from. No one knew how to answer them, and all they said was that he was an inoffensive crazy, that he liked to beg for food, that he would cry rivers of tears at the slightest pretext, and that he also liked to insist that he was a great artist. One of the men making inquiries concluded: he's nothing but a bum, one of those useless men who don't even have a history.

THE VERY FINE rain coats the houses wrapped in mist. It is a timid rain that forms ashy phantoms as it falls. The large drops slide down the window panes as though the houses could feel nostalgia. The streets shine like dirty mirrors lit up by the beams of the automobiles. People go by with their heads barely sticking out, their ancestral memory urging them to seek the cave. Skinny dogs go by with their backs arched, looking like they have five feet and whining like sick children.

It's cold and Doña Candelita is standing on her corner, holding a basket of merchandise. She no longer sells lottery tickets and is now trying another branch of commerce. With the day so nasty, she feels more like her eighty years are a hundred. Her ancient insides, which will soon pay for their gluttony by feeding the womb of the earth, bear her along through the streets in search of money she can exchange for bread and milk, even if for only a small glass of the river that flows beneath the crags.

On the opposite sidewalk a young man is walking with a lost expression, looking like a blind man who has lost his last guide.

TOMORROW WAS THE FIRST DAY *of creation, and yesterday will be the dawn. I feel as though there were no longer any watches, as if all the clocks had burst from a heart attack, as if all the clocks were hanging from their trapezes, dead, like paralyzed pendulums. No, I can't see! The ash blinds my eyes, and how heavy is the load of marble I'm carrying on my back!*

"Hey you, old lady, with the basket of flowers, come over here, please."

"You come over here, sir. The way those longhairs are whizzing by in their cars, they'll run me down."

"Wait for me, Grandma, I'll come over."

"Just look at you, sir, you're sopping wet."

"My God! Your eyes are shut. How did you see me from so far away?"

"I saw your hair floating in the wind. It looked like a sheet or like a very large bouquet of white flowers."

"What do you want, sir?"

"Make me a crown from every flower in your basket. They're so pretty! I'll pay you for them, Little Grandmother. They're for a dead friend."

"But, sir, these are not flowers. I'm selling something else."

"You think I don't have any money. Aren't those roses I'm looking at? Daisies and lilies . . . "

"Ah, how funny you are, sir. These aren't flowers, but rather bunches of rosemary for making tea, sir. The women who sell themselves buy them from me. Everyday they wash themselves with rosemary because it makes them tighter."

"My God . . . "

"Why are you crying so hard, my son?"

"I'm all alone."

"Don't cry. Be strong. I gave birth to my children, I saw them grow, and I closed their eyes one by one. My offspring have been in the grave for a long time now. I took to the street to find charity, and I see everything as though I were standing on a strange planet. That's why I'm not even ashamed to offer what I'm selling. At times I walk through these streets filled with people and I feel the same way I would if I were in an abandoned cave. No one shouts my name any longer or rushes to embrace me. Everyone turns to stone on me. The words I hear in my mind are not even those of the past. . . . They're the words of the future, son, because not even in death will I be so alone, unless the souls are this cruel too. This is a strange world, son, and there are times I even forget what it's called. . . . "

"My last friend died."

"No, son, don't cry for your dead friend. Listen to what I know as an old lady: it's your illusions that are no longer alive. . . . "

"How pretty the flowers in your basket are."

"Let me touch your forehead. Are you feverish? You're ice-cold! Cold, my dear sir! How long have you been walking around dead? Go, son, go find a cemetery where you can rest your bones."

THAT NIGHT HE SNUCK into the Rose Windmill, the most luxurious of the brothels. And for a luxury brothel, of course, luxury whores! The young ladies of the Rose Windmill are very attractive, and there's someone for every taste in a variety of different races, even French girls who, according to what people say, conjugate better than anybody else that most popular of verbs. And there is even a little gringo who's in love with classical art, not to mention the mulattoes who are so full of grace. The majority of the nymphs who work at the Rose Windmill are Mexican girls with aristocratic manners. He snuck into the Rose Windmill thanks to the carelessness of the doorman. Since it's a decent whorehouse, undesirable types are not permitted. The prices?

High as the sky! That's why anyone who enters such a place ought to be well heeled and extremely well dressed in the bargain. It would be appropriate to say that the service is select and unique. The setting is presided over by a very quiet and attentive harmony, such that any member of the best society would feel himself to be in an exact replica of his own world while in the brothel. He walked toward the back, excited to be contemplating such a majestic palace. What an attractive interior! He stopped and smiled, stunned to see that three people were greeting each other with ample ceremoniousness and phrases of mutual adoration: the lawyer Flaminio Jarandas, who had become wealthy from quickie divorces (Hollywood actors, who change partners quicker than dogs in heat, had afforded him millions), the speculator Hércules Flores, bald, with his little eyes placed well above his nose, and Dr. Canelo Robinhood, who had a gold mine of fetuses in the "decent" girls who prefer not to have babies out of wedlock. He felt himself under their influence. He walked over to the group of honorable professional men and bowed with supreme courtesy.

"Gentlemen, it's a pleasure. . . . "

The whores and the clients who were standing behind him laughed out loud. The seat of the man's pants was ripped. They kicked him out. Outside they hit him so hard that he could barely take off up the street at a run. It was drizzling. He collapsed exhausted in front of a very elegant mansion. Between the drapes he could see Mr. Mario Miller de Cocuch; he was wearing a very fine gold-colored gown. There was such beatitude and devotion in his gestures that he seemed to be conversing with a divinity. In reality what moved him with such emotion were the gorgeous notes of a Schubert serenata Doña Reginalda was drawing forth from the piano under the magic of her noble hands. Terrified, he saw the image change suddenly. Mario Miller de Cocuch laughed hysterically as he rolled all over the floor in a pool of vomit and blood, while Doña Reginalda, dressed in silver, banged away at the piano with gnarled hands, bursting her lungs singing a shrill song that sounded more like an animal braying. Streams of worms poured out the orifices of the wealthy couple. He followed the gully until he reached the crest of the craggy hill where he often went. He sat down on the edge facing the city. It must have been dawn

when he made out the transformed city. It had grown enormously
and a bright glow emanated from its heart. He could see a group
of very attractive buildings among which a multitude was coming
and going with a quick and lively gait. Dawn came slowly. Sud-
denly he saw something very strange. An eight-year-old came up
carrying a very heavy box on his back. He placed it at his feet.
"*What are you doing here? A child out at these hours. . . .* "
"*I've come from down there where all the lights are.*"
"*What's that?*"
"*It's for you from the university.*"
"*Who's the gift from?*"
"*It's not a gift. . . . It'll cost you dirt!*"
"*Dirt?*"
The box contained some printed papers. He held them close
to his eyes until there was enough light to make them out. He
read: Fragile. Difficult to construct. He tried to lift the box but
couldn't. How heavy it was! He saw the little hand of the child
holding a key out to him. He opened it, and then covered his face
with consternation. He sobbed, possessed by a mortal sadness.
The box was full of nails. The dawn was now turning blue. He
could see the child. He was wearing worn-out adult's clothing, cut
down to his size. His dirty face was streaked by tears. Holy God!
The child had the same eyes as he had when he was a child, the
same face of his own childhood. It was him when he was a child!
The child threw himself into his arms, and he tried to embrace
him lovingly but he vanished into thin air. He turned to look at
the box and it had disappeared.

He jumped up suddenly with the rapidity of a cat. He had the
impression that a gigantic explosion had blown the dawn away
into burning bits that were swallowed up by the sky. It was the
dawn bursting forth and uncovering furtive clouds that scurried
away in embarrassment. There was only a fraction of a second in
which he thought in ecstasy: What beautiful golden boats I'd like
to have!

He heard the same celestial music again. He looked at the
bottom of the ravine and among the crags. He could only make
out the rounded stones that the sun salvaged from the darkness by
making them shine like pillows or maternal breasts.

The sun woke him, and he was burning with thirst. He went
into the city looking for a drink. He spent hours that day with-

drawn, his wings shattered, alongside Peluchi, who sold chicken tortillas from a cart, the same crafty little fellow who buys the rabbits for three pesos that have been shot to death and for one peso those that have been run over by cars. One of his clients complained with his mouth full of a taco. He was complaining about the cloud of drunken flies that were flying around like crazy, looking like tired planes back from a bloody mission. Nevertheless, the greedy eater was using all ten fingers. There was always some jerk to claim with a knowing air that the filthy insects contained protein, but all he got was a hard look from twelve offended eyes that looked on him as dirty and lacking in manners. Someone else joked that they should put rubber stockings on them. The street vendor asserted that when a lot of flies come around, it means someone who's standing nearby is going to die soon. He heard the word die and remembered his childhood. A cow had fallen into a canal and they had taken it out already dead. He came out from behind the foliage of the *tápiros* and could see without being seen. Two brothers were seated on the arm of a recently fallen tree, their chins resting on their fists. They had no other cow. A child of eleven held a leash that was tied to a dog, and the dog had his snout buried in the cow's guts. The child looked at the sky with a face full of purity and saintliness. What a beautiful child! Suddenly he realized that the two brothers were immortalized. The child was ecstatic. The dog was an idol with a red snout. The water of the canal was glass that did not flow. A single silence of birds and trees. The cow . . . the cow . . . did not move her eyes, could not get up, did not moo. It was the first time that he knew time is used to standing still, that over a fraction of a second, hours, years, and even centuries pass. . . .

THE LAWYER Espíndola Fernoch stood up with the solemnness of a statue. He instinctively banged the desk. An old woman and a little man wearing a threadbare suit were standing in front of him. The man's suit had been mended so many times that his appearance evoked a compassionate smile. He stretched out his right arm pretending to hide the display of a shining gold watch. He was the one who'd found the body in the craggy ravine.

"Your neighbors have been summoned by my office with the objective of establishing the identity of the man who died today and whose name is a mystery that, out of pure formality, we are trying to clear up, either with your help or that of someone else."

Espíndola Fernoch, Esq. had a physique that matched his name: pointy whiskers, a squashed little nose with large nasal cavities, and thick hair falling down over his forehead. He spoke in a self-satisfied manner and with the affectation of functionaries who believe themselves to be the tentacles of government.

"Madam, what are the general facts about you?"

"Ay, sir, at my age, what would I be doing with military men?"

"Madam, I'm asking what you go by."

"The only thing I go by is not to have to die of hunger."

"Madam! Your name."

"Oh, my name is Doña Candelita."

"Excuse me for interrupting, sir; I'm looking for loose pieces of paper, manuscripts, personal effects of the man who died by his own hand. I will continue to rummage around."

"Well, Miss Betty, leave them on the desk. I will take a look at them in a minute."

Betty Pérez, secretary for many years, showed that she had spent her life sitting down. She had constantly developing buttocks, skinny arms and legs, and a small head which made her look like an ostrich when she walked.

"According to the information I have, he lived next door to you, a relative, surely. Let's talk about that, and tell us his name."

"Ah, sir. I don't really know his name. I found him yelling in the street, burning up with fever. He knelt down and called me grandmother, me, who's nothing more than a poor unfortunate old woman. Well, it melts your heart. I took him to an abandoned adobe room where I live. I gave him a corner and a cup of soup. He told me that a friend of his had died. I know about these things because I'm an old lady, and I said to him: "It's not that anybody has died. Your illusion is what has died, son. Then he fell silent."

"Did he continue at your side?"

"He would return home drunk at dawn, hungry, and I had to throw him out. I barely make enough to eat with what I earn."

"What do you sell?"

"*Pionilla, chuchupate,* orange blossoms, rue, rosemary, Indian root, medicines for all kinds of things."

"Come on! Indian root. What's that good for?"

"Well, sir, Indian root allows women who haven't been serviced by their husbands to have children."

"OK, we're here to establish an identity."

"My only crime, sir, is to be an old woman. Let me go."

"You're not being accused of anything. You can go."

"Your name, sir."

"My name is Vicente Gabaldón, but everybody calls me Chente and Chonón as well. When my wife gets mad at me, she calls me Cholo the bastard. I tended nanny goats for a while. Now that I'm an old man I take care of turkeys."

"Well, well, now we know your story. Miss Pérez, prepare to write the report that I will dictate to you."

"Califa, on the etc., etc., etc. On the basis of the declaration of both witnesses, it was established that, the first witness having gone to the nearest grocery store, that is corner market, with the name Abarrotera Universal, he saw some seven vultures which, guided by their voracious appetite for carrion, had gone down into the bottom of the ravine, a fact that attracted his attention and led him to believe that it had to do with a goat that had gone astray and was dead, and he went down to see what the predators, which the bad-mouthing witness compared to politicians, were feeding on, and he forgot that his objective was to buy flour to make hotcakes. This witness swears to tell the truth and nothing but the truth, for he's a firm religious believer and goes to communion often, so much so that he blesses the animals which, in the opinion of the declarer, are much nobler than humans, for example the dog and even the burro, not to mention the lessons to be taken by the stoic billy goat. He states that his name is Vicente, that he is called Chente, and that they often call him by the nickname of Burro because of his white hair. The witness expounded on how the aforementioned hotcakes were for his wife, that because the woman is pregnant, she gets irritated and takes advantage of her state by coming up with the most absurd stupidities. When he had descended into the ravine, the vultures tried to fly away quickly, but they were so clumsy from their gluttony that he could well have, if he'd wanted to, caught one of those dirty birds. He said that he saw in the macabre image the amusement with which the aforementioned politicians satiate

themselves . . . (correct that, I meant to say vultures). He went
up to the top, being the first to bring forth the news to this authority. He states that on the way up he told the story to so many
who invited him to have a cup of coffee and relate the morbid and
horrifying details, such as whether the sockets had been picked
out and whether or not there was a nose left, and which side the
vultures liked in particular. When the authorities arrived, they
corroborated what the loquacious witness had said, it being agreed
that the evidence points to death by the victim's own hand, or
better, suicide. It was determined that the deceased, whose name
is unknown, who had gone to that area for reasons unknown,
whose days went by rapidly, spent his time partying at the expense
of whomever he could get to provide for him, and it is apparent
from the papers found in his pockets that the unfortunate man was
a fabricator of verses of haughty and disdainful muses. These authorities having testified, the very deteriorated body of the young
man was exposed (damn vultures!), having thrown himself among
the crags from a height of thirty-some meters. The aforesaid witnesses agree in that the picture was . . . terrible, no, better if you
write, horrifying . . . no, better tragic . . . let's see . . . leave
that, Betty, and we'll finish this report in the next few days. Did
you say that among his papers there is an "Elegy to my friend the
poet"? Very well, let's see it.

ELEGY TO LORENZO LINARES, MY POET FRIEND:

LORENZO, it would have been better for you never to have left San
Jacinto de las Nubes.

Lorenzo Linares went down from San Jacinto de las Nubes along
roads of crystal, woven with creepers, where the shadow of the dry
leaves sounds like the clinking of the iron grates, green sirens spread out
under the footsteps of the shipwrecked.

The sun tore the hymen of dawn, and the seas and the mountains
became blush colored.

Dew, chlorophyll; an afternoon of emeralds; the blue, the wind, and
the gold of the mornings.

The nets outstretched, he sought to catch the silver of the stars
that sleep in the water, fishes, moon, breeze. His feet swollen from

geography, with his steps drained of color, sunken in the dust, the desert of Sonora. . . .

His gaze slithered along over the sinuous back of the specter of nature, a cemetery of colors, the paleness of a dead woman.

Lorenzo Linares fell on his knees speaking the name of God. The roads disappeared before him, blind from maps, an orphan of the shining stars, the lord of dead paths. He was found by the stars when his star was consumed by the shadows. His blue rivers became shadowy clots without the bubbles playing the collapse of the globules, conquered armies of white and red.

He was unable to compose his poem. He had the sea, the moon, the sun, the sky, and the sand. But in order to rhyme with life he lacked water.

Water! Wat, wa, w . . . The projectiles of sand overwhelmed the word, which rose again, trembling with anguish, pain, and rage!

Wwwa . . . te . . . r! Until the final "r" flickered out, matterless. Ay, Lorenzo Linares! The sky is the dust of blue pigeons that went after the stars.

In San Jacinto de las Nubes it was raining hummingbirds with winged and transparent kisses, gardens of enchanted damsels, white, blue, lilac, purple, and scarlet, a purple green ground that colors the mirrors of the afternoon. The land and the jungle, water that ran quickly down the neck of the ravines overflowing the womb of the lagoons.

Chorus of frogs, a mass of toads.

In Lorenzo Linares's shack, eyes fixed on the fantasy of the absent one, raining nostalgia.

Come back, Lorenzo Linares, do not enter that sterile plain of deceit: imaginary lakes formed by the fever of the banished, a green mist of the dying demons.

Crosses and knives; mirrors and pieces of glass; bloodless, anemic, avid vampires.

The red wail turning into liquid, the unborn and beheaded adolescents.

The sea is a round river, a mirrorlike lagoon.

The seas are the eyes of God. The deserts are the basins where inexistence is to be seen.

The Yuma Desert. How it burns!

Lorenzo Linares, my friend, was a torrent of happiness and joy, channeled in a river of nostalgia. He wished to make the desert flower with poems. Ecstatically, he went forth to plant metaphlowers and fountains with jets of polychrome letters, his red blood, lakes, jungles, and the vivid irises of his fantasy.

On the canceled page of creation, he heard the cries that silence buries.

A man without a country, his Indian forebears had already died. . . .

Poet, your bitter destiny, surrounded by the nimbus of unknown galaxies and cosmic milky torrents.

The sand dunes are souls of millenary voices that weep over the fronds the wind does not stir.

Cursed desert! You have drunk the language and the breath of my people of yore, Nahuatlaca majesty. Heavenly Faaather! Lord . . .

Yuma . . . Arizona. . . . How cruel you are to my people! Shrouds in the cottonfields, calvaries of lettuce. Vines covered with bunches of tears!

God intuits, God does not think: God intuits the fire with which he fashions the planets. Ashen tails mark out his fire.

Lorenzo: long before you died, you were always a memory.

The desert of Altar covered itself with fleeting fronds.

Leaf storms without autumn, the wings of buzzards happily screeching responses to the carrion.

Lorenzo Linares, poet friend, stripped of your putrifying clothes you are now a bony smile that rises above the shining stars, singing with the wind, caressed by the sand dunes, lulled by small voices in cathedrals that will never again stumble on memory. Swollen choruses scream at the top of their lungs in the eternal labyrinths of silence!

Looreeeenzooo, Looreeeenzooo.

THE SKY WAS ASHEN and the air was blowing like a train calling everyone on board. It was a playful air that blew the hats off the poor and played with the witches, howling through cracks in the windows and worn dentures. Since there was no dirt, it made whirlwinds out of obscene words that flew suspended in the atmosphere. Without the nostalgic melancholy of the flowering afternoons, without the prodigious glory of a jeweled space, the darkness fell like a blind sky impaling itself on the rays of the city's glow. It was autumn and winter when people look like they're in a hurry with an air of mystery. They rush in and out of the stores buying many things as though they were getting ready to hole up for a long period of hibernation. Loreto saw him coming out of a brothel, the Olympic Seraglio, and knew he was going to fall. Later, his soul would become afflicted with the blackest anguish when he learned the enormous tragedy of the little drunk.

Frankie Pérez stumbled toward the old carwasher. He came to a stop, waving his arms in the air. His knees became stiff. He took a few more stumbling steps like a newborn colt. He stretched his neck with a glow in his half-burned-out eyes to see if old man Loreto was a living being or the statue of some legendary Indian. Scrawny and childlike, he looked fifteen at the most. Nevertheless, he had recently been initiated as one more cell into the glorious gringo army.

"Hey, fella, you seem real neat to me. You're a great buddy, you know. Just like you were my grandfather."

He was about to fall, and Loreto held him up. He saw that he was dark, with a big nose and the features of a Yaqui. The old man trembled, shaken by a burst of tenderness.

"Where are you from, boy?"

"From California, pops."

"Are you a Chicano?"

"Yes, pops. I'm a Chicano!"

Frankie burst into tears.

"They bug the hell out of me just so they can beat me up."

With his resistance disarmed, the lethargy of the alcohol submerged him in dreams that vanished without engraving themselves in his memory, inconclusive images, dispersed voices that he could not assemble in order to understand and erase the cursed questioning that crawled like rats across his forehead, that dug at his eyes and chest, that filled his head. No matter how hard he moved around and rubbed his hands, the rats and the uncertainty would not become dislodged. His life, as brief as the life of an adolescent can be, arose as he conjured it up. Although he was just beginning to live, his conscience already was demanding an accounting from him, a justification for the absurd drama that destiny had set for him. He, his family, the war, prejudice, slavery, school. Spanish is not to be spoken! Hunger. Spanish, no! The

grapes, the cantaloupes, cucumbers, cotton. Without medications!
I told you. Don't speak Spanish. Dark people are worthless. Get
to working hard, hard, hard. Listen. Speak English. The war, the
war, ah, ah, the wa . . .

His childhood in the sight of the symmetry of the fields, where
he had stood deep in thought so many times, channeling the nostalgia of mysterious epochs that he only intuited beyond the walls
of lettuce and the bitter beds of the cotton fields that stretched
out like vast shrouds. The cursed vineyards that imprison with
their tentacles. And that oven! The infernal oven that squeezed
streams of sweat from them, sweat that coated the watermelons
and cantaloupes, while they, the Chicanos, became dried out like
leftover cane stalks. His tragic joy of an undernourished child had
only recently been alleviated, living in the filth imposed by poverty, breathing a humid, living breath that drew its greenness from
the plants that grew vigorously, growing like soldiers. Like soldiers? My God! From then on the rigid discipline sealed in routine
nature, also green like the Chicano soldiers. Now he moved his
arms in the jungle of bitterness, when his perspective as a dreamy
child had been so different.

They carry them off to Asia, so they say, my friend. Tender as
can be, the poor things, with the story that they are going to
defend I don't know what the fuck, and then a little bit later,
there they are, back again, either in bed or wounded, all kicked
out of shape, with their soul full of knots at having seen so much
shit. Ah, my friend. . . .

Frankie Pérez hunched his shoulders together, trembling. Don
Loreto realized that Frankie was cold so he took his overcoat off
and took a few steps to cover him with it. Each step was accompanied by a creaking sound. He bent his left knee with difficulty
and, stretching his right leg out, managed to cover him. His right
leg was made from a very rough wood. He had to use it tempo-
rarily and, finally, it became permanent. The fact is that his
buddy Chayo Cuamea was the one who made it, out of ironwood.
What a demon colonel! He worked the wood with just machete
blows. He even remembered that Colonel Rosario Cuamea had
told him: you're going to turn out to be a real live wire, pal, because this is the wood I used to make tops and ball-and-cup toys
when I was a kid. Every time the squat Loreto remembered the

colonel, he laughed out loud. Chihuahua! What a scamp of a
man that Chayo was. Because, who, aside from Colonel Cuamea,
had been able to go after Death for himself? What a devil of
a guy! All he did was hear him swear. Clean off! And there was
the leg rolling on the ground, boot and all. If he understood
anything at all, it was because someone was shouting: "Get
Loreto Maldonado out of here! A burst of machine gun fire
slashed his leg!" Right away it began to rot from the sun, and
there was a cloud of flies that buzzed stupidly around because they
had eaten their fill. A nice little guy of a doctor named Mariano
sawed it off. But there was no doubt he was wrong in his predic-
tion: "This Yaqui will never eat quelites with atole again." Since
there was no anesthesia, the unfortunate warrior sweat blood just
hearing the hacking of the saw. But he didn't give out. Later he
told his buddy Rosario Cuamea, "Ah, pal, giving birth would
have hurt less."

"Agua . . . water . . . agua, please."

"Frankie! Come on, buddy. What's going on? No, not that,
no. Don't give up, no, come on. . . . Frankie! Frankie . . .
look. . . . "

"Watch out, pal, be cool. These guys'll get you even under
water, guy, just like they were turtles. Keep your eyes open out in
the brush, man. If you think what you're seeing are branches,
you're dead wrong and they'll kill you. Be careful of even the
toads, my good friend. Now if you're careless and fall in a hole,
well, your number's up. You'll end up impaled on stakes this big,
stakes dipped in poison to boot. Don't be a fool! If you get yourself
a chick to be all lovey with and screw, you know what I mean,
brother, after a while you'll be yelling at the devil through a small
hole because the Asian clap will rot you right down to your soul,
little brother. No, listen, it won't rot you, it'll make you burst like
a watermelon shot full of holes, and penicillin won't do you a
damn bit of good. You know what, my friend, what's going on in
Vietnam is so frightening that if you don't smoke grass or do coke,
you'll go stark raving mad from fear. The soldiers in Vietnam, I
want you to know, don't use hot rice to shoot with."

How beautiful the grapes are. They look like little jugs in min-
iature, all full of wine. In the morning, they look like little
lighted crystals and then they turn into little silver bubbles. They

are pure gold in the afternoon until the sun goes down. And
then . . . they're like tears.

His dad had a mean heart. He didn't buy them good food. The
hovel where they lived was made from the worst kind of wood,
and it didn't even have a floor to drop dead on. Poor old guy! He
didn't realize at the time that the father he loved so much worked
hours on end and that the money the owner paid him wasn't even
enough to fill the cavities in his teeth. My poor dad. So many
years spent walking the furrows, and he had to wander back and
forth, eternally looking for an ending which the falseness of the
circle would mask as infinity.

That's right. He'd watched his old man talking to himself,
clapping his hands angrily. Shit! His kids, without schooling,
would end up in the same vicious circle, part of the same herd.
But some day . . .

It was past midnight. Frankie sat down trying to remember the
place. He looked at stubby Loreto. The latter, on his knees, put
his arm under Frankie's head, trying to hold it up so he'd drink
something. Frankie gulped down a whole ocean of fresh water
with the voracity of a sand pit. Then he fell into a deep sleep. It
sounded like death rattles rather than snoring. The crippled Indian continued for several seconds in the same position. He had
lived a similar scene far away, very far away, as far back as his
youth. He sat down on the cement wall contemplating the Chicano and the past. All the avenues of his life had led to sadness.
Suddenly, his tired heart began to pound like a train full of revo-
lutionaries. . . . Memories that frantically tore away the yellowish
webs of oblivion, in shreds, hacked away with a machete blade,
the loud voices and the fever, the fever and the cannon shots that
assaulted your eardrums . . . those damn cocks that destroyed your
brain with their pecking. Cockadoodledoo. Long live Villa! The
frightened horses fled in droves through the doors of death. The
shouts, the stampedes, and the neighing, men blown to smith-
ereens became fixed in blinding flashes that imprinted the ephemeral silhouettes as though a stamp of history marked the end of
living pages in a vertiginous trance. Chaca, chaca, chaca, chaca,
auuuuu, auuuuuuuu. Let the reactionary troops go fuck their
mothers! What's this, Cuamea buddy? Who the hell knows, but
we're going to kick them in the balls. The popping of the bullets

burst like red popcorn. Colonel Chayo Cuamea. What a devil of a Yaqui! The only guy in the world who's screwed Death.

The draw of life . . . it was fate that old Loreto Maldonado hold a symbolic wake over the body of Frankie, because nine months later, when he fell in Vietnam, no one accompanied his lifeless body. The Chicano was left behind while Pánfilo and Magui were living with Jesús on their lips, their mind on nothing but their son. When Magui would burst out in tears for her absent son, exposed to so much danger, Pánfilo would say to her: "Well, the kid'll be back and then we can go to Magdalena de Kino, down from Nogales on foot, to give thanks to St. Francis." A party of his American soldiers removed the metal tags with his identification number when all that was left of him were bones in the middle of the jungle where the one who'd been Rosario Cuamea's lover reigned.

Surrounded by all the sounds, he and the young Chicano were like an island of silence. The old revolutionary soldier noted suddenly that the little Chicano was not moving or making any noise. He anxiously drew near him to observe him and saw that the kid's eyes were open, lost in his own divagations.

Frankie was drawing his Texas hometown in capricious dreams, a group of adobe houses with mud roofs. When it rained, the roofs turned green with growth. The straw they used to make the adobes grew like hair with the erosion of the dirt. At night, the light from the petroleum lamps tinted the doors and windows with a flickering yellow. Over the years, little by little, the wind and rain ate away the walls as though they suffered from leprosy. An eternal dust storm coated the houses. Men of dust, cemeteries of dirt and dust, a sun avid for sweat . . . In the background, the blurred parade of bent human beings carrying hoes over their shoulders. His father, Pánfilo Pérez's bosses. How good they were! They never forbid him to look at their dream palaces and how considerately Mr. MacCane always greeted him: "Hello, Frankie Boy!" His father loved Mr. MacCane a lot, because when the mister spoke to him, Pánfilo Pérez always answered, "Yes, sir!", eyes cast down out of respect. Pánfilo went out every day at dawn. He returned from his labors when it was already dark, with his feet swollen and his eyes all red, dragging his feet and looking like a rag doll. He sat down, angrily pounding the table with his fists because his wife

only brought him tortillas and beans to eat. Then he would sit by
the door, hour after hour, just looking toward the hole the sun
dipped into. His wife would cry silently, and he and his little
brothers would hang on her skirts, shaking with fear. Often their
father would get mad and beat them. Other times he would kiss
them and was tender with their mother. It was terrible when
someone got seriously ill. Pánfilo would cry like a child with his
face in his hands. He would rush out into the street and would
come back hours later with packets of chamomile, *chuchupate*,
mint, and other infusions, which he would give them with sugar.
True, at times the colics and fevers were so bad the children
would die, despite the chamomile. How different the MacCane
family was. How proud of them Frankie felt. They had oil wells
and private airplanes and a lot of land. The MacCanes were important protectors of the Chicano. Anyway, they employed a lot of
them. . . . In the first place, they were profoundly religious. At
meal time, with the whole family seated at the table, Mr. Mac-
Cane read the Bible. With a strong voice and pointing with his
finger, he seemed to give off sparks. Then, everybody bowed their
heads with respect, and it was something to see such a pretty picture, giving thanks to God for their daily bread. With what gen-
erosity the divinity paid that beatitude, for the MacCanes' table
was heaped with all kinds of delicacies. Their beloved cats glowed
with health, and the dogs were fed ground meat so they wouldn't
hurt their teeth. They ate so well their noses always glistened.
What a holy family! At night the MacCane house seemed
wrapped in a mist of saintliness.

While the eyes of the little Chicano filled with tears that
slowly streamed down his face, the peg leg philosophized as
though he had slept years and years, and someone had just
plopped him down there. There he is, for those to see who do not
believe that destiny is often like a puppeteer, like those guys who
make the dolls dance any which way and, in the process, make
fools of them. Taking care of the cars of the gringo tourists! Loreto
Maldonado, his pal Rosario Cuamea should see him now. He remembered the letter that Chayo sent him a little while before he
undertook the deed that gave him so much fame. Death may have
a lot of tricks, but his buddy Chayo made Death lose the title
of Miss.

Maldonado, buddy: Along with a troop that includes my three sons (the other one is sick), I'm about to topple the supreme government. Come join us, Loreto buddy, with whatever you can. We're going to raise Zapata's flag, "Land and Liberty." You already know it's not a question of balls. Your pal, Rosario Cuamea.

WHAT A SCAMP that Chayo was. They say that Death resisted three days by putting fomentations between her legs. How many times did the pedestrians walk indifferently in front of Loreto's rigid, dark copper figure? Because he cast himself into the vanquished time, situating himself time and again with stubbornness in his earliest days, reconstructing his life with sick delight. Coming out of his withdrawal within himself, he looked at Porfirio Díaz Street with a tenuous, ironic smile that came from his most intimate bitterness. His eyes could no longer stand looking toward any future. He saw everything as a backdrop in the mirror of water in a very deep well. With many wounds and a leg that had been eaten by the vultures, what did he have left to take his mind off his hunger, other then to remember those times?

How lucky Pánfilo Pérez was to work for the MacCanes. When he could handle seven days, he made as much as 25 dollars a week. How much in a month? It must have been around one hundred dollars. What a pile! How much candy we would have been able to buy with that capital. But his father gave money for candy on so few occasions! One day his hellraising buddy Choni showed up. Come on, Pánfilo my friend, let's set off for Arizona. Pánfilo was afraid, but Choni egged him on. Let's go try our luck, pal, we couldn't be any more fucked up anywhere else than we are here. Well, what do you say? So the whole circus set off in Choni's jalopy. Frankie remembered that he'd gotten into a fight with Chililo, because the latter had said that his dad's boss, Mr. More Sany, was richer than Mr. MacCane. Frankie was very sad to leave the place where he'd been born. That's why Frankie would always remember the words of his godfather when he said by way of goodbye: "From now on, why the hell do we need these sons-of-bitch owners?" Choni was a real ingrate and foulmouthed. His wife said to him laughing: "They're going to burn your face with a brand." Then came the long days of picking and picking, cantaloupes, watermelon, grapes, cotton, and whatever there was to be picked. It's no little thing to have the sun beating down on your neck like the blade of a machete or to carry it on your back like a burning coal cutting into your kidneys.

Frank Pérez left for the war when the metamorphosis from youth to puberty promised an order that would save him from chaos, from the confusion and solitude so intimate that he came to believe that no one would ever get to understand his strange world. He made a supreme effort to find his place in an unexplored world, because the world of his previous eighteen years was a handful of the broken glass from his first mirror. Frankie set off with new eyes that picked up the landscape, provoking discomfort in him. He wanted to take everything in, drinking in the countryside with his eyes. He shuddered every time his nerves jangled and his spinal chord was invaded by a strange pleasure half-anguished and half-expectant. Frankie Pérez marched off to war when his life was a flower full of pollen. He reddened with emotion with a thought that illuminated him like a burst of fire: When I return I'll get married or take a lover. But the rapid and ravenous jaws of the cruel god of war demanded their tribute of blood and tears, no longer the traditional holocaust of a few victims, but raging rivers that would inundate the world with suffering and spread seeds of hate throughout the land. Meanwhile, the priests, perpetuators of the bloody ritual, sent victims to the sacrifice, caressing white doves in front of their people and speaking with inspired words of justice.

Thus it was that Frankie Pérez, a Chicano, became acquainted directly with what war means. With great difficulty he overcame the indescribable terror that threatened to burst from within him, as though he himself were a grenade. But no sacrifice would be small. He had the sacred duty to defend his country. His beloved country, so just and generous with all its sons. He recalled the ancient noble and just patriarchs, with their brave hawklike profiles who, full of pride and with apostolic echoes, had begged him: "Defend us and defend our people, if necessary with your life. Our advanced age keeps us from fighting." Frankie cried with emotion just to remember such distinguished men. The valiant hawks could not take up arms, but they remained behind to suffer in pain and anguish, imposing great sacrifices on themselves and reducing their salaries as public officials and apostolically aiding the needy. What great patriots, what honored and noble men. They did not bear arms but encouraged their people with words full of serenity and wisdom by being, above all else, examples of reason, justice, and loyalty. For this reason the multitudes came out by the hundreds of thousands to praise them, cheering them until their voices went hoarse, saluting them with perfume and flowers, profoundly grateful for the honesty and wisdom with which they guided their people. The long watches and the despair of danger made Frankie stir up his ingenuity as a child for some extraordinary help from his imagination to calm the terror of the imminent massacre perpetrated by a determined and cruel enemy who did not give up in his aggression. It was then that he invoked the legendary idols that inhabited the heart of his countrymen. Superman destroying planes in midair by merely spitting at them, lifting convoys with his baby finger, winning the war in a wink. Batman with his genius and strength overcoming the stupid Asians who did not know how to fight because they're cowards and short on smarts. And if these ultrapowerful beings did not dominate the unjust enemy, ah!, there was the great, the sublime, the invincible, and moreover exquisitely beautiful Great Cowboy! The most grandiose legendary hero of his country. Alone, mounted on his spirited horse, with a pistol in each hand, he had vanquished and eliminated thousands of Indians, liberating territories and caravans of religious men and women predestined by God our Lord to colonize these lands, as fertile as they were vast. What is more, he had punished all of the evil Mexicans, killing them like rabbits or humiliating them just by looking at them askance. Frankie saw him come up mounted on an enormous horse, with pistols in each hand and a whip wrapped around his waist. A few curls fell limply on his forehead under his Texas hat. With his toothpaste smile and his lips colored a pale, lipstick red, he was singing a ballad. His ballad, full of emotional and poetic voices, sang about how in a battle against thousands of Indians and after containing them for hours, first with bullets and then with just a whip and finally by slapping their faces, he had had to flee because his arms had grown tired. He sang such an inspired melody, and, in order to save time, he had fled hanging onto his horse's tail. His ballad was so moving that the little birds that lighted on his shoulders were cheeping out their tears, and the forest seemed to fall silent just to listen to such a peerless hero. He concluded by narrating that his horse ran so fast that all you could see was the wake it left. His beautiful voice bordered on tears when he clarified that when he stopped such a vertiginous race, he had lost his clothes and was left stark naked. With theatrical whoops he sang that his buttocks had suffered for days from the bruises of the projectiles that the hooves of the cyclonic horse had raised from the ground.

Frankie looked at the Asians who were frightened by the appearance of the Great Cowboy. Their feet flew up as far as their necks as they ran filled with fear and waving little white flags. But no, the resources of his fantasy were far from being reality. Such miraculous entities did not materialize, despite his efforts to conjure them up. They, the weaker beings: What a great privilege! They had the distinction of dying, in a higher percentage, sacrificing themselves thus for their noble country and honoring the slogans of the distinguished, wise, and glorious hawks. All praise to the valiant hawks!

Dawn was coming. The human vampires flew to seek refuge in their coffins, covered in red. The butterflies awoke, rubbing their thousand cosmetic hues, dropping overcome with sleep, irreconcilable to the pallid masks fabricated by time and the inertia of their suffering with the rush of laughter, tears, and vain words, a whole foamy adventure that dissipated beneath the earth or floated off on the winds. The cocks plucked out the threads of the dawn, sharpening their claws and beaks in order to attack with fury the sun which had begun to come out again. Just a few hours ago it had played dead in order to enjoy the responses intoned by nature before a cosmic altar cloaked in supreme royalty. In his years as a peasant, Loreto learned to determine the hour just by looking at the sky. But ever since he earned his living among the nightclubs, in the middle of a lighted city, he knew dawn as that hour in which the worlds that spring free from the temples of vice become damp and smelly and as repulsive as dirty insects, looking for ears in which to nest. Loreto Maldonado had lived the night without sleeping a moment, taking care of the little Chicano. It seemed that the old Yaqui was making an effort to stay awake in order to cover, in the little existence he had left, the entire world that reality and dreams had woven for him in an infinity of paths.

Loreto observed Frankie, who remained stiff as though his bulk
were an empty copper pot instead of flesh. Months later Frankie
would be in the same position, but quiet and with his head destroyed. Just seeing the poor boy, the squat man suffered, as
though something were allowing him to understand that he was
symbolically paying Frankie his posthumous honors.

A seizure of tenderness and a deep sadness sent him back toward the beginning of the century. Once again he ran right into
his terrifying buddy. What a wild Yaqui!

"Buddy, buddy, what's your name?"

"I . . . don't speak . . . Spanish."

Christ! What an imposing Yaqui. Tall, with the slenderness
and elastic elegance of a panther, unruly hair, with small black
eyes so full of energy and intelligence that even the officers knew
he was a man to respect. Later he got around to learning Castil-
ian, and even though he had never been educated, he got to be a
colonel. Damn! That was something. What he lacked in brain
learning, he more than made up for in the influence he had
among his companions. The general himself, as though it stymied
him, couldn't believe it, but he couldn't deny it either. Son of a
bitch Yaqui! It looks like he's steel-plated—a bullet or a knife
couldn't penetrate him. The rain of bullets and machine gun fire
would begin, and there he'd be, laughing like he was out for a
stroll. Damn Chayo. It seemed . . . as though he wanted to throw
himself into the arms of death.

Rosario Cuamea had grown up right in the very heart of the
Bacatete Range. For many centuries it was a question of going
after the white men or fighting them every time they tried to
claim the rich lands that, by natural right, belonged to the Yaquis.
It was the second decade of the century. Cuamea, along with
many of his brothers, had refused to get involved in any peaceful
settlement, having decided to fight body and soul for the Yaqui
Nation. In those days, the Yaqui tribe had been fighting for about
four hundred years against being joined to the yoke like the rest of
the Indians, despite the sadistic cruelty with which Porfirio Díaz,
someone named Torres, and a couple of other carnivorous animals
assassinated their sons. There has never existed a race that fought
with such determination and courage for its land as the Yaquis

did. Ready to die for their soil, to die with all the crudity which the term in reality signifies. They covered their hills with bones, and sometimes they would commit suicide by the hundreds in the depths of a precipice that freed them from the white men. They bore from the womb the rage to fight and the rancor that fires the desire for vengeance. Neither women nor old people were excluded from the struggle to death for the land that the white men grabbed from them like pulling their nails out. With the terrible cry of the Yaqui, *"Yori sáncura!"*, the hills would quake with the battle cry, the swollen riverbeds would roar, and the lightning would strike mightily. But dogs and coyotes would be happy, and the skies would cloud over with the black warning of the vultures. Written history, a breezy coquette, disdains them like every whore who only concedes favors if she feels the weight of gold. Diego de Guzmán, according to reports much more bloody, raced over the Yaqui River along about 1533. He was accompanied by thousands of Indian reenforcements because by that time he had already made the rest of the Indian groups jump through the hoop. It looked easy for this hyena, why not! They planted the flag of Spain in Yaqui territory. With horses covered by the hides of dead cows and some rifles that spit fire, they descended on the Yaquis shouting "Santiago!"—the battle cry of the Spaniards. And they came off like real fools. The beating the Yaquis gave them was so great that for seventy-some years they walked past each other not even saying hello. About that time, another Diego showed up, more or less like the first, with the difference that this one turned out to be named Hurdaide.

The man pretentiously believed that his great army was ready, but Diego de Hurdaide got blasted too because the Indians beat him as much as his wet nurse had kissed him. He spent a year regrouping and returned, determined to get his revenge.

"Take your revenge!", the Indians told him. And there the captain goes in his failure, dragging shreds of glory. To make the story short, from that time on the brave Yaquis fought and fought. Porfirio Díaz, a mestizo from Puebla who rolled in the ashes in order to look like a white man but who in reality was a jackal with the pretentions of being a patrician, also tried to finish the Yaquis off. He drove them toward Yucatán, selling them like slaves. The Indians fled for their safety to the United States.

In sum, the Yaquis, by dint of their guerrilla efforts, did not allow themselves to be beaten. The Revolution broke out in 1910. It didn't take long for the politicians to turn to the Yaquis and beg them to participate in the struggle, swearing that it was a question of beating those who had abused them, that once the latter were beaten the government of the people would redeem all the Indians and respect the Yaquis. They believed it, so much so that even the wild ones came down from the hills with their bows and arrows, overjoyed to fight for the justice of the poor and the guarantee of respect for the Yaqui Nation. Among these wild men was Chayo Cuamea. And that's where he met his friends: Elpidio, from over by Tecoripa, and Loreto Maldonado, from near Vícam. With his whole life as a guerrilla fighter, tanned to the core by all the rigors of the bloodiest of battles, fighting in the Revolution came naturally to Rosario Cuamea. The Yaqui barbarian was in love like a burro, as only he could be, so much so that not even the bony lady was able to escape from him. When the ungrateful woman least expected it, she was already a prisoner in the arms of the tremendous Chayo Cuamea.

The first days Frankie Pérez sobbed in the middle of the jungle like a lost child. He went crazy from panic, a feeling of abandon that drove itself into the middle of his breast like a stake. After a few weeks, when his cries and shouts were lost without an echo in the bottomless pit, his eyes dried, sinking even more into his mute face which showed the signs of suffering. Frankie Pérez's mind had never before been exposed to meditation. What he had seen put a rusty machine in motion that had not been used for a century. Returning from each excursion, he sunk into meditations that wounded fibers of his soul, which until then he didn't even know existed. The horrendous slaughter of the bombardments, thousands of children, women and old people burning like coals, impregnated with napalm and screaming horribly. The massive extermination of the villages: "Don't leave a single living thing moving." The constant death of his comrades in arms, pieces of iron battering their bodies, bayonets sticking into them, traps of gangrenous stakes hidden underground, the disguised death of toads, lagoons, trees, a thick atmosphere of hatred, terror, shame. No! No, it was no longer only a question of his small suffering as a child-man, as an adolescent. He was now invaded by a deeper pain. The suffering of man! Of his species. Universal Suffering. Of man throughout his history. His intimate suffering, which no longer fit in his soul, was now the suffering of everyone, of his friends among his people, the Chicanos. Even of his executioners. Poor suffering Frankie Pérez. Standing on the earth, over a world inhabited by human beings, seeing the moon, large and luminous, the dark moon that illuminates with the look of the deluded, seeing the stars while his heart beat, among the living thicket, alongside the water painted like an unbreathing canvas of jungle and moon, hearing the musical murmurs of the night. Poor suffering Frankie Pérez. Standing on the place of the earth that has existed for millions of years, exactly at the instant of an opprobrious death whose scream of pain joins the echo of the massacre. Frankie was enthralled looking at the moon. When he sought in the moon a reason for his anguish, a cosmic giant, armed with an enormous club, came along and struck it with such violence that the moon cracked as it bounced. Ah! Poor little moon. Foaming cracks gave off fountains that covered its once luminous face. The moon, its face covered, grew dim from its suffering. A dark cosmos began to swallow it up. It fell . . . fell. . . . Until the final little light . . . went out! Then it sank into the red water borne by the cursed riverbeds. Frankie called out, Mommy, Daddy, but his shouts turned to marble. He was unable to bear the jungle which cried all night long, nor the responses of the toads that shattered the silence with such a high-volume uproar, as though wanting in a single night to denounce all human injustice. How the rivers moaned, how the roots of the plants writhed in pain, with what suffering the wounded beasts roared over the death of their offspring, with how much terror the little birds looked at the skies flashing with blood and fire. The winds that traveled from the past, from every direction and era, how disconsolately they cried. The very beasts in their instincts seemed to understand in their startled panic that the earth was inhabited by a being that was all cruelty and viciousness.

Part Three

The beasts of the sierra disappeared rapidly among the smooth crags, the depressions in the soft earth, and the bushes. The rails provided occasional cushions for their hooves and paws. They fled terrified by the distrust inspired by the human beings pursuing each other on the steep slopes, ragged and barefoot men who fled pursued by soldiers with miserable clothes, scarce rations, and the tragic slogan to kill their brothers. An enormous whitish rock, gray on its hidden side and dislodged by one of the two bands, came rolling down from high up. In its vertiginous fall it knocked over an intrepid saguaro, amputated an ironwood, wounded its other arm, and eliminated little animals who were sleeping trustfully. It ended its descent by decapitating cleanly a swollen barrel cactus and avoiding a palo verde by sheer miracle. Many beautiful fragrant plants were left trampled and wounded.

He was walking in the direction of San José de Guaymas. His feet, accustomed to climbing the hills, were hard and insensitive to the thorns and gravel there where every surface becomes a bed of coals. They were hard like the hooves of the deer and his anguish and fear were hidden beneath the thick cloak of hate. He always carried with him a macabre offering to the Yoris. In order to avoid them, he had even turned into a mesquite bush or into the dry arm of a palo verde. His were also the red spots of the *garambullos* bushes, and when the Yoris surprised him on the plain, he dug himself into the ground by sticking out his head which was thorny like a barrel cactus. He was going to seek revenge in San José de Guaymas. On the side of the hill they killed his father as they fled. His breath had run out before his blood had. Rosario Cuamea saw his blackened father, wrinkled like an accordion, just like the cracked earth, dry and sterile. Not one tear. Father! Daddy. He felt the waterfall like an inner channel, a cliff where a river blindly crashes below in the very core of one's soul. He was going in search of revenge. He stumbled on destiny and its tricks.

When Rosario Cuamea woke up, the storm of the Revolution was already bearing him along. He was joined by Elpidio, who became his assistant, his shieldbearer, his shadow and inseparable buddy. The latter was timid, asthmatic and a sleepwalker. The

first man he killed left him upset, and he became a scared little
boy, sleeping fitfully in a sweat, but the rest, as the expression
goes, "came easy." It didn't take him long to believe he had
rights, as he said, "since this was for our country and liberty, after
all." When his next one fell on his face, he turned him over with
his foot and contemplated him with scorn in his face and viciousness where before there had been compassion.

Rosario Cuamea was a wild Yaqui in a state of barbarianism.
His first contact with "civilization" was the war. . . . He was educated in the Revolution and, thanks to his vivaciousness, his
boldness, and his fury, he got to be colonel. He fought with the
rancor and rage of his tribe, which was painfully dispossessed of its
territory, ripped like flesh from the body.   .

The day he was promoted, after a victory, the officers joined
the general himself, a guy with a chubby face and haunches like a
horse.

So, we've covered ourselves with glory. . . .

The glory at issue was in a field of blood mixed with shit,
mashed guts, stinking flesh, severed heads, a massacre among human beings so cruel and vicious that not even the dogs and
wolves had seen anything like it in their most ferocious moments.

He began to hear the first greetings of "Colonel, sir," and he
smiled with satisfaction. Then a certain sadness darkened his face.
Suddenly he burst out laughing, which made those around him
shudder. He had lost his best friend in battle that day, his buddy
Elpidio. When he went to him, he saw that his friend had been
turned into a piece of Swiss cheese. He picked him up in the
midst of the fray, shot through with holes by a machine gun. He
felt him hum like a buzzing beehive. Dripping honey, he gasped
for air in his arms, and he said goodbye bubbling words and clots
of iron: for them . . . the children . . . the genera . . . tions. . . .
He saw the Skinny Lady over to one side, and he shouted at her
enraged: you carried off my buddy, daughter of a whore! He would
then see her everywhere, multiplied, as though each dying man
were a pool of blood representing her.

Old Cuamea had to get drunk, like every combatant, on gusts
of madness. After the slaughter some longed with anguish for their
childhood, avid for a regression that would free them from such a
horrible present. There were those who cried for having been

born, and the voices of others jumped out, their minds turned into a box where every memory floats around with no notion of time. Old Cuamea went in another direction: he had the idea that he saw death, "the Skinny Lady," as he came to call her familiarly. On a certain occasion, in the worst part of the battle, he saw the Skinny Lady occupied in her task of providing for the vultures and the dogs. Her back was to him and she was busying herself with eviscerating the soul of an abject being which, tangled up in his guts, was rotting as a single jumbled mass. The Indian Cuamea cackled crazily, permitted himself the luxury of embracing her with obscene intentions. The Skinny Lady turned around and slashed at him with her sickle, which he sidestepped thanks to his feline agility. Without a hat or a rifle, blandishing his machete, he pursued her, obsessed. The Skinny Lady fled, looking at him out of the corner of her eye, not without great distrust and covering with automatic modesty what is the summit of the fork formed by her legs.

Colonel Chayo spoke incoherently. Taciturn, his face began to show marked moments of sensuality. The truth is that he had reached the point of falling madly in love with the Skinny Lady. Such an absurd, outrageous, incredible passion devoured him that he swore to make her his lover.

The fratricidal war gave impulse to abstract reasons of always absent justice and liberty. The initial hatred overflowed, satiating the snout of the filthy beast. One mass killing after another in a wake of millenia marked the line of a destiny full of bloody tragedies. . . . In the midst of the cruel scenery, praised only by interest, Colonel Rosario Cuamea and She! met once again. She noted with surprise that the terrible warrior did not have the deep sadness of those that sense her to be near, nor the terror of those that see her close by, nor yet the resigned melancholy of those who receive her trembling and barely able to believe in their obvious mortality, nor the attempt to flee of those who vainly try to cling to the struggle. His calming and enchanting look made her feel strange, a feeling that increased as she observed that there were fires in the eyes of the Yaqui, and he mumbled an amatory response with his arms wide open. Her surprise turned to open terror when she saw him advance lasciviously with the lustful gesture and the determined step of the rapist. She knew this was not the moment to strike him down with the dull edge of her knife, and she fled in fright before the battering ram of the frustrated pursuer who like a shepherd chased her for the second time. It could well be said that if the Skinny Lady had any hair at all it stood up on her like the antennae of a puritan female porcupine. He also enjoyed watching her that day when she revealed on her angular face a gesture of repugnance and anger when she saw General Cajetes contenting himself with clouds of marijuana, the general with the happy little eyes always thirsty for blood. He had reached the troop when dusk was falling. Victorious, the troop was leading a bounty of more or less 300 prisoners. How tired they looked. Once they had put them in the pen, they sat down in small groups. Their lips did not seem to move. Nevertheless, from the very place they occupied there arose a murmur of tired voices. They looked more like they were coming back all worn out from work with that gesture of the peasant who looks upon the field where he has left his soul and then at the sky, quizzically, and with the painful foreboding of having worked in vain. They had joined the Revolution because they sought justice: land and liberty, according to the slogan. But the terrible game of the Revolution turned into a game of roulette for them, and it was their turn to lose for having chosen the wrong leader. Now they were going to be shot by other peasants just like themselves who had entered the Revolution to fight for the same thing, only that for the time being the same game of roulette made them the winners. General Cajetes ordered the execution of all the prisoners. They walked to the firing wall with the same step with which they had followed the plow for so many years with the sad face of the Indian, where happiness lies sealed like in a tomb. That day, General Cajetes drank rivers of blood with his eyes. Colonel Chayo Cuamea witnessed the executions. But he contemplated in a sad daze his beloved Skinny Lady. When she had gathered up the soul of the last field laborer to be eliminated, he approached her tenderly and speaking words of love. "You are mine, mine." He wasn't able to embrace her because he stumbled over a pyramid of the dead. She turned toward the noise, still with tears in her sockets. When she saw him, she bared her teeth and opened the hollows of her jaws half frightened and half out of modesty. And she ran, crossing space with a string of souls on her shoulders, while the loving colonel invoked her from a distance. "You will be mine, mine, because I love you madly."

The tremendous fratricidal war ended. The leaders grabbed up the bounty in a silent struggle in which money and power were to be had. The people heard speeches in abundance in a high-sounding and emotional language in which liberty and justice were once again insistent, one-note songs of deceitful sirens. People assassinated each other in betrayal and viciousness and with exterminatory zeal, where intrigue and astuteness sought an alliance with luck.

Colonel Chayo did not understand this struggle. It did not have to do with firing machine guns. He was soon discharged without honors, without money, and with his memories as his only glory. Frustration, like a slow fire, made his soul boil, and then . . .

Several years had passed by then. Colonel Chayo had not seen his "girlfriend" again. He was satisfied to marry a replica of the original, a woman as tall as a reed, fleshless like Lent, teeth like a corncob row of spurs, breasts as flat as a skating rink, and lacking in lactating mounds. The manifest absence of buttocks gave her pubic triangle an arrogant prominence like the forehead of a billy goat ready for the attack charge, and her bones could be counted in a wink with the naked eye. They had four children: Chayito, the first, just like his father; two nondescript ones followed, indifferent and with the seal of displeasure, as though they might have refused to be born; and the fourth, a poor being, half stupid. He trained his sons like guerrilla fighters once they had grown up. The old tiger threw himself into the battle followed by a half dozen dazed kids. He didn't know that wars elsewhere had brought about vertiginous scientific advances and that the military weapons and strategy required highly trained men. The lowest officer had to cram himself with knowledge as much technical as scientific, and it was not unusual among them to find a large number of queers, not like in his days when any illiterate with determination and a butcher's instinct ended up leading armies.

His troops did not waste any time in decreasing in number. The battle reduced itself to a cruel version of hide and seek. The soldiers carried out their orders with the maniacal morbidness of

those who have the license to kill cleverly. He and three of his
sons tried to get lost by hiding among the thorny thickets.

The first to fall was Chayito. The patrol got him, while the
other Cuameas turned into a handful of flies. A little officer who
was a presumptuous dandy with an elegant uniform and just out of
the Military Academy, ordered him hanged without delay. But
first he spit out at him, "But why the hell are you up in arms in
the first place?"

"Well, to defend the Revolution which has been betrayed, sir."

"Which revolution? Revolutions are social aberrations that
come in cycles and end in bloodshed. . . . "

"Sir, I don't understand anything you're saying."

"How the hell could you understand? Son of a bitch!"

"Son of a bitch" seemed to be the agreed-on sign. They pulled
the knot. Chayito stuck his tongue out at them, and with an animated step he did the "ragdoll gig." A thick shroud of clouds, a
somber frond of the tree that covers black thicknesses in vain, the
dark figure of the hanged man swung back and forth invisible to
all eyes, like the rhythm of a second hand marking the time of the
dead man, a blind negation of the existence without luminous
wisps in the sky, a frigid antithesis of the concept of "universe."
He hung there looking like a strange sign from some gray language
told to the shadows. . . . The malnourished trees simulated the
resigned weeping of women who have just given birth to stillborn
children. The squalid trees gave off a distant whistle like a train
disappearing into the distance far beyond the rails and the
earth . . . as though everything were disappearing without leaving
a trace. The three remaining Cuameas arrived two days later at
the sprouting tree which, according to what people believed,
should have dried up. The pious vultures had picked Chayito's
eyes out so that he would not see his own tragedy. The old man
threw himself on his son, embracing him by his feet with tenderness and warmth. It was a useless softness . . . when he was still
in the cradle, when the child wanted to feel the sky of tenderness
with his little arms, there was only a stony land without flowers or
rain. It was a tardy outpouring of sentiment. The old tiger cut
him down, and he slipped through his arms covered with a gray
and slippery paste. With pernicious irreverence, the birds, although each was the abode of a winged poet engaged in continu-

ous cheeping, had covered the decomposing body with shit. The little Indians lowered their eyes in silence. The tired genealogy demanding a respite, tired of violence, already showed in them. They understood profoundly that they were doomed from birth, but not for the crime of being rebels. Being Indians meant being forgotten, being censored, being scorned, receiving the iniquitous sentence of the worst kind of poverty and insulting disdain for their dark skins. The old man began to turn instinctively in circles like an imprisoned feline.

The other two glum ones were victims of a vile trap. They dulled various knives which went from being dry and brilliant to colored, rusty, lusterless when dried. The rifles also responded to the mission of their manufacture with fountains of expansive bullets. In this way their lives slipped away like pools of oil colored by the light of dusk. The setting sun and its shootin grays added the reds in a glorious flash. Two nights concluded: one tragic and without tears; the other, a skylight of the universe, fixed, firm, full of stars.

THE YAQUI LORETO survived the unfortunate Frankie by two years. They found him already dead in the little house that he had constructed in the neighborhood alongside the dried-up river. That neighborhood is situated on the bed of a dammed river. People who go there have no roof over their heads; the sand serves as their bed. At first they went there only to sleep, with no walls other than the four winds and the sky, which the hungry say is as lugubrious as the fabric used to line coffins. The dried-up river neighborhood soon became populated with the sorriest of human beings, some with a limb missing from their bodies but with a surfeit of malice. Others were dirty, old, and scrawny and were looking for someplace to die decently. Thieves and trinket peddlers and even food vendors were not lacking, in addition to the presence of hippies, strange youths whose bodies only half responded, divorced from their spirits. It was as if all the scum had been gathered together, arriving by the dozens. At first they smiled at each other and said good evening and invited each other to share their crumbs. Their domains did not take long to become defined, just as happens with the birds and the animals. They would get into fistfights in order to become the owner of a small plot. Some saved up rocks to be used to smash skulls. Rusty kitchen knives inspired terror in throats, and the variety of weapons included baseball bats, police clubs, switchblades, and slingshots. Even the old cripple everybody called Coffeepot was stabbed to death. The venerated title of mother was dragged through the mud and was also used as a weapon. At last, after a bloody battle, crying and cursing their having been abandoned as orphans, the most defenseless fled in shame. The same was true of the almost paralytic and the blind, in addition to those who could barely move their bodies, cemeteries of cells in themselves, bent under the weight of so many years and the assault of a force of gravity that already licked the bones it would swallow up. Loreto, the old revolutionary, also lorded over what would be his territory and where he would fashion his house with the patience of an ant. The photographers would not take long in coming around to take pictures which, when published in magazines, would serve for many readers to use as a frame and background for their own belongings so they would glow brightly. When the old cripple left the pavement of the city to walk the dirt of his neighborhood, anyone could have followed his trail up to his doorstep because he left a track consisting of a footstep and the depression from his peg. During the final days only his footstep left a clear impression, next to a line that would stop every little bit. The news was brought by the intolerable stench. At first the neighbors didn't pay much attention, thinking that it had to do with one of the many skinny dogs of the kind that drag their fleshless bodies through the streets dodging stones, dogs that are always dying whenever they please. It was Peluchi, the owner of a cart, a rolling restaurant. "Come and get your tacos with hot sauce," and he'd blow his whistle. "The body doesn't belong to a dog. Hell! The dead man is the peg leg, he's checked out."

The news was taken to the authorities by the old woman who sold lottery fractions, the one who according to wagging tongues used a football to simulate a humpback. The cops didn't get there until the next day. Although what had occurred was very clear to the garbage men whose job it was to pick up the body, the same ones popularly known as bichigetters. According to the Academy of Popular Speech, which explains such obscure sayings, a *bichi* is one of those tiny little hairless dogs with no coat. Thus when they die, whether violently or naturally, their owners toss them in the garbage lot. And it's there where they're found by those who dedicate themselves to scatological undertakings. As they go around in their vans picking up refuse, they also pick up the *bichis*, which logically gives them the name of bichigetters. Now, it would not be inappropriate to clarify that *bichi* in the Yaqui language means someone who's naked. With respect to bichigetter, it should not be forgotten that the clean-shaven, that is men who have neither a beard nor a mustache, are called with an undeniable lack of respect "butt faces." The fact of the matter is that there were five bichigetters. They pulled up in such a beat-up truck that it looked like a Martian laboratory. For masks they wore dirty handkerchiefs dipped in mezcal and tied around their necks, covering half their faces. The one with the death certificate stood off at a distance. He wore a wide tie and a jacket whose owner had been much smaller. Since he blinked continually, they called him Lightning. The head of the party gave the order:

"Go get him, you bastards!"

They surrounded the fragile construction, ready to lift the whole thing up along with the body of the Yaqui Loreto. The place consisted of one eight-by-eight room, five feet high. It was made out of empty cans and cartons picked up now and then and here and there, wherever. The north wall was almost red, made almost exclusively of Tecate beer bottles. The south one, in addition to various boxes, had a large poster with the photograph of a woman showing off her rear end and drinking Poca Cola. Others advertised Nabisco crackers and there was a large box with a hungry kid eating Bimbo Bread. There was a make-believe window with the portrait of a callous, skinny elected official with little snake eyes and a simian mouth with a loose lower lip. For the east wall he had used sheets made from cans of Enca shortening and from cans of Fedo dog food sold to fancy people like Doña Mariana, the aristocratic lady who was the wife of the owner of the superbrothel known as the Little Pill. It is said that the old lady in question, as is frequently the case among the wealthy, took better care of her dogs than she would have of her children if her being barren had not prevented her from having them. She put them to sleep in luxurious beds and dressed them in little rubber panties with pictures of butterflies. In the morning she sang to them with maternal sweetness while she cleaned up their poop. Since she was always kissing them, the breath of this distinguished lady smelled like a dog's, although her husband was a dog in his very soul, being a greedy and corrupt politician. The front part of Loreto's house and more than half the door, with hinges made of bent cans of Spam, were covered with a box with the legend "Enjoy meat cooked over the coals" and with the picture of a steak that was so real that you could almost smell the aroma. The wall was finished off by foil that exhibited delicious Oscar Molla Wienies, and a sheet of tin stood out showing a fried chicken with such an authentic appearance that any schoolteacher who happened to see it would start to cry. The Indian had also placed on the front wall the laminated advertisement of a large ham whose magnetic force was a threat to the most solid denture. There was another sheet with the portrait of a famous fairy who played the part of a cowboy in the American movies. The base was made up of boxes of Phobia soap, and in a prominent place there was the picture of an ice-cream cone.

One of the bichigetters looked at the chief and asked:

"What do think this guy kicked the bucket from?"

"It sure wasn't from indigestion. Death must have been from hunger, pure and simple; you know that, so don't act dumb."

Since the construction was so fragile, it didn't take long to get it into the garbage truck. They wrapped the remains of the dead man in a rotten tarp. They lifted the bundle up and placed it on top of the remains of the home of the miserable Indian. His peg leg came loose and fell on the head of the runt, Nelson Ortiz, who quickly dedicated a rosary of dirty words to the dead man. (He even called his mother a whore.) The taco vendor, whose forehead, eyebrows, and nose were of course red from wiping away the sweat with hands covered with sauce, felt he had certain rights because he had discovered the body, and he asked the head bichigetter:

"Where are you going to bury him, sir?"

"How the hell would I know!"

They found no effects of the dead man and much less sign of food, with the exception of an overcoat as stringy as cheese soup and some raggedy pants that looked like leather overalls. But there was a real uproar when they discovered a small chest in good condition, and they all fought over it, shouting and shoving.

"I saw it first, you fuckers, give it here."

"It's mine, you assholes, I've got it now."

"Calm down, you jerks, sons of bitches."

"Even-steven for everyone, and anyone who makes off is a dog's fart."

"Swear to it, crisscross your heart and hope to die."

"Fair deal, and whoever runs off, may his dick dry up and fall off."

When they opened the chest they took out a handful of yellowing papers, a photograph of the Indian Loreto in uniform, still young and healthy. Standing on his right was the general himself, with tiny little eyes shut with laughter, and anyone could have seen goodness itself in his round face. But it was well known that General Cajetes loved to drink pools of blood with his eyes. To one side stood the dashing Colonel Chayo Cuamea, his eyes brimming with malice, the very Chayo Cuamea who would become famous for being the first and only man to win Death with his charms. There were several other documents also.

"Look at this! Who'd have believed that that fucking dude was a general. Look here, so you won't think I'm making it up!"

"Well, he must have been. . . . Look, it's probably true."

"Come on, let's get going."

The Indian Loreto died at the end of June. It was at that time that they celebrated with great fanfare in his lands the first cresting of the Yaqui River. It was Midsummer's Day when all the rivers are named Jordan and carry holy water, when the water that baptized the just man fertilizes the fields that so generously yield up their fruits to all men of good will. . . .

THEY LET COLONEL Chayo live. Cruel vengeance: without teeth and nails, full of age and fury, he remembered that he had a pup left and he trotted off home. The poor idiot was contemplating a lagoon where the toads were entertaining themselves in a perfect paradise, free from rationing and useless moral ideas, and with no shadows on their joyful liberty, intelligent beings exclude sin from their codes by refusing to think.

"They killed your brothers and made fun of me. Only you can avenge us."

The old man was overcome at what he heard: "Papa, I'd like to be a four-eyed toad." His disenchantment was replaced by a crafty little laugh and the astute glow of his tiny eyes.

"Really, son, would you like to be a four-eyed toad like that one?" He cleverly slid a pair of batrachians toward a dry spot, and the one on the bottom began to jump with her passenger on her back. The crazy child was surprised to see that in reality they were two toads practicing equestrian jumps.

He began to tremble with excitement. The old man yelled imperiously: "Do you want to be a frog, son? Do you really want to be a frog?"

The crazy child was overcome, and he kicked the romance of the ingenuous animals apart.

The astute old man, with his years of experience, did not take long in bringing an Indian woman around for the imbecile, who had reached the age of uncontainable fury that overflows the bounds of puberty, thrust suddenly into an explosive state in which nature asserts obsessively her irrefutable demand.

The old man went down to the lagoon every morning to enjoy his terrible illusions, down where the beasts used to go to drink, and under the skeletal shade of an old mesquite he would stretch out. And on more than one occasion his air of a tiger would frighten the animals. One morning, slipping through the bushes, the old man lay in his usual place. His firebrand eyes glowed and he happily contemplated the lagoon bubbling with tadpoles and tiny toads. He also made out the buds of new arms, terrible arms they would have to be, machete wielding, remorseless, bloodthirsty. The Indian woman assumed the conic shape of those wrappers used for portions of peanuts bought from a street vendor. What the devil! . . . The Indian woman looked like quintuplets! His perverse imagination converted her into a Trojan horse. He had to take revenge against the cursed traitors of the Revolution. He remembered when he had tried to see his former chiefs. He was hungry and they lived in palaces, and the irrigated fields and all the wealth belonged to them. The concept of "revolution" had swept everything before it: little can-do politicians, pernicious freeloaders who had all they wanted just for the asking like fortunate little pigs. The colonel, a great narrator of his past as a fighter, soon woke up to his false dream. He noted anguish, hunger, and a profound disillusionment in his brother Indians. His people had been put down. What the centuries, the soldiers, and the weapons had not done was achieved by alcohol, which had taken over, thanks to the systematic help of profitable publicity. That and cursed hunger. He went forth determined to make a personal claim on those who governed, fellows in arms in the majority and even buddies. It was useless. They did not recognize his name, and no door answered his knock, nor was there a single plea that could yield the most insignificant favor. He returned to his mountains, his hideout, and his hole, dragging behind him physical hunger and consumed in spirit by the other hunger, which is cancer, bitterness, rancor, hatred, and the unbreakable idea of avenging himself. He remembered obsessively the splendor of the mansions inhabited by his former comrades, his awed imagination overwhelmed by fantasies from *The Thousand and One Nights*. They would not even receive him. He clawed at the earth like a wild bull, yellow spittle on his lips and bloody hatred in his eyes. Traitors, sons of bitches!

The truth. The old colonel was not frustrated because of noble ideals, very much his own, that had been cut down. Through the strange power of self-suggestion, the old tiger had deceived himself into believing that he was a seeker of justice. Like all fanatic idealists, trapped in his own world, his suffering, his anguish hinged on deceptive facts. But they filled his mouth with the pride of not being counted among the pack of scoundrels that buzzed all over the map of the republic and helped themselves at their own discretion to the wealth of the land and the broken will of its inhabitants. His aspirations, perhaps hidden, of being a feudal sire collided with hapless reality. He began to scream crazily: I will rise up with my grandsons and I will take the knife to all of you, you pack of thieves! He tried to stand up, fell to his knees, arching his back like a furious tiger, and he instantly collapsed. The inopportune and noisy fluttering of birds and their rapid flight, the blind stampede of the cattle urged on by fright, the howling of the dogs despite the absent moon, and the silent and quiet profile of the vegetation made him jump up agilely and gaze into the pool. . . . The afternoon was coming with a midnight silence. The itching

from trampled ants invaded his flesh, and the avenues of blood
overflowed their borders, hot, as it had been then . . . very hot.
He whirled around instinctively, fixing his gaze on a point. Before
his reason, the floodgates of his subconscious vibrated, and he
shook from a strong electric jolt to his spine, which flooded down
to his toes and hands. The muscles of his face and arms moved
involuntarily. The grinding of his teeth sounded like the galloping
of a horse. Trembling all over, he felt a pinprick in each of his
pores. There!

On the banks of the lagoon there stood a roadrunner five
times larger than normal. She pretended to concentrate on something else, but he noticed that the roadrunner had both eyes
twisted toward him, staring at him intently out of the corner of
her eyes. He fixed his tiger's eyes on her, and saw her go hide
herself solemnly behind a *barchata* clump with an unnatural gait
for birds like that. Without seeing her, he knew that she was siz-
ing his humanity up and gauging how much life was left in him.

It was her! His great love, his lively passion, the romantic
dream of his life, the most seductive object of his desire, a tremendous desire that all he had to do was see her to start to tremble
like a volcano coming back to life. He was invaded by a warm,
soft tenderness. He was in love! His eyes turned red from the ur-
gent, blind, unconquerable compulsion. Mechanically without
thinking about it, he took his clothes off. He stretched out on his
back, pretending not to have seen her, crafty, feline.

The Skinny Lady, cautious, circled about, overcome by a fear
that verged on panic. She wanted to desist, go on her way, but
no, not even she could miss the appointed hour. . . . Never had
her duty upset her more. When she felt her strategy to be the
most secure, thinking that it was only a matter of an instant to
free herself from such a unique spectacle of erect beings, she
dropped her guard. The hapless woman did not foresee that she
should have approached such a stallion wearing a chastity belt or
with her sex full of sandy dirt, like hotly pursued Indian women of
yore did whore fused to yield to the deceitful stranger. What a
stupid Miss Death! Her treasure of tricks was unable to inspire her
with the necessary ability. . . . The respect produced by the
wicked man made her forget that Colonel Rosario Cuamea, more
than bloodthirsty, brave, astute, and bestial, owed his greatest

fame to his indefatigable character as a belly squasher. In every town taken by the depraved colonel, the women fled in despair no matter what their age and condition. They flew rather than ran, like chickens sentenced to die. They pulled cruelly at their breasts, as though they were really mature pears and he a hungry bird. Any woman he did not get by deceit slipped half-naked through his hands and legs, and he always saved a piece of torn underwear and a handful of hair.

The Skinny Lady observed him stretched out on his back, in agony, in that time without space or planet, apparently dead. Thinking she was safe, she made a horrible grimace that could be translated into a satisfied smile that said "Aha." But she discovered a strange glow in Colonel Cuamea's eyes, and she sat down astride him to blow them out completely. In her anger she felt a sharp object like a dagger tear at her insides. . . . Full of rage and pain, she brought her hands to her groin, seeking desperately a way to free herself from the enormous mast that deeply invaded the interior of her body. But all she could find was a sack of cantaloupes that hung down like a lock. She turned around quickly bellowing with anger and pain, and she furiously dug her claws in the chest of the perverse Indian. Deeply she pulled, pulled with an exact strength, pulling out the tough roots until from the farthest reaches of his very insides, with the mystery of darkened centuries, she yanked out all the roots from which life hangs. Colonel Cuamea gave a terrible death rattle, stretched his body gasping, and felt an intense, very intense orgasm. . . .

The body of the Indian colonel remained there in the field, rotting like an animal. Protruding eyes like large tomatoes adorned the carrion banquet.

PÁNFILO PÉREZ and his wife looked at each other torn by anguish, reconstructing the omens that had reached them on the wings of birds. A letter that they thought would be happy had been sung to them by the tecolote as tragic. Pánfilo quickly became reanimated.

"Momma, the tecolote could have sung to the neighbors. Doña Chonita is so old. . . . "

His wife took up the same illusion, and husband and wife became absorbed in the hope of taking flowers to their ancient neighbor. Why not? Drink coffee with a cinnamon stick, chatting at the wake about ghost stories, scattered episodes in the life of the dead woman and a couple of those dirty stories. They fell asleep with the drowsiness of the dream that fed their exhausted bodies. Pánfilo dreamed that he was in a strange field, covered with saguaros, ocotillos, an entire desert in bloom. At his side, his beloved absent son, asking him questions. No matter what paths Pánfilo's mind took, like a lamp that suddenly lights up and wants to find out everything, everything like a mountain of questions that he wanted to decipher by rubbing his forehead in order to think deeply. But before God, Pánfilo was also a child with lots of questions.

"*Papá, what are we?*"

"*Mexicans, son.*"

"*Mexicans and we don't live in Mexico. Are we Americans then?*"

"*Yes, my son, we are also Americans.*"

"*Why then do the Mexicans call us Pochos and here they call us Mexican greasers?*"

"*My son, what things you say. . . .*"

"*Papá, I'm sorry about that day I refused to speak Spanish. In school they hit me so I wouldn't speak Spanish, and I thought it was a bad crime. . . .*"

"*Losing your native tongue, son, is like losing your soul. We have been losing it little by little, burdened down by the work of beasts, as though we were subhuman beings.*"

"*Like the slaves, papá?*"

"*That's what we are, my son.*"

"*For how long, daddy?*"

"*Until life no longer means anything to us.*"

Pánfilo wrapped the tender dialogue that had flowed over his feelings so many times in the dreams of his illusion, dreams that he had never communicated to his son because his anguish and his desires could not express themselves in beautiful words. The ones he used were rough and harsh, just like his exhausting days at work, like poverty itself and the rabid impotence that made him distrustful of even pleasant things. That night his absent son's spirit seized him. He got up after midnight to walk through the fields. At the edge of some trees that were friends, in peace with the vineyards, he stopped beside a water ditch, seeking white voices in the murmurings of the water and the lullabies with which the wind rocks the sleeping birds in the branches. He looked at the living stars of light, like every man who feels anguish. Knowing that they tell the story of God, he wanted to turn them into messengers. Pánfilo cried, because words often spring forth from deep within, from the same depths where tears are born. From the heart of the humble peasant the innocent figure of his beloved son glowed forth, asking him, like he always used to do, about things that not even he could explain. Precisely now that he knew him to be far away and in danger, he allowed the dialogue to flow like the clean water that passes by tinged with blue or adorned by the glowing stars.

His wife woke him up regretfully at dawn. The day, radiating light and happiness for other beings, demanded from him with the cold heart of a moneylender the tribute of another exhausting workday. Pánfilo showed up for work like he was used to doing every day. He noticed that the sky was strangely ashen in color and the song of the cocks was very sad. So when they yelled at him to go home, that he was needed, he knew immediately what it meant. He dashed off toward his house, wishing secretly that he would never arrive. His neighbors were standing around both inside and outside his house. He saw various fellow laborers, silent, bent, wringing their straw hats in their hands. Pánfilo entered his home. The hidden screams of the ancestral Indians swelled the pores of those present, wounding and explosive. It was accompanied by a chorus of tears in a lower tone, with knowing respect and deference to the mother who, crazed with suffering and refusing to accept reality, was calling for her son. With a sacrilegious gesture she demanded of the Supreme what right He had to dispose cruelly of the lives of the innocent. The women surrounded her, rubbing her with alcohol.

"Console yourself, woman, you have your husband and other children to look after. Frankie is already in heaven."

The women paused, talking low and sniffling.

"My Ernest is already sixteen."

"My Robert fourteen."

Pánfilo moaned hoarsely, wounded, accepting the tragedy as one more thing that weighed him down.

"The boy and I had thought that, when he left the army, he might have the chance to go to college with the government's

help. The kid was real clever, and I never would have had the
money to send him or even to get him an old jalopy. The school
bus doesn't come this far for the kids. Maybe if he'd been in college he wouldn't have been drafted."

The old woman who lived in the third cabin came in, Doña
Chonita Urías. She bore all of her many years stored away in a
hump that was getting the best of her. The octogenarian came in
wrapped completely in a black shawl, mysteriously finding her way
over to the suffering mother. Three steps before she reached her,
she half opened her shawl at the level of her eyes and began a
weak but prolonged crying, a uuuuu that come out faintly, from
who knows how far away. The women embraced, joining in a
raised cry and seconded by the wailings of the children.

Choni pulled his buddy Pánfilo aside.

"Come over here, pal. Have a drink, your suffering is so heavy
you need it, buddy."

Choni handed him a bottle of tequila. Pánfilo served himself a
stream of fire, drinking desperately. Choni had to grab the bottle
away from him by force. The man who had been stabbed by destiny sat down with his eyes wide open. He smiled, moving his
lips. He saw a herd of horses stamping the ground and bucking
with men wearing hats on their backs, carrying machetes and .30-
30s. They suddenly turned into the border patrol galloping behind
hound dogs in hot pursuit of a wetback. Then they turned into
skinny men with beards, dressed in iron with swords and lances,
angrily challenging the mountains and the giants to beat the shit
out of them.

His buddy Mingo came in at that moment.

"He doesn't recognize you, Mingo. It looks like the blow has
sent him out of his head."

Shouting loudly, Pánfilo pointed to his buddy Mingo. "Cut the
horns of this goat; I will be responsible."

The scene had its comic note, and some smiled discreetly. Various youngsters burst out laughing. Suddenly Pánfilo's conscience
came alive, and a sob that sounded more like a death rattle tore at
his chest. Choni, his faithful pal, looked at Pánfilo and his one
hand with a fist made from the other.

"And I brought him with me, buddy, truly believing that leaving Texas, a prison for our people, would allow us to warm a cor-

ner for ourselves here where we could live like human beings. And now they've taken your son away, only to bring him back dead. Damn sons of bitches."

Pánfilo took another swig from his buddy Choni's bottle. He drank the liquor like a thirsty sandpit. It was at this moment that the metamorphosis began, in which Pánfilo Pérez became an enormous bird with black wings.

WITH HIS POWERFUL WINGS, *Pánfilo Pérez began to fly all over the far corners of the Chicano lands, the vast stretches of Arizona, New Mexico, and Texas. Everywhere he fixed his eyes on his people, and there was a moment when Pánfilo was unable to see a thing because his eyes were full of a downpour that was so thick that it was as if his soul had turned into a sea. There went the flying Chicano, beating his wings every now and then, and then stretching them out serenely, floating even higher than where the celestial lambs graze. He flew until he encountered a mountain high enough for him to be able to see the teeth in the man in the moon. How Pánfilo cried for all he saw from the sky: his Chicano people reduced to the worst of humiliations, enslaved in the fields, the mines, the cities, denied their rights and dignity because they were dark and weak. Thousands of children segregated in the schools with the label of mental retards because they didn't speak English. His Chicano people massacred in the war with a greater number of casualties in relation to their number in the population. His copper people begging for justice at the top of their voices in demonstrations of suffering by the thousands, only to hear the tragic response of the bullets with which the authorities answer in the form of a police force that acts with brutality against the orphans of social justice. Pánfilo Pérez cried so hard that tears ran down his long face. He turned back homeward. On his way home Pánfilo Pérez did not fail to make some pirouettes in the air, taking advantage of his condition as a bird. In his navigation through the regions of blue he was entranced to see the stars so enlarged that it was a real find to discover that they are piñatas in reality and not phosphorescent billiard balls, as they seem to be when seen from earth. If Pánfilo Pérez did not smile when he looked down, it was because his mouth was not made for such gestures. The rivers snake their way across the earth, prodigious in their knots and contortions, looking just like varicose veins. Simpleminded Pánfilo was amazed to see the forests thick on the cheeks of the ravines, weaving themselves through the mountains. And there were little clusters of mountains wherever he looked: stupid earth, furry and full of pimples. Since Pánfilo was not a poet, he exclaimed as he passed over the Yuma desert and saw the immense stretch of land. Damn! It looks like the Apaches have been here. There were eagles in abundance, along with other kinds of birds that joined his flight out of a desire to look him over. When he had them by his side, Pánfilo turned around and, seeing him so strange looking, the gossipy birds took fright and dropped like lead, more than anything else from hearing such an unheard-of bird talking like a Christian and calling after them: "Hello, there, you chunky birds!" The singular bird is now flying into the atmosphere of the Imperial Valley, falling to earth burning like a meteorite with the brilliant flash of the infernal region. His Chicano people bustled about below like ants, glowing like mobile raindrops from so much sweat and from working so hard. Pánfilo said to himself: "And they still call us lazy, seeing as how we produce the food for so many lazy bastards." The idea came to him in a flash: "Since I'm so close to this so-called sun, I'm going to go right up to his ears and tell him a thing or two." He soared up so high that he felt his beak warp as though it were made of molasses, and little clouds puffed out of his wings. His claws became soft like the hands of a newborn baby and his eyes as brilliant and fiery as two white-hot coals. When he had the sun within spitting distance, he shouted at him: "You smart-ass son of your sunny mother! Look how you treat my people. You brand their kidneys as though they were your own beasts of burden. See how you suck the innocent little kids dry, just to see their parents cry when they bury them. You shout at the top of your voice that you come out for everybody, that you are democratic, and that you light the way for the rich and the poor. You hypocritical, truculent liar. How little respect you have for their humble homes. Because these are poor people, and you turn their houses into ovens. Ah! But you only caress the powerful when they come out half-naked to stretch out like puppies. You toast their backs and caress them morning and evening. Then you wink your servile eye and say: 'Take refuge over there, my lovelies, where you won't get hurt, because I'm about to begin to heat things up for the humble.' Be more just, you damn little sun. Can't you see that there are a lot of us poor people and that one day we're going to cast a shadow on you and your face is going to get even dirtier? Do you hear me, son of a bitch?" The sun got so mad because of Pánfilo's nerve that it swelled up red and spit on him. Pánfilo felt the blow and fell in agony, filled with tears: "This is how they must have killed my little Frankie, you heartless people."*

THE AFTERNOON HAD FALLEN on the silent tears of the Pérez family, filled with their memories. The majority of those present surrounded Pánfilo, waiting for the miracle of seeing him conscious. He remained quiet, with an imbecile look, trying to say something with strange gestures and incoherent words. Pánfilo half came to, held up by Choni and Mingo. The women looked at him with profound respect, but some children laughed in his face, seeing how he arched his arms like an eagle and made faces and sounds imitating the birds. A stream of tears fell from his reddened eyes. The profound suffering of the crazed man joined hunger and despair with tragedy. A few days later some men dressed in white picked him up in a sort of ambulance. They brought some straitjackets that they didn't even have to use. They took Pánfilo away, drooling and doubled over with laughter as though he were a little child. The bosses said that he had gone crazy because he was a real drunk. In part they were right because Pánfilo certainly got drunk from time to time to alleviate the frustration of so much despair, but he also went mad from working like an animal, unable to replenish his energies with abundant food, and more than anything else, from seeing his family, which he loved so much, sunken in the cruelest of poverties, and, the last straw, because of the death of his Frankie in the war. Poor Magui was left alone with the rest of her children, condemned to beg for help in the labyrinths of bureaucracy, as though she were a beggar going from office to office. They refused her with excuses. She smelled bad, stank, and besides she was a long way from fixing her hair and dressing in style. The employees could assume with her an authority that they did not have. The base servility with which they dealt with their superiors became toward Magui the most despotic of behavior. The children of Magui and crazy Pánfilo were left at that point to drink rivers of bitterness, and later they would drink booze in the vain attempt to erase unpleasant memories. And it was only one step from there to delinquency. Pánfilo Pérez, like the majority of Chicano farm workers, was not covered by social security, and much less by a pension or retirement fund. Like so many Chicanos who work in the fields, he lived out his life forgotten by the laws that protect every worker. He was like a subcitizen of the basest category, with a salary and working conditions that only legalized slavery can inhumanly impose by turning its back on every principle of true justice.

"My good friend, what a miracle to see you here, man."

"Well, here I am. If you'd come five minutes later, you wouldn't have found me."

"Don't tell me you're off on a trip."

"Yes sirree, friend, I'm off to my homeland. Can I get you anything there?"

"Well, just have a good trip, friend, have a good trip."

"From Tucson I go on to Nogales, and from there I follow the main highway to my town."

"Well, where are you from really?"

"I'm from down there by the Yaqui Valley, right in Sonora."

"You don't say, I was through there in the 30s."

"You must not have been down there in a long time."

"Let's see . . . Alemán was still president, the one who was always smiling. It's been about 25 years. How time flies! When I came up from there, I didn't have a single gray hair. Now, my friend, I look like a negative of a picture from when I was a youngster. And the damndest thing is that my kidneys are not doing well."

"Do you remember that in 1955 we worked the cantaloupe together? Remember?"

"I'd rather forget it. We couldn't drink any water until we got to the end of the rows. Damn! How long they were. In the afternoons, all we did was drink water. I tell you, that's all we did, drink, drink, drink, and our guts would never get their fill, no matter how much we drank."

"I didn't earn enough from harvesting cantaloupes to starve on."

"Well, that's the time I talked to you about an idea I had."

"Yes, I remember that, just so you can see how things are. You were going to set up a business in your hometown with the dollars you'd saved up, and I told you that I was going to buy machinery so I could work the land I'd left behind. . . . Which, of course, I lost."

"I'd be satisfied now with a basket to sell ice-cream cones in my town."

"Same for me with regard to a little piece of land, just so I'd have something to call my own."

"But the family grew, and now I've got eight, all big now."

"And I've got seven, friend."

"You know . . . I don't understand my children, they barely speak Spanish. Besides . . . they're all longhairs and say they're Chicanos. What do you think about that! One of them got the bright idea to put patches on the seat of his pants and on the knees. Real weird, friend."

"Look, I don't understand them either, and I was always fighting with them, until the oldest one took me aside and explained one thing and another to me. And if you think about things, you see they're right. You and I and many others have lived with the idea of returning to our land some day, and the rest has not mattered a wit to us, which is why we've allowed ourselves to be beaten. But they were born and raised here, my friend, and they couldn't stand being treated like animals, refusing them jobs and schooling, killing them in wars just because they want to. Not a bit of it. My son already made it clear to me: 'Papá, we're going to live here until we die, and this is where our children are going to live. Since they've filled our shoes with tacks, they might as well beat the shit out of us for what is just; otherwise, we'll always have their boot on our neck. And as far as what I wear goes, get it straight, boss, your days are over.' If you look at it that way, you start to think and then you see the kids are right."

"I guess so. . . . Certainly, but you'd like them to feel and think like you do. . . . But no, the world goes on turning. Friend, you really make me think."

"Buddy, the bus is ready to leave."

"Look, what a piece of luck, that's the one I'm going on."

"I'll go with you as far as Yuma, yes sir, my friend. That's where Rosemary, my daughter, lives. She's the second oldest. You probably remember she was a little runt, but you should see her now."

"I'm going now, my friend. I no longer have any ambition to have a business in my country. I'll just be happy to die there."

"Will you be back soon?"

"God willing."

"Goodbye and good luck."

"Why shake hands, if I'll be back? Tell our people I'll be back. So long."

THUS THE STORY, like a bad dream, left us stranded suddenly in the island of forgetfulness, prisoners. Not only that, but the genes that guard our culture, the essence of our history, have been left chained up, clogging the arteries that carry the impetus of the blood that animates the voice and soul of our people like rivers. Neither dignity nor education for the slaves, the masters said, only ignominy, prejudice, and death. At best, the tragic slobber of demagoguery, the counterfeit money of the perverse. When amnesia began to sow shadows in our memory, we went to our ancient lakes, seeking in the depth the faces we had lost. We saw through the mist of the ages that they were blurred and no longer the same. We reached the ancient bed of a river, facing the mountain of granite. We shouted for the echo to give back to us the names and the voices that had departed . . . leaving us empty. We came down from the hills, along all the trails and roads, dragging our roots against the thorns, the snow, and the fire. We inquired after our destiny, but no one wanted to understand us because our signs were so strange. . . . We descended to the bottom of the sea, where the stars descend to their nests, to ask if the heavens know where we are headed or where we come from. . . .

RETURN BEYOND THE CROSSROADS. Break the silence of the centuries with the agony of our screams. You will see the fields in bloom where you planted your children and trees that have drunk the sap of the ages, petrified trees without songbirds and without owls, there where the voices of those who have succumbed dwell. Destiny is history, and history is the road stretched out before the footsteps that have not existed. Who has made you believe that you are lambs and beasts of burden?

Tiger knights, eagle knights, fight for the destiny of your children! Know, those who have been immolated, for in this region you will be the dawn and you will also be the river. . . .